A Witch's Holiday Wedding

by

Tena Stetler

The Lobster Cove Series

A Witch's Holiday Wedding

Cover Art by *Kristian Norris*

The Wild Rose Press, Inc.
PO Box 708
Adams Basin, NY 14410-0708
Visit us at www.thewildrosepress.com

Publishing History
First Black Rose Edition, 2016
Print ISBN 978-1-5092-1181-4
Digital ISBN 978-1-5092-1182-1

The Lobster Cove Series
Published in the United States of America

A strong arm whipped around her waist,
the air whooshed out as she squealed. She balled up her gloved fist as a large warm hand wrapped around her wrist. "I've seen you defend yourself. Not going to chance it." A deep voice chuckled behind her.

"Lathen—I'm going to…"

He spun her around and covered her cold lips with his warm ones. Werewolves run several degrees warmer than most of the population, one of the things she loved about him. She relaxed into him. Their parkas making a *wisping* sound as the material rubbed against each other. "That's better," he murmured against her lips.

All at once the lights in the square blinked on. Low positioned red and green laser light decorations sparkled over the snow-covered ground and onto the gazebo, complementing the white lights. From the other direction, a blue laser sprinkled tiny snowflakes across the building. Evening fell quickly in December.

"This is absolutely beautiful." She breathed against his chilled cheek and whirled out of his hold taking in all the lighted decorations not visible earlier then pointed toward the bulletin board. "I've been reading the town's holiday events. Lobster Cove really embraces Christmas."

"Told you," Lathen said smugly. "Even some of the boats docked in the harbor are decked out with colored lights."

Praise for Tena Stetler

A DEMON'S WITCH was the All Romance Best Seller and The Romance Reviews Readers Choice 2016 Nominee.

"I thoroughly enjoyed this sexy paranormal story with excellent world building and well developed characters. The author has created a clever setting by making the headquarters of the demon a trendy hair salon in Washington, DC. An excellent debut novel that I recommend!"

~Lana Williams, Author

~*~

CHARM ME was The Romance Reviews Readers Choice 2016 Nominee.

"This is a great book, a wonderful story full of surprises and will keep you reading long into the night. I am looking forward to reading the next book by this great author."

~L. Collins

~*~

"Just finished *A Witch's Journey* by Tena Stetler. What a great book. I had tears in my eyes, tears of happiness for the people in the book. I LOVE when a book takes you away with emotion and makes you feel you are part of it. Thank you, Tena, for an amazing story. Can't wait to read more of your books."

~J. Gray

Dedications

To my family and friends,
who are so supportive.
~*~
To my husband, Bruce,
who rocks my world!
~*~
To my editor, Lill,
who makes my books the best they can be.
~*~
And to my readers,
I can't thank you enough!
~*~
To the wildlife rescue and rehabilitators,
whose tireless efforts
make the world a better place,
a heartfelt thank you!

Chapter One
A Change of Plans

Fingers poised over the keyboard, Pepper glanced down and smiled admiring the morning sun glinting off her emerald and diamond engagement ring. Thoughts of her fiancé intruded into her morning, despite her busy schedule. Her computer chimed indicating the arrival of a new email. She clicked on the email to open it, her body stiffened. Her mother was at it again.

The office door banged open. Pepper jumped as a frigid blast of air hit her square in the face before the door closed. Her office shared space with the lab and supply room of the Lobster Cove Wildlife Rescue and Rehabilitation Center. It was located on the family property she'd inherited under somewhat interesting circumstances. Pepper built LCWRRC with the help of former Navy SEAL, Lathen Quartz, her now fiancé. The Center filled a badly needed resource for the community and fulfilled her lifelong dream.

She glanced up from the computer screen and grimaced. Lathen, his cheeks rosy from the cold, surfer blond hair tousled as usual, stomped his snow-covered boots on the mat. Tonk tried to squeeze in between his legs. He grabbed the wolf pup rescue that had become his shadow by the harness. Dylan Foster, a vet in town, had brought the pup to the Center. A vehicle had hit the gray wolf in Arcadia National Park, shattering his jaw and hind leg. Dr. Foster pinned the jaw, put a rod in his leg, and neutered him because even with rehab, it was apparent he wouldn't be suitable for release.

"Halt." Lathen's aqua-marine blue eyes sparkled against his bronze skin. "You track mud and snow in Pep's office and we'll both be sharing your kennel tonight. And I have other plans." He waggled his eyebrows at Pepper, gave her a lopsided grin, which faded at her stormy expression.

"What's wrong?"

Despite her frustration, Pepper's heart did a flip-flop as she stared at the tall, muscular man she was due to marry in a few weeks. "My mother."

Tonk, his thick tawny fur covered with glistening snow, tilted his head up, flicked his ears and shook. Snow flew in every direction. Lathen frowned. "Tonk, sit."

Pepper hopped up from her desk chair, almost knocking the chair over, grabbed a roll of paper towels and tossed them to Lathen. Ember, a chow/mutt mix, lifted her head but remained curled up on a rug in the corner behind Pepper's desk watching from beneath it. With her shiny black coat and bright eyes, Ember was a far cry from the matted, skinny, skittish dog Pepper had rescued upon her arrival at the cabin months ago.

"Good thing your parents left when they did or they'd be snowbound here." Lathen glanced at Pepper before bending down, wiping the floor and Tonk's paws. He released the wolf who promptly loped across the room to join Ember on the large fluffy rug in the corner. Tonk bowed down, his butt in the air, yipped, and grabbed the frayed edge of the rug. He tugged, eliciting a low growl from Ember as she curled her lip in warning.

"Knock it off you two," Pepper said firmly. Ember laid her head back on her paws, and Tonk let go of the rug and raced across the room to Lathen's side. "He's not going to save you, boy."

Lathen grabbed him by the harness again and commanded, "Sit. Stay." The wolf obeyed but not without loud complaint. Lathen crossed the room, wrapped his arms around Pepper, and brushed his cold lips at the base of her warm neck. "Now what about your mother?"

Pepper squealed. "You're freezing. And you did that on purpose." Shivering she shoved him away.

Feigning innocence, he shrugged. "Who me?"

"Most certainly you." She laughed in spite of herself, helped him out of his coat, and kissed him affectionately on the mouth. "You want something to warm you? There's fresh brewed coffee." She motioned to the coffee maker on the counter to the left of her desk. "Or I have French vanilla tea bags. Hot chocolate might take a little longer." Taking a sip of tea from her steaming mug, she watched him over the rim, tamping down the irritation at her mother.

"Not exactly what I had in mind, but coffee will do...for now," he said in a low, seductive rumble.

When she tried to ignore his innuendo, heat flashed through her body. The man never failed to arouse her at the darnedest times. Memories of a recent night in the hot tub only fanned the flames of desire. Pepper shook her head, attempting to dislodge such thoughts and address the business at hand with little success.

With a slight smile, she recalled the first meeting with Lathen when she inherited the cabin and property in Lobster Cove, Maine, from Aunt Ashling, her father's sister, whose ghost still inhabited the property.

"Hey, where'd you go?" Lathen stood beside her waving one hand slowly in front of Pepper's face, while the other rested on her hand holding the coffee pot that hovered dangerously over the mug.

He tipped her hand so the hot coffee streamed into the mug, then took the pot and set it on the warmer. "How's it going this morning? I assume you've heard from your mom? Did they get home all right?"

"Yes, they did. Take a look at this." She stalked around the desk and jabbed an index finger at the screen.

Lathen stood behind her chair, hands resting on her shoulders and read the email. "She's only suggesting a change to the Thanksgiving plans. If you calm down and think this through, it might not be a bad idea."

"You're siding with her?"

Lathen blew out a breath, keeping his voice calm. "No... I'm considering all you have to do with the Center, our upcoming wedding, Christmas and New Year's celebrations that maybe spending Thanksgiving with your parents would be a good idea."

"She's always trying to run the show, take control. That's why I seldom went home, nor invited them to my place very often. I didn't have the inclination to listen to her criticize my career path. You know, she always hated that I followed in Ashling's and my dad's footsteps."

"Whoa, there. You two got along great the two months she and your dad were here. They were a great deal of help to us with the Center as we got it up and running. Especially when we took the unexpected trip to Alaska to attend my father's wedding and clear up that family mess."

She chewed on her bottom lip and nodded reluctantly.

"Remember you told me to give my dad and the pack the benefit of the doubt. You were right." He chuckled and rubbed his cheek. "About most things. There was that incident at the community center in Alaska…with Sofie."

Silent for a couple beats, Pepper's cheeks warmed. "Okay, I guess I flew off the handle without provocation. It's just…there's so much to do between now and the first of the year. I don't need her interfering."

He rubbed her shoulders. "I wouldn't call it interfering. I think it's a good idea."

"Even if I agreed to Mom's plan, which I'm not. It's only three weeks until Thanksgiving. That is not enough time for your family to change reservations."

"Well, since they are taking Dad's plane, I don't think that will be a problem."

"Your dad has a plane?"

"He is a tour guide in Denali. Of course he has a plane and a pilot's license to fly it."

"But you never mentioned a plane when we were there."

"You didn't ask. Reuniting with my dad, the pack, and the wedding consumed my waking hours. Getting around in Alaska is a lot easier by plane than other modes of transportation, weather permitting."

"What about Kaylee, Tonk, and Ember? I don't want to leave them here on our first Thanksgiving together."

Lathen snapped his fingers. "Leave that to me. As far as the rest of the creatures here, I'm sure Alec will be happy to care for them while we're gone. He can also call in the two teens that help out in the summer, if necessary."

"I hate to leave all that up to someone else. It's our responsibility. The animals are dependent upon us to care for them until they are well enough to take care of themselves."

"That's true, and why we hired Alec. He's experienced enough to handle the chores for a few days. We won't be gone long. He can have the week before Christmas and New Year's off in exchange for working Thanksgiving week. Seems a fair trade."

Pepper chewed on her bottom lip, a habit she'd had since childhood, when nervous or considering a problem and nodded slowly.

"The rest will do us both good before the whirlwind of the wedding and holidays. I plan to enjoy the season with my new bride." He leaned over and kissed her, with a whisper of movement he grabbed her parka off the hook by the door, held it out for her. "Bundle up, let's take a walk around the property, you need to clear your head." Lathen released Tonk from the place by the door where he'd finally settled. The wolf pup stood, arched his back, and pushed his front paws forward then stretched his back legs one at a time. "Ready for a run?"

Pepper whistled for Ember to follow. "Let's go back to the cabin and let Kaylee out of her aviary to follow us." She slipped on her boots, wrapped a scarf around her neck, pulling part of it over her face, and shrugged into the parka.

Pulling on his jacket, he opened the door, ice crystals sparkled on the crisp air that swept into the room. "You didn't let her out this morning?" Lathen closed the door behind them. Tonk and Ember raced up the snowy path, barking and tumbling over one another on the way to the cabin.

"Nooo…fed her from the fish holding tank. Kaylee was okay with it." Pepper finished zipping her coat up. "While a wild osprey would be able to hunt and fish in this weather then hunker down in shelter somewhere and survive, she never learned those skills, due to her injuries as a chick." Pulling her gloves on, she sauntered down the path. "Being my familiar, a magical creature, she bonded to me rather than looking to return to the wild. She's done much better here than the eight years prior at the Salem Wildlife Sanctuary."

"Hey—I wasn't questioning your abilities or judgment, only whether or not you let her out this morning." He raised his hands, palms up in a surrender gesture. "A little touchy this morning?"

"No. I was doing just fine, until the email arrived." Pepper huffed.

He arched an eyebrow. "Really? You've tossed and turned every night since I proposed a week ago. Maybe I should have whisked you off without warning to get married, instead of asking you to be my wife at the gathering of your family on Halloween night." His lips twitched, and he ducked anticipating her reaction as she swiped at him. "As long as we are on this subject. Your ghostly aunt appeared by the pond the other morning as I passed by on my way to the seabird aviary."

"Do I really want to hear this—now?" Pepper peered up at him, her lips pursed.

Lathen shrugged, the corners of his mouth kicked up in a devilish grin. "Ashling wanted to know if you planned on getting married at the pond. I asked if she was out of her mind, us warm-bloods would freeze. Your aunt hooted and said the ghosts wanted to create a magic bubble over the pond and surrounding shore to accommodate those attending the wedding. Apparently most of the spirits that were here on Halloween plan to return to attend our wedding and feel most comfortable at the pond."

Pepper groaned and rolled her eyes. "Not them too. Whose wedding is it anyway?"

"Just my two cents, but the idea intrigues me. The town knows you are a broom toting, cauldron-stirring witch after the occurrences on All Hallows Eve. No problem there. My family or pack may howl at the moon—outside, but they won't think anything about the magic. In fact, Dad and Amy kinda like having a witch in the family, not to mention my brother and sister-in-law."

Her hands fisted on her hips, she slid to a stop in the middle of the path to the marine habitat on the ocean shore. "Broom toting, cauldron stirring…strong words for an alpha male werewolf that howls at the moon and likes…"

He roared with laughter as he scooped her up and silenced her tirade with a searing kiss, one that warmed her down to her toes. She sighed. *He always knows how to relieve my stress.*

When they reached the fork in the path, Lathen took the one that led to the Seabird Aviary. Once inside, he lowered her until her feet touched the ground. Whistles and screeches permeated the air as Kaylee sailed in behind them, banked, and landed on a perch specially designed for her. She whistled to the birds and they quieted down.

"Hey, I thought we were walking the property."

"Oh, we will in a moment. I wanted to show you where I'm going to construct the temporary flight for the falcons." Lathen pulled out his tape measure and handed one end to Pepper. They discussed the size, shape, location of the structure and gage of the wire needed. After reaching an agreement, Lathen pulled a note pad out of his pocket, scribbled something, then snapped the measuring tape back, and stuffed it in his pocket. Holding open the aviary door for Pepper, he whistled for Kaylee to follow, closed the door after she soared through and out into the cloudy sky.

Gloved hands entwined, they meandered along the path that ran through the property, discussing everything except the wedding and holidays. As soon as they reached the expansive pond, the mist settled along the ground grew thicker at the water's edge and crept up the trunk of a nearby tree.

Pepper crinkled her face and blew out a breath. "Not now."

Ashling floated out of the mist, her form solidifying in her usual jeans and sweater. "Nice to see you two again. That was a nasty piece of weather that blew in here night before last. Did Klaren and Duncan get home all right?"

"They did. Thanks for asking." Pepper narrowed her eyes at Lathen.

"I'm glad you stopped by." The ghost hesitated for a beat her gaze sliding between Lathen and Pepper. "I wanted to talk…"

Out of the corner of her eye she saw Lathen give an almost unperceivable shake of his head.

"Is anything wrong?" Ashling asked.

"No—As long as you're not going to meddle in our wedding plans." Pepper settled on the bench that Lathen had created out of enchanted wood on the property. Steam rose from the bench as it warmed her damp coat and chilled body. Lathen slid in beside her and wrapped an arm around her shoulders.

"Of course not dear. Just wondered if you'd picked out a location?"

"Not exactly. Why?" she asked, as suspicion crept into her voice.

"Well…as I suggested to Lathen…earlier…maybe we, meaning the McKay spirits could provide a welcoming venue for your family and friends here." She spread her arms toward the pond.

Pepper began to shake her head.

"Now, dear, just hear me out. We could cast a spell, invisible to the mortal eye, warming the pond and surrounding land long enough for the ceremony to take place at the water's edge. Another consideration would be for you to be wed under the arbor Aidan McKay created for his first daughter's wedding in the 1800s. The arch has since returned to the tree from which he carved it, but at your touch, the arbor will be viable again. Wouldn't that be a memorable way to begin your married life? Especially after the true facts of his life and marriage came to light."

For a few minutes, Pepper sat speechless, then she wiped a solitary tear from her cheek remembering Aidan's tale of a young Irish immigrant, alone in America. And his rescue of a young woman, Dusty, who fled the Salem witch trials in 1793, where her mother was condemned and burned to death for witchcraft. He protected her. They fell deeply in love and married. The loving union produced six children and lasted sixty-two years.

Until recently, rumor had it that as a young man, Aidan Duncan McKay enslaved Dusty, stripped her magic to strengthen his own, enchanting the land and cabin he built. The same one Pepper inherited. Aidan and Dusty's spirits set the record straight on Halloween night.

"Yes, Auntie, I accept your offer of such a venue, but..." She leveled her gaze at Ashling. "No shenanigans, from you or other McKay ghosts. Is that clear?"

Her aunt nodded. "Agreed. Not that I would ever consider doing such a thing at your wedding. I'm a little hurt that you would even..."

"Sorry, but Lathen's family and his pack will be here, and I don't want to have to explain anything to anyone. I will leave it to you and the other spirits to handle the details. Subject to my approval on everything." A cold sensation spread across her cheek as Ashling kissed her.

"No problem. It will be a magical day for you both." Ashling gave two thumbs up as she turned toward the pond and faded.

Pepper looked across the water, but there nothing there except fog floating across the surface and an occasional tendril of mist rising into the air. "Thank you." Pepper rose from the bench and took Lathen's arm slowly retracing their steps until they reached her office. Kaylee whistling overhead, they opened the door, she dived between them, a wing tip nearly caught Pepper's cheek. "Kaylee, you know better," she scolded. The bird whistled softly from her perch.

"Change of heart?" Lathen asked enveloping her in his arms and holding her tight.

She rested her head against his chest for several minutes in silence, listening to his steady heartbeat and enjoying his warm embrace. Not caring that Tonk and Ember were leaving muddy paw prints all over the shiny office floor, she merely closed her eyes. "Yeah, I guess. We need to contact your family. See if they're okay with a change of Thanksgiving plans. Do you think they'll mind?" Pepper murmured against his coat. "But I really want them to see the facility we've built together."

"Nope, not at all. Bet they'll be here early enough in December to tour the facility and attend our wedding on the Winter Solstice. Maybe we can even talk them into staying through Christmas and New Year. The pack has had them long enough over the holidays. They can spend this year with us."

She tipped her head up to meet Lathen's gaze. "Oh, I'd love that. Family together for the holidays." She sighed and snuggled closer, breathing in his rich spicy aroma mingled with brine and an outdoorsy scent. "I'll contact Mom and Dad right after we talk to your dad and Kolby."

Kaylee whistled softly from her perch in the office and looked out the window toward the cabin.

Reluctantly, Pepper released her hold on Lathen, stood on tiptoe, and kissed his lips. "I better head up to the cabin and feed Kaylee." She glanced at the trails of muddy paw prints.

"Don't worry about those, take everyone up to the cabin with you, I'll be up in a few, after I clean up your dog and wolf's mess." With a warm smile, he reached across her desk and turned off the computer. "Work will still be here tomorrow." When he turned to face her, his smile morphed into a mischievous grin. "Unless you've hired elves to help with the paperwork."

"Naw, more trouble than they're worth." She snickered and motioned to Kaylee, Tonk, and Ember to follow her.

Chapter Two
It's One Damn Thing After Another

Lathen watched out the window as his tall, willowy woman with wavy strawberry blonde hair cascading to her waist made her way to the cabin. The osprey soaring above her, wolf pup, and black dog trotting behind her.

If someone had told him six months ago that he would be mated to a green-eyed beauty and planning a wedding, he'd probably hauled off and punched them. Or laughed manically. But here he was.

The family problems he'd experienced for years, most of his own making, settled. The pack had welcomed his return with open arms. Thanks in part to the wonderful woman trudging up the path.

His brother, Kolby and wife were expecting their first child. He'd be an uncle. Still wasn't sure how he felt about it. Life had taken so many twists and turns, flipped upside down that he wasn't sure what to expect next. He eyed the roll of paper towels on the desk, then went in search of a bucket and mop from the supply area of the building.

After cleaning the floor, he plopped the mop in the bucket and settled into Pepper's chair. Her scent of lilac and roses mixed with light citrus still clung to the fabric. He inhaled deeply drawing his phone out of his pocket, tapped the screen, and put it to his ear.

"Hey, Lathen. What ya up to?" Kolby's booming voice came over the phone.

"No good, as usual. How's Hayley and my little nephew?"

"Who said it was a boy? Could be your little niece. But Hayley is great. She can finally function in the morning without praying to the porcelain god. Been rough on her, but seems to be over."

"That's good to hear. You're flying down here with Dad aren't you?"

"Yeah, we'll split the cost of fuel, still cheaper than all of us flying commercial. Why?"

"May have a change of plans, if you guys are all right with it. I haven't talked to Dad and Amy yet. Thought I'd see how Hayley was doing first."

Kolby hesitated, his voice concerned. "Is something wrong?"

"No, no, not at all. Pepper's parents in Colorado want to have everyone for Thanksgiving at their house. Pepper was against the idea at first, but I convinced her that it wasn't a bad idea. She's been losing sleep over planning Thanksgiving, our wedding, Christmas, and New Year."

"Makes sense. Sure we're included?"

"Of course. The other thing is that after the wedding, we'd like everyone to stay on with us in Lobster Cove for Christmas and New Year."

"But Christmas is a Christian holiday. Pepper's a witch, so…aren't her traditions…" Kolby said.

"Oh, we worked that out and decided to celebrate all traditions. What she…we really want is to celebrate our wedding, Christmas, and New Year's with family. A new beginning for both of us."

15

"Wow. Okay. How long we stay will all depend on when the baby decides to make an appearance. The doctor said Hayley is safe to travel over Thanksgiving, but after that, wolf genes dictate a shorter gestation period. Hayley thinks the baby is due end of January, so we should be good to go."

"Great. I'd love to talk longer, but gotta call Dad, and Pepper is fixing supper up at the cabin. I just finished cleaning the muddy mess Tonk and Ember made in Pepper's office. Thought I'd give you a call to make the arrangements before confirming with Pepper's parents."

"I'll hold you to it, bro."

"Give Hayley our love. Tell her take good care of my nephew to be. Talk to you soon." When Lathen hung up, he was a little surprised at the excitement that curled in his belly. He tapped in his dad's number and waited for him to pick up. A female voice answered the phone. Lathen glanced at the screen to make sure he'd called his dad's cell. "Amy?"

"Yes, who's this?"

"Lathen...Is everything all right? Where's Dad?"

"In the shower. Elijah...your dad...always leaves his phone with me when—unless we both...well."

"That's too much information, Amy." Lathen laughed as his original concern melted away. Lathen's mom had died giving birth to him. His dad, Elijah, alpha of the werewolf pack in Alaska, had chosen to raise his sons alone. Last summer, Elijah had fallen for a woman, Amy, he met while guiding a tour in Denali. She was from a pack in Montana and didn't take any of his dad's shit, wouldn't let him push her away. Lathen and Pepper had attended their wedding the end of

August, and he was thrilled for his dad and Amy. On that same trip, he and Pepper had spent time with Kolby and Hayley at their home in Anchorage. Pepper and Hayley hit if off right away.

"Have Dad call me back when…oh, never mind, I'll just tell you. Pepper's mom has offered to host the family Thanksgiving in Colorado. Kolby and Hayley have no problem with the change of location. I wanted to make sure you and Dad didn't either, before we give the go ahead to Pepper's mom and dad." He went on to fill her in on all the details.

"Hey Lathen, hold on, your dad just got out, and he's dripping all over the floor." There were muffled sounds, and Amy squealed. "You're buck naked. Lathen is on the phone. Talk to him. Change of plans for Thanksgiving."

"Too much information again," Lathen said with a hardy laugh, waiting for his dad to come on the line.

"Son, your timing…"

"Oh, Dad, I'll only take a minute of your time." Lathen brought his dad up to speed with the change of venue for Thanksgiving holiday. Promised to have Pepper's parents call with directions, the location of the nearest airport to their home, and gave his dad Duncan and Klaren's number. Afterward, Lathen and his dad shot the shit for a while before he ended the call, anxious to tell Pepper the news.

He wrung out the mop and rinsed out the bucket before heading to the cabin. The night was clear and cold, but the storm had passed. His breath formed a fog around his head while he walked to the cabin. Ice crystals fell from the trees wafting through the crisp night air as he walked up the path.

"Pepper... I talked with... Wow...where'd you get that almost teddy? Com'on over here, sexy." His hands were ice cold, hell his whole body was frigid, except the growing ridge beneath the crotch of his jeans. He shucked his coat on the floor and grabbed her around the waist pulling her warm body to his frozen one. *God she was hot.* She squealed, nearly splitting his ear drum. *It'll be a while before I hear out of that ear.*

"Later... Go warm yourself by the fire while I finish dinner." She laughed shoving at his chest to no avail.

"To hell with dinner, I got exactly what I want right here." Nuzzling into her warm fragrant neck, he tried to kick off his boots. He breathed a kiss and flicked his tongue at the scar left by his claiming bite at the juncture of her shoulder and neck. *Mine.* He was going to have to unlace his boots before taking off his jeans, so he reluctantly released her. "Tease!"

"Oh, no that's a promise for later this evening. Thought we could heat things up in the hot tub." With a twitch of hip, she flounced off to the kitchen. She stopped in the doorway and blew him a saucy kiss.

He groaned bending over to unlace his boots, toed them off, and set them next to the door. Undressing next to the fire, he seriously considered stalking her in the kitchen and have his way with her on the table as an appetizer, but figured his skin was still chilled in some areas, and she'd just squeal again. *To hell with it.*

Silently, on the balls of his feet, he stalked to the doorway, and leaning against the wall out of sight, he waited. Pepper sashayed though the doorway, and he pounced. He scooped her up in his arms, kissing her surprised full lips as they formed an O, taking advantage of her parted lips, his tongue thrust inside. Stopping only once to deepen the kiss, he carried her down the hall and into the hot tub room, closed the door with his bare foot.

A couple hours later, the door swung open and Lathen stepped out followed by Pepper, less the teddy. "Ever eaten in the nude?" he wanted to know.

"Not as I remember, but things are about to change." She giggled and sprinted into the kitchen, opened the oven door, and the delicious aroma of pot roast, potatoes, and carrots filled the air. "Good thing I anticipated your appetite." With potholders, Pepper pulled the roaster out of the oven and set it on the ceramic trivet in the center of the kitchen table. Plates, glasses, silverware, and napkins were in place. She lit the candles and whirled around to face him.

"Which one?" He chuckled wrapping a hand around her neck, slipping a finger under her chin, tilting it up so he could ravage her mouth once again.

"Both," she murmured against his lips, curving her torso into the contours of his naked body. "Shall we eat before round two? Or let it get cold?" she whispered as her cell phone song split the quiet.

"Don't answer it," he urged, lifting her up on the counter, slipping between her legs. His large hands gently cupped her face and gazed into her emerald green eyes, thumbs caressing her cheeks. "I love you Pepper McKay, more than I ever thought possible."

A quick glance at the screen and she let it go to voice mail, returning her gaze to Lathen. "Mr. Quartz, that's quite a declaration…but…I love you more." She wrapped her arms around his neck, brushing her lips over his, then vaulted off the counter into his arms as her stomach growled loudly.

Lathen chuckled and let her slide down his body until her feet touched the floor. "Guess we better feed you."

She hesitated only a beat then reached for the homemade rolls in the bread warmer, walked to the table, and set the basket next to the pot roast. "Dinner is served."

Lathen checked to make sure Ember and Tonk's food bowls were full and added fresh water to the other bowls. He pulled out Pepper's chair, waited for her to be seated, and sat down in the chair beside her. After finishing the meal and he was completely stuffed, Pepper pulled a pumpkin pie from the lower oven. Lathen groaned. "You could have told me we had dessert."

Grinning she served the slices of pie with a heaping helping of whipped cream and set the plates on the table with a flourish. "You don't have to eat it."

"Oh, no, never turn down homemade pumpkin pie." He scooped up a piece of pie on his fork, slid it into his mouth, closed his eyes, and savored the flavor. "This is the best damn pumpkin pie I have ever tasted."

"And just how many pumpkin pies have you tasted?"

"Lots. The women of the pack used to bring entire dinners over on the holidays. They were trying to get Dad's attention. The ladies were great cooks. Dad was never interested, but we sure reaped the benefits when I was growing up. But none match the flavor of your pie."

"It's my gram's special recipe."

"Well, it's delicious. I talked to Dad and Kolby

earlier. They're fine with spending Thanksgiving at your parents. I told Dad we'd have Duncan call him with the nearest airport location and directions to their house."

As if right on cue, Pepper's phone chimed. With a mouth full of pie, she checked the screen, put the phone to her ear, and swallowed. "Hi, Mom."

Lathen pushed back from the table, leaned the chair on its back legs, and put his hands behind his head.

Shaking her head, Pepper pointed to the floor and narrowed her eyes. The chair dropped to all four legs, and he stood. Walking over to the fireplace, he stirred the embers and tossed several logs on the fire. Within moments, flames raced over the dried wood. By the time Pepper finished talking to her mom and joined him on the sofa facing the fireplace, the fingers of flames had transformed into a roaring fire.

"Wine?" She set the crystal stemware on the table in front of the couch and poured red wine into both glasses. Lathen picked up a glass, swirled the crimson liquid in the glass watching it wink in the firelight. Then he brought it up to his nose, sniffed, and took a sip. "Excellent."

"It's your favorite, but thought you might be too full for wine."

"Never."

"Mom was thrilled when I agreed to her plan. I gave her Elijah's phone number and instructed her to have Dad call with directions. Didn't want your family winding up in Alabama or worse. When my parents first moved to Colorado, Mom swore the mountains moved, and she wound up calling Dad for directions to get home numerous times, to hear him tell it." Pepper roared with laughter until tears streamed down her face. Lathen's puzzled expression turned to disbelief. In between fits of giggles she said, "Really, she did. Navigationally impaired that one."

He stretched his arm around her shoulder and drew her close, leaning his head against hers watching the flames bounce and weave in a strange dance casting shadows across the room that had warmed up nicely. "We are going to have to have dinner in the nude more often."

Chapter Three
Wedding Plans, Dresses, Flowers, and Catering—
Can't We Just Run Off and Get Married?

Pepper sat at her computer in the office scrolling through wedding dress sites Gwen emailed to her. Nothing but fru-fru dresses. Pepper hated fru-fru dresses. All she wanted was a nice shimmery, cream dress; she wasn't a fan of white. The gown had to fit her curves, Lathen's words not hers, and be comfortable. One that didn't mop the floor with a disagreeable train. Not so tight that she couldn't bend over or a skirt so full that she couldn't sit down and knocked over everything the dress came in contact with. Was that too much to ask?

She skimmed a few more dresses. Moved her mouse to the little X in the corner of the page and clicked. Nothing there. Also, she had no intention of squishing her poor feet into pointy toed, four-inch spike heeled shoes like on the other website Gwen suggested. For heaven's sake, she was nearly six feet tall.

Nope, plain and simple was her intention, and if she couldn't find something in the next ten minutes, she'd wear jeans, a nice sweater, and tennies to her wedding. A soft laugh in the corner of the room made her jump as the computer chimed another email's arrival. With her fingertips, she rubbed her throbbing temples and glanced over top the computer screen to see Ashling fading in and out of view.

"Is there something I can do for you?" Pepper grumped narrowing her eyes as fingers continuing to massage her temples. "Aren't you out of your element?"

"Not really, just prefer outdoors rather than inside a stuffy building. Haven't seen you at the pond for a while and wanted to discuss flowers for the wedding."

"None, not going to have any. Going to run away in jeans and get married."

Ashling snorted atrociously unlady like. "Okay. I'll do as I please." She disappeared leaving only a wisp of mist curling in the corner.

"Ashling come back here," Pepper demanded clicking the new email icon on her computer. She chewed on her bottom lip as the email opened on screen. In the center was a picture of a shimmering cream dress, floor length, with matching ballet type slippers. A simple tiny deep purple bow topped each shoe. In the email, Lathen's step-mother, Amy, described the material as unbelievably soft and stretchy. The dress was well within Pepper's self-imposed budget for a dress she'd wear once. Her lips twitched while she emailed Amy for the location of the dress.

As it turned out, one of the women from the pack had seen the dress in a magazine and thought it was perfect for Pepper. One of them recreated it in what she thought would be Pepper's size, and presented it to Amy, with the condition that she would only accept payment for the price of the material if Pepper loved the dress. Amy also indicated the shoes were available in a little store in Alaska, what size did she take?

Pepper scooped up her phone and touched in

Amy's number. She answered on the first ring.

"Got my emails, huh? Don't you love the dress?"

"You have no idea. It's like you plucked that dress right out of my mind. The shoes too. I wear eight and a half. Any chance they have that size?"

"As a matter of fact, they do. I checked the shoe and sizes before emailing you. Figured about now you were pulling your hair out," Amy said with a soft laugh.

"Exactly. I was contemplating running away to get married. But couldn't do that to our families. You're a life saver."

"Well, thanks. I still remember going through the same thing putting together Elijah's and my wedding, not so long ago. I'll just purchase the shoes, pack them and the dress with us at Thanksgiving. Will that work?"

"Sure. Send me the receipt, I'll reimburse you."

"Not necessary, my gift to you. You have no idea the change in Elijah since he talks with both his boys on a regular basis. We know you are responsible for Lathen's transformation to some extent. Besides, us non fru-fru girls have to stick together," she said on a laugh.

"Thank you so much." Pepper's shoulders relaxed as she slid down in her high-back chair.

"One more thing. Another lady in the pack makes lovely floral tiaras with trailing vines down the back. A deep purple rose tiara would go great with the dress and shoes, if you haven't gotten a veil yet."

"Veils haven't even crossed my mind. Wasn't going to wear one, but what you describe sounds perfect."

"I'll take care of it," Amy said.

"You've been a huge help."

"I'm glad. Love to you both. Call if you need

anything. See ya soon," Amy said in a cheerful voice.

"Love you too." Pepper touched the screen ending the call. The door banged open, and Lathen strode in, mist curling behind him, Ember and Tonk scooting in as he closed the door.

He frowned at the door. "Gotta get that fixed," he said more to himself than to Pepper. "Seems we have a very disgruntled ghost at the pond," he said forehead still creased. "Scratch that, I believe she's followed me here." The mist formed into a woman's shape.

"Ashling, I'm sorry. It's just that…well…tell me about the flowers," Pepper said then held up an index finger.

Lathen shrugged and leaned against the door frame. "That was easy."

"Amy is the greatest person in the world."

"My dad would agree with you wholeheartedly. Me too. But I'm curious, what has she done now?"

"Only found the perfect wedding dress, shoes, and tiara." Pepper beamed.

Making three check marks in the air, Lathen said, "That's three fewer things to stress out about." He winked at her. "I think your aunt has some great ideas about the flowers, let her handle the setting at the pond." He opened the door and stepped outside before turning around to admire her. "Just my two cents." Tonk bounded out in front of him, while Ember curled up in the corner on her blanket. He closed the door quietly.

"All right Ashling, you have my complete attention." Pepper smiled as she remembered the same stance she was seeing now long ago, from Ashling when she patiently waited to discuss something.

"We've decided if you approve, that blooming rose bushes will be conjured around the pond and climbing roses at the base of the arbor." Ashling went on to explain the exact details.

"That sounds great. Go for it."

Ashling smiled wide, then frowned. "There's a hawk of some kind hanging around the pond since last night. It's dragging one wing. You might want to take a look. I was going to tell Lathen at the end of our conversation, but he didn't give me a chance, just strode up here quick as you please." Ashling made a clucking sound. "A bit bossy that one."

"Thank you, I'll check it out." Pepper shrugged into her parka. Ember looked up, stretched, and padded to the door waiting patiently for it to open. Ashling's filmy form trailed behind Pepper and Ember.

When Pepper arrived, Lathen already had a crate and blanket on the bench. He was talking softly to the frightened bird. He looked up at Pepper's arrival. "Believe it's got a busted wing but won't let me get close, not without risking my digits." He held a hand in front of her and wiggled his fingers slowly.

Closing her eyes, she connected and reassured the bird as she moved toward it. "What happened to you sweetie?" she crooned. "Let me take a look at that wing." Pepper bent down and carefully lifted the wing slightly. The bird screeched and lunged at her as she released the wing. "Yep, it's broken."

Lathen handed her the blanket. Pepper wrapped the bird in the blanket, careful to support the wing and tucked the bundle next to her body, hurrying to the seabird aviary. Lathen followed with the crate. Once inside, she placed the bird on the examining table and taped the wing to its body with vet wrap.

To help the bird relax, she administered a painkiller and placed a call to the vet's office. Dylan wasn't in, but Pepper left a message for her to stop by when she had a chance and gave a description of the bird's injury. Lathen transferred the bird from the table to a heated cube, then lowered the lights.

"He should sleep for a couple hours, then we'll see if Kaylee can get him to eat. The hawk is in pretty good shape physically, except for the wing. Too soon to tell if he'll be able to fly again."

"Where is Kaylee? Haven't seen her all morning."

"I let her out early. She came back with a big flopping fish and flew in her aviary before I walked to the office." She shrugged. "I held the door open for her, but she tilted her head at me then resumed tearing into her fish from the perch. She may have a bit of arthritis in that wing and leg that bothers her during the winter storms."

"Oh, could be." His arms enveloped Pepper, and she leaned into him. "You love this, don't you?"

"Yes, it's all I ever wanted to do. You're not so bad at rehab yourself. Need to work on your mental communication with the creatures."

"Hey, I'm not the creature whisperer, you are."

"But you have the ability, and you should start honing it. Could be very useful." She winked at him, wriggled out of his grasp, and looked thoughtful.

"Oh, no… I know that look." He groaned holding his head with both hands.

Ignoring his antics, she said, "I'd like to put wireless cameras in the seabird aviary and connect them to the computer in the cabin. That way we can keep an eye on the injured birds without running down here several times a day. In fact..." Tilting her face toward him, she peeked at him from under her long lashes.

Lathen shook his head and sighed. "You'd like them installed in all the habitats, eventually."

"You read my mind."

"Of course." Pulling a pad of paper and pen out of his coat pocket, he scribbled a few notes and tucked the pad back in his pocket. "I'll check our inventory before ordering the cameras on-line later today. Next time we head to town, I'll pick up whatever else is needed for the install from the hardware store."

"Sounds great. I appreciate it and you." She stepped away, blew him a kiss.

"It's a good thing you had the foresight to fall in love with a handyman."

"Yep, that was fortunate, but don't forget computer guru too." She grinned. "Let's head back to the office. There's still work to be done. Those invoices are not going to pay themselves."

One final check on the hawk and they strode toward the exit. The heavy wooden door gave a loud nails on chalkboard sound when Lathen yanked it open. Pepper winced. "Damp and cold got to the hinges."

"I'll work on it, later." He pulled out his pad again and jotted a few notes.

She sashayed through, waited for him to close and latch the door, then tucked her hand through the crook of his arm. They wandered up the path toward the office.

Pepper stomped the snow off her boots and wiped them on the rug. Lathen followed suit before entering the office. She sat down at the computer while he strode into the supply room. A light tap on the door had Pepper jerking her head up as Dylan stuck her head inside.

"Got your message. I was in the neighborhood, so I stopped in." Her gaze wandered from the inbox to the pile of files next to Pepper. "Looks like you're inundated. I'll check on the hawk and be on my way. She's in the converted barn?"

"Yes. Thanks. I'll go with you." Pepper pushed up from her chair.

"No need. If there's a problem, I'll be back."

"I appreciate it." She eased into the chair.

There were emails from the caterer, the bakery, and the stationery shop. The wedding invitation proofs were ready for her review. The cake decorator wanted to know if Pepper was sure about the purple piping and roses on her wedding cake, and Love Caters All had the menu ready for the wedding reception. Could she look it over? Pepper opened the attachment and printed it out.

On the corner of her desk, stacked neatly in her inbox were today's unopened mail and invoices to be paid. Pepper picked up the invoices, logged into her bank's site, and systematically entered the bills to be paid. Synced the bank transactions to her accounting program, then drew a line through that task on her to-do list and picked up the menu printout.

Tool belt cinched around his waist, Lathen swept into the room and knelt behind the door. He installed a door stop, squirted lube into the hinges, then he touched up the paint where the door handle had nicked the wall. "I ordered eight cameras, that should do for starters. Checked our stock of batteries and wiring and I believe we are set. The cameras will be here in a couple of days so I can install them and perform a test run before we leave for Colorado. In fact, the system will be accessible by computer and smart phone anywhere we have Wi-Fi or cell service. I'll add security patches to the system so only authorized users can get in."

"That's wonderful. If you've got a minute, could you go over the menu for our reception?" She held out the three-page document for his inspection.

He took the menu from her and looked over it. "There is nowhere near enough food to feed those folks coming from Alaska. Better double the amounts. If we have leftovers, we'll freeze them or serve them as snacks. I believe several pack members are planning to attend the wedding but leaving immediately afterward. Only Dad, Amy, Kolby, and Hayley are planning to stay through New Year."

"So what you're saying is we better stock the freezer before the wedding. I only ordered one five-layer cake. Should I order a couple sheet cakes too?"

"Wouldn't be a bad idea. Since we'll have guests throughout the holidays, I don't think food will go to waste. Gwen is coming for the wedding, and she will be staying with us. Dad and Amy can stay in the visiting veterinarian quarters on site. Hayley said she was going to book the same suite at the Sea Crest Inn that they had in August."

"Yeah, Mom and Dad made arrangements to stay in the cottage they rented this fall beginning the first of December through January. Dad mentioned purchasing a cottage in Lobster Cove. I think he and Mom reconnected with several friends when they were here for the LCWRRC grand opening celebration. It'd be nice to have them closer once in a while."

"Your dad liked helping out around the rescue while they were here."

"He sure did. I'm also going to try to convince Hayley and Kolby to stay in our other spare room."

Lathen shook his head. "Good luck. She loves the Inn."

"But she can't sit outside on the balcony or at the beach…so we'll see. Okay, back to the menu. I'll have the caterers double the menu and add two full sheet cakes with the bakery. Do you think deep purple piping on the white cake is odd?"

"No. I think whatever you want is fine. It's our wedding. It doesn't matter what others think. But I'm not sure Ember is going to like wearing that purple bow you have for her. Tonk is not going to cooperate with the purple bow-tie you got for him."

"They both will cooperate after I promise a special treat," Pepper said smugly.

"Oh, I see, bribery it is. If you're ready to wrap this up, let's release Kaylee and take food to the hawk. Then we can return to the cabin and relax the rest of the evening."

Pepper blew out a breath. "I still have the wedding invitations to proof, then I'm done." She clicked on the email attachment, and a picture of the invitation filled the screen.

Lathen bent over the back of Pepper's chair, laid his cheek on the top of her head staring at the image. "We should drive into town tomorrow and physically see the wedding invitation before we order them. The screen version looks okay, but the real thing could look quite different. Don't you think?"

"You're probably right."

"You haven't made the plane reservations for Thanksgiving yet, have you?"

"Not yet. I did look up flights, but I still don't feel right about leaving Kaylee, Ember, and Tonk on our first Thanksgiving together." On a sigh, she asked, "Want to take a look at what I found?" She half-heartedly handed him several sheets of paper with different flight times and dates.

His lips twitched as he took the papers. "No, why don't you leave the transportation to me." Lathen tossed the schedules in the trash. "I think you"—he touched the tip of her nose—"Kaylee, Ember, and Tonk will appreciate my creative travel arrangements."

"Lathen we can't drive to Colorado in November."

"Who said anything about driving? Don't worry your pretty little head about it. I've got it covered. Now turn the computer off, and let's go home." He waited for her to get out of the program and click on the shutdown icon, then tugged her out of the chair, and turned the light off. Dog and wolf waited anxiously at the door.

Chapter Four
The Next Couple of Weeks Would've Put a Whirlwind to Shame

The next morning after checking on the rehab creatures, Lathen and Pepper drove to the stationery shop in Lobster Cove. They approved the beautiful wedding invitations with deep purple trim and lettering on cream textured paper. The manager said the invitations would be ready by week's end. They returned to the truck.

Lathen stopped in front of the bakery and turned to her. "I have a few errands to run. Do you want to ride along, or would you rather take care of the cake and the other items on your list, and then we'll meet at Maggie's for lunch?"

"Since the sun is still out, I'll take care of the cake arrangements and a couple other things right around here, then walk the block to the diner and wait for you. Looks like the predicted storm will roll in by late afternoon. I'd prefer to be at home when it does."

"Fair enough. See you in about an hour."

She started to push open the door and slid out, when he grabbed her arm.

"Not so fast. There is a two kiss minimum to get out of this truck." He laughed and pulled her to him, taking her mouth with his in a lingering kiss, then brushed his lips lightly over hers and released her.

"That will do for now, but it's only worth a kiss and a half. You have a half kiss deficit."

"You know you're crazy. Right?"

"Crazy about you," he confirmed.

She slipped out of the truck, turned, and brought her fingers to her lips. She blew him a sassy kiss with a wink. "There, we're even." And she closed the door.

****

After finishing his errands in Lobster Cove, Lathen put his phone in the hands-free cradle and turned the truck onto Highway 3 toward Bar Harbor. Using his index finger, he tapped the hands-free control and said "Call Jay." Then he glanced at his watch. *Yep, just enough time to catch him at the office.*

"Hey, you old dog, what ya up to?" Jay answered good-naturedly. "Is it true?"

"Hi Jay, not much—same ol' same ol'. Is what true?" Lathen checked his speed and glanced at his rearview mirror.

"Heard you're getting married next month."

"Geez...who told you?"

"A better question. Why didn't you tell me?"

"I was just heading your direction to do exactly that. You going to be around the office for a bit? But yes, it's true. The wedding is set for the afternoon of December 22nd, on the Winter Solstice."

"Marrying the McKay witch, if my sources are correct," Jay said in a smug voice. "Her name Pepper? Right? Built the Lobster Cove Wildlife Center on the McKay property."

"Yep. If Q & A time is over, now, I'd like to stop by and discuss a situation with you, maybe hire your services."

"Sure. I'll be here for another twenty minutes or so…"

****

Lathen yanked open the door to Maggie's and strode into the diner. A breeze ruffled the blue and white checked window curtains as he settled into a blue vinyl booth facing the street to wait for Pepper. Jay had cut him a heck of a deal, and the arrangements were complete. Resting his head back against the booth, he closed his eyes for a couple beats and hoped fervently that today was Kate's day off. When footsteps approached and stopped beside him, he opened his eyes to Kate standing beside the cream and chrome table tapping her pen against her order pad. *Shit.*

"Afternoon Kate. It's been a long while." Lathen shifted in the seat and checked out the window for Pepper. *Not long enough.*

They'd made a point to patronize Maggie's even though Kate was put out that he had chosen Pepper over her. Not that there was a chance in hell he would have asked Kate out in the first place, except in her wildest dreams. The scene a few months back in town square gave the town fodder for gossip but hadn't lasted long.

"It has. Heard you and the witch set a date," Kate said setting two glasses of water on the table then examining her hot pink nails.

"We did."

A bell above the door jangled as it opened. Lathen twisted in the seat, then stood while Pepper made her way to the booth. She kissed him and scooted into the booth. He slid in beside her, arm around her shoulder.

"Lathen confirmed congratulations are in order," Kate said matter-of-factly.

"Well, thank you, Kate," Pepper said cheerfully. "I was finishing up a few last minute wedding details before the Thanksgiving holiday."

"Do I need to give you a few minutes, or are you ready to order?" Kate said in a bored voice.

"We're ready." Lathen peered at Pepper, who nodded her head. "We'll have two burgers, fries, and coffee for me, hot chocolate for Pepper."

"Oh don't forget…two pieces of the homemade blueberry pie, *à la mode*. Please. I've been looking forward to pie all day." Pepper smacked her lips and grinned.

"Got it." Kate put her pad back in her white apron and flounced toward the kitchen.

"You don't want Kate to feel like she's won, by staying away, but I don't think…" Lathen said.

"It was supposed to be Kate's day off. Sandy said she'd be working the afternoon shift. Besides, they have the best lobster burgers in town. Kate doesn't bother me anymore. You?" Pepper spread her napkin on her lap.

"No—she never really did. Hated how she treated you. That's all." Lathen swirled his glass of mostly ice and tried to get a sip of water. Ice cubes shifted and fell on the tip of his nose, water splashed on his face.

Pepper pressed her lips together to keep from laughing. In the end, a giggle slipped out. "Did you get all your errands done?"

Taking the napkin, he wiped his face. "Yep, I did. Tied up all the loose ends. Looking forward to seeing everyone for Thanksgiving without interruptions. I can't wait to visit your parents' spread in Colorado."

"Yeah, I'm kinda looking forward to it myself. When they retired a few years ago, Dad was tired of living in the city, and Mom was okay with whatever he wanted to do. So they bought land near Evergreen, Colorado, and built a house. I haven't visited since their new house was finished. Come to think of it." She glanced out the window. "The plans and framing I did see from pictures, looked a lot like our cabin, less the additions."

"That doesn't surprise me." He reached for her hand, covered it with his. "How about you, everything set?"

"Yep. Took care of the cakes and doubled the menu with Maya's mom. She runs the catering business now. All that's left is to address and mail out the invitations before we leave. If we leave. Getting kinda late to get reservations."

"Oh, we're leaving. Travel arrangements are made." He glanced around. "Tell you about them on the way home."

The bell chimed again when Sandy sprinted in the door, her cheeks red from the cold. She glanced in Pepper and Lathen's direction as Kate took off her apron and pushed past. Sandy walked over to the table. "Sorry about that Pepper. Damn car wouldn't start this morning, had to have it towed. Asked Kate to cover. I'm going to regret that. I would have been here a lot sooner but the mechanic…" She raised her hands and made chattering motions with them. "Talked and talked then made me wait while he wrote up an estimate. He's never done that, but whatever."

"No problem. We just placed our order, and Kate was mostly pleasant." Pepper shrugged. "If it wasn't for your lobster burgers…"

"She better be, or Maggie will have her head.

Besides, Kate's dating one of the dungeon masters from the Red Club, so she's moved on. What a hunk…uh…if you like that kind." Sandy's cheeks pinked. "I better get your drinks. The usual?"

"That's more information than we need." Lathen laughed. "Yeah, hot chocolate for Pepper and coffee for me."

Eyebrow raised, Pepper leaned over and whispered, "Bet he's got nothing on you." A seductive smile curved the corners of her lips.

"That depends—" Lathen whispered, a sly grin tugged at one corner of his mouth.

Sandy came back with the drinks and a tray full of food. "Hot off the grill. Enjoy." She served the burgers and hurried off to wait on a table of boisterous men who just pushed through the door and sat down.

Famished, Lathen took a big bite of the burger as Pepper dabbed her french fry in the ketchup and nibbled on it. The storm clouds rolled in, and the wind howled around the diner. He chewed thoughtfully watching townspeople pass by the window leaning into the wind. Some stopped and waved, others came into the diner to discuss holiday plans and ask about the wedding. The diner was the hub of community gossip. The men were worse than the women at times. Still the tight-knit community was what drew Lathen to set down roots and start his business after drifting over the country for a couple of years doing odd jobs.

Pepper took the last bite of blueberry pie with the last dab of ice cream and glanced out the window. "Guess we better get going. I left Kaylee out along with Ember and Tonk. Didn't think we'd be gone so long."

"They'll be fine. If the weather gets too bad,

Kaylee will settle into the greenhouse until we get home. Tonk and Ember will use the dog door into the mammal habitat."

The wind tugged at Pepper's scarf as she exited the door Lathen held open for her. The minute they got into the truck, Pepper shifted in her seat to face him. "So what are the transportation plans?"

Lathen chuckled as he turned the key in the ignition and put the truck in gear. "Just can't wait. Talked to a buddy of mine, Jay, he owns an air charter service. Come to find out, he's headed to Denver to spend the holiday with his sister and her family."

"Makes it convenient. He's okay transporting a dog, wolf, and osprey?" She cocked her head in his direction.

"We'll be flying out of Bar Harbor the Sunday before Thanksgiving and returning the following Sunday. He has a booking that week." Lathen twisted in the seat and waited for traffic to clear before backing out of the parking space. "Tonk, Ember, and Kaylee will need airline approved crates, but they are welcome to accompany us. I spoke to your dad yesterday. He indicated there is plenty room on their twenty acres for them to run and the acre of property around the house is fenced in. Kaylee can hunt the area as well."

"I can pack frozen fish in dry ice for the trip too. Lathen that is perfect!" She wrapped her arms around his neck and claimed his lips with reckless abandon.

He put the truck back in park and surrendered to her appreciative attentions. With demanding mastery, he smothered her lips caressing them with his tongue until he heard several footsteps crunching on the gravel parking lot. "I think this best wait until we get home.

But I appreciate your enthusiasm."

The color crept up her neck, spread across her cheeks when the group of construction workers from the diner passed by the truck. One guy let out a wolf whistle closest to her window then grinned waving at Lathen, his hand raised in a meant no harm gesture. Lathen waved him on, backed out of the parking space, and turned onto the highway home.

Upon their arrival Tonk and Ember raced up the driveway to greet them, but Kaylee was nowhere in sight. After ear scratches and kind words to the wolf and dog, Lathen unlocked the door to the cabin then followed Pepper around to the greenhouse.

The osprey was perched on the edge of the corner shelf situated high on the wall. Pieces of a dead fish lay on the ground below Kaylee, she blinked sleepily at Pepper and ruffled her feathers…twice.

"Well, I guess she made herself right at home." Sheathing her arm in leather, she requested the bird to step up. Lathen grabbed a shovel and scooped up the dead fish parts depositing them in the compost bin and securing the barrel's lid.

"Usually, she doesn't bring her fresh caught food this far up."

"Oh, she's unhappy with us, and that is her way of showing it." Pepper stroked the back of her hand gently over the bird's wing. "We have a great surprise for you." She crooned to Kaylee.

Inside the cabin, Lathen tossed several split logs in the fireplace, then walked over to the stack of newspapers. Pepper laughed and flipped her hand toward the logs. Orange, yellow, and blue flames raced up the raw edges of the logs.

"Show off." Lathen grunted and dropped the papers he'd crumpled back on the pile. Pepper went down the hall to Kaylee's attached aviary. He picked up Tonk and Ember's food and water bowls, filled them and placed them on the navy mat in the far corner of the kitchen floor when someone pounded loudly at the front door.

Chapter Five
Wounded Owl, Poachers, and a Moose, Oh My

Tonk and Ember diverted their attention from the food bowls to the front door, rushing ahead of Lathen growling and barking menacingly. Pepper sprinted up the hall, paused to backtrack and close the aviary door into the cabin. He saw her stop out of the corner of his eye as he checked the computer monitor on the far wall. Before he reached for the door handle, he commanded dog and wolf to step back and sit away from the door's path. Once they obeyed, he opened the front door to Rocky and Janice, neighbors a few miles down the gravel road.

Rocky's old jacket had what appeared to be new rips on the arms, and Janice's hand was bleeding.

"What the hell happened to you two? Come on in." Lathen opened the door wide. "Pepper, can you grab the first aid kit?"

"Sure thing." She scurried down the hall in the direction of the bathroom.

"Let me get a look at that." He reached out to grasp Janice's hand when she pulled back.

"It's really nothing. But the huge owl in the back of our car, hopefully still wrapped in a couple tarps is hurt badly. I think." Out of breath, she sucked in air and continued. "Knew the vet clinic wasn't open this late. So we rushed over here."

"Okay. Pep, we got an injured owl in the back seat of Rocky's car." Lathen called down the hall then reached into the crate of supplies they kept next to the door and yanked out a pair of leather gantlets, stuffed them in his back pocket. He glanced at Tonk and Ember, commanding, "Down and stay."

Pepper came sprinting around the corner, handed the first aid kit to Rocky, and jerked open the front door with several bath towels draped over her arms. "What is an owl doing in the back seat of your car?" She directed the question to Rocky but kept moving out the door with Lathen at her heels. Through the car window, she saw a lump moving slowly under a tangle of blue and green tarps. She closed her eyes and breathed deeply, attempting to connect with the owl. Lathen observed her while opening the car door slowly.

"Anything?"

She shook her head. "All I'm getting is panic and pain from the owl. No real connection." Pepper gingerly put her hand on the tarp a few inches from the moving lump.

Lathen shoved her arm out of the way. "You're going to need stitches too if you don't let me handle this bird."

Pepper swung around then noticed the leather gloves on Lathen's hands. She backed away, glanced toward the doorway where Janice and Rocky still stood watching. Turning her back on them, she murmured a couple words, her arms and hands became immediately encased in leather. Her warm breath swirled around her head like smoke, as did Lathen's in the frosty air. Carefully, Pepper poked at the tarp and was able to distinguish where the bird was as opposed to the extra bunching material.

"It's okay. You're going to be fine. No one is going to hurt you," Pepper sing-songed soothingly. Her words and abilities of calm won out, and the bird relaxed just a bit. Lathen was able to hold its wings against the body and back out of the car, ripped pieces of bloody tarp hung awkwardly from his arms while he held the bird firmly in front of him. "It's a big one."

"Let's go directly to the seabird aviary. Not going to want to try to move the owl again."

As they passed by the open front door of the cabin, Pepper stopped and quickly explained what they were doing to the waiting couple, asked one of them to call and leave a message for Dylan. She reinforced the stay command to the canines, then closed the door.

Catching up with Lathen, she said, "I left Tonk and Ember in a stay. We don't need them sniffing around and scaring the owl any more than it already is. Rocky will join us as soon as he gets Janice bandaged up. She may need stitches but is refusing at the moment."

"Heartbeat is slowing, so panic may be subsiding." Lathen shifted the bird's back against his chest for a better hold.

"That's good. It's not going into shock."

Lathen rested the owl on the examining table and with caution peeled the layers of tarp away from the bird. "The feather patterns on its neck and back are barred crosswise, and its belly is barred lengthwise, no ear tuffs. It appears to be a Barred Owl."

"There you go fellow. It's not so bad." She reached for a light sedative then moved away after looking at the bird's dark brown eyes and examining a lump forming on its head. "Must have sustained a hard blow to the head."

"I thought the same thing when you touched the raised area on its head. Feathers are caked with blood over the lump, wing edge is sliced, and there are abrasions above its talons."

"I don't think those are serious. We'll clean him up, administer antibiotics per Dylan's instruction sheet until we hear from her. Can we get him on the scale, get a weight?"

"He's a big boy. I'd say that wing span is well over three feet." Lathen maneuvered the bird onto the scale and let go for a beat. Looks like a little over two pounds."

"Thanks." She cleaned the bird up with warm water then drew the drug into a syringe. "Hold him still." She stared into the owl's eyes then administered the shot. The bird jumped and gave a shrill hoot.

"We can put him in one of the heated cubes with a few towels. I'll stay out here with him tonight."

"No, we'll stay out here with him," Lathen corrected.

The heavy wooden door to the aviary, which used to be an old barn, squeaked open when Rocky strode in. "Is the bird going to be okay?"

"Yeah, I think so. What happened?" Pepper's cell phone rang in her pocket. She held up an index finger and looked at the screen, frowned. "It's the DIFW (Department of Inland Fisheries and Wildlife)."

"What do you suppose the wildlife department wants?" Lathen asked as Pepper put the phone to her ear.

"Well, that was what I was just getting to…" Rocky paused glancing from Lathen to Pepper. "The owl flew into the side of a pickup truck when the driver was using a spotlight toward the forest. We were following the truck on the way home and heard shots. Suddenly, the owl hit the truck. Must have been blinded by the spotlight. They didn't shoot it. Did they?"

"No, there are no gunshot wounds on the bird, mostly scrapes and abrasions from hitting the truck. Hell of a lump on its head. Your story explains a lot of its injuries."

"Anyway, Janice called the DIFW, reported what we saw. The driver gunned the truck, took off, and the poor owl lay quiet for a couple minutes then started flopping on the ground. We couldn't leave it like that. Got the tarp out of the trunk and threw it over the bird. That's when it really came to life. Gathered it all up, but its foot came out of the tarp and clawed Jan pretty bad."

"Next time call us; we've got equipment to transport birds of prey safely. But you did good, probably saved its life. It could have flopped onto the road and gotten run over."

"That's what we thought. So here we are." Rocky shrugged.

Lathen turned his attention to Pepper as she said, "We'll be there ASAP. Got to stabilize an owl, and we'll be there. Don't shoot it! Sounds like it was only grazed, a little rest and antibiotics, he'll survive." Pepper tapped the screen ending the call and turned toward the guys, the color drained out of her face. "A young male moose has been shot, a mile down our road. The officer thinks it's only a few months old. No sign of its mother or herd. Sounds about the same place you found the owl."

"I knew it. They were poachers." Rocky cursed. "How bad?"

"Hopefully, not life threatening, but won't know 'til we get there."

"I'll hook up the trailer and meet you out front." Lathen strode to the door and yanked it open. "Rocky we'll probably need your help."

"I'll let Jan know what's happening and see if she wants to wait here for us or go on home." Pepper tossed medical supplies into her bag, grabbed the tranq gun, then sprinted out the door and up the path toward the cabin.

Lathen hitched the trailer to the truck, and Rocky climbed in the back seat of the truck's crew cab. Pepper barreled up to the vehicle and hopped in the front seat. "Hurry." She slapped her hand on the dash.

"Yes, ma'am." Lathen put the truck in gear and sped down the road, throwing rock and gravel in his wake.

As he slowed to a stop beside the DIFW vehicles, Pepper jumped out and sprinted across the field. Lathen turned the ignition off and bolted after her. It took about five minutes to find the officers, who pointed to an area where a young moose lay, breathing hard. Pepper stared toward the wounded creature and began walking toward the young moose.

An officer grabbed her arm, without a word, she wrenched away and continued walking. Lathen shook his head meeting the officer's gaze. "She's got this."

****

The animal's head swung around, and he stumbled to his feet. Pepper heard the animal's rapid breathing and heartbeat. It could be going into shock. Using the tranquilizer gun was a risk, but there wasn't another option. Glancing around she counted four big strapping men. They could hoist that moose into the trailer. Raising the gun to her shoulder, she fired. The moose took two steps, paused to look at her, and crashed to the ground. She rushed to where he'd fallen.

After men loaded the moose into the trailer, the wildlife officers followed behind Lathen's truck back to the cabin. They helped unload the unconscious animal into the small stable attached to the mammal habitat. Dylan Foster was waiting at the cabin and ran down the path to the building. The officers said their goodbyes. Lathen thanked them for the help and walked back into the stable.

Dr. Foster completed a thorough exam and turned to Pepper. "Barring infection, the young moose should make a full recovery."

"Sorry I had to tranq him, but I didn't see any other way to move him without someone being injured," Pepper said.

"No, you did fine. The bullets only grazed him, but they did cut into the flank muscle pretty deep and his panic caused him to fall, so his left side is pretty scraped and bruised. It will be several weeks before we can release him into the wild. Do you have room to keep him here?"

"Yes, we do but were planning to be gone over Thanksgiving. Meeting Lathen's parents and his brother's family at my mom and dad's house in Colorado. But I guess we could…"

"No problem, I'm staying in town for Thanksgiving. I can stop by a couple times a day to check on him. Who's watching the rest of your animals?"

"Alec is. He will be on site while we are gone. Speaking of others, there is a Barred Owl I'd like you to take a look at. It was injured during the same incident. Blinded by the damn spotlight and flew headlong into the truck. Appears he hit sideways to the truck and slid to the ground. Lots of bruising and lacerations but that's about it. A huge lump on its head with a laceration, but pupils are normal and responsive, so hopefully no serious head trauma. Going to have a bad headache for a while, I'll bet."

Dylan picked up her medical bag. "Lead the way, we'll go check him out."

By the time Dylan left and Pepper made sure all the creatures were secure for the night, it was well past midnight. Lathen let out a jaw-popping yawn. "The cameras are supposed to arrive tomorrow. I'm going to call Alec first thing in the morning and see if we can't get them all installed before we leave."

"That would be great." She stifled a yawn with the back of her hand. "We don't have to stay with the owl, Dylan said he's resting comfortably, pupils are responsive, no indication of concussion, or injury to neck or spine, only the lump on his head. Her guess, it was a glancing blow, not a direct hit."

"If you want to stay, we'll haul out the folding cots. Not a problem."

"If Dylan isn't worried, we don't need to be either."

"Okay. Back to the cameras. I know you would feel better about leaving if you were able to keep tabs on everyone."

"I have complete faith in Alec to handle it while

we're gone, but it would be nice to check in once in a while." Pepper smiled sleepily. "I'm going to print out mailing labels for the wedding invitations. I can't see handwriting all the envelopes, still having time to pack, and making sure everything here is done before we go. I know it seems a little..." *Unless...maybe I could use an alternative...*

"Sounds good to me. Don't worry about it. I doubt anyone will care how the invitations are addressed, just that they get one." Lathen chuckled. "If they don't like it, they don't have to come."

Pepper swiped at him, but he sidestepped her scooping her up in his arms. "You, young lady should be in bed."

She wrapped her arms around his neck as he carried her up the stairs into their bedroom. After they took a quick shower, he pulled the covers down, she plopped onto the bed, and he crawled in beside her. Resting on his side, he pulled her to him. She snuggled into him, nibbling at his neck as her fingertips caressed the contours of his back. He relaxed, her fingers slowed, then stopped as her breathing became shallow and regular.

****

The sound of a sonar ping penetrated his sleep muzzy brain. *What the hell?* Then he remembered leaving a message for Alec last night. Lathen rolled over, reached for his phone, and tried to focus on the screen. It was eight o'clock, and Alec's text said that he'd be over by nine.

Pepper rolled over and breathed a kiss at the base of Lathen's throat. "Good morning."

"And a good morning to you." He tilted her chin up

and kissed her full lips. "I'd love to finish what we started last night, but Alec is on his way over."

"Why?" She blinked at him sleepily.

"To help me install the cameras." Lathen tossed the covers off and rested on the edge of the bed. "I'm going to take a quick shower." He shoved up from the bed and padded into the bathroom leaving the door open.

"Okay." She waited until the water splashed in the enclosure, slipped out of the bed and tiptoed into the bathroom, opened the shower door and stepped inside. "Want me to wash your back?"

"Sure." A seductive smile spread across his face. She took the bar of soap from him, lathered her hands and began massaging his chest, abs, and her fingers slipped lower…

He moaned and took the soap from her.

As Lathen turned the shower off, the sound of tires crunching up the driveway caused him and Pepper to scramble out of the shower, and rush to get dressed.

"I'll bring breakfast out to you," Pepper said breathlessly. "I'll fix enough for Alec too." She pulled on black jeans and snagged her bra and plaid flannel shirt from the back of a chair.

"Sounds like a plan. He reached for her caressing her naked breast with his fingertips as she tried to put on her bra.

"You're not helping."

"I know, but…"

A loud knock sounded on the front door. A short pause then another. "Hey, you two. Are you up?"

"Yeah, I'll be right there. Hang on." Lathen yanked on jeans, pulled on socks and boots before dashing down the stairs. He yanked open the door and grinned at Alec. "Come on in, kinda slow getting going this morning." He closed the door.

"So I see." Alec raised an eyebrow. "Heard you had some excitement last night."

"Yeah. Got a couple new additions that will be with us for a while." Lathen shrugged into his coat and opened the door just as Pepper bounded down the stairs and a delivery truck pulled up out front.

"It's going to be one of those days." Pepper yawned. "After I check on the new additions, I'll get breakfast ready and bring it to you. Alec, you hungry?"

"Always."

Lathen ushered Alec out the door and closed it behind them.

****

An hour and a half later, Pepper stuck her head out the door of the cabin and glanced around. Tonk was nowhere in sight. Ember was ambling up the path from the mammal habitat. "Where's the guys?" she asked Ember. The dog stopped and looked back at the stable.

"Thanks." She donned her parka, covered a tray full of hot food, mugs of coffee, picked it up, and hurried across the path carrying breakfast. Ember stuck her nose in the air and sniffed, electing to follow Pepper and the food. Inside the mammal building, she found Lathen with a hand full of wire and Alec up on a ladder. "Breakfast."

"Mmm that smells fantastic," Lathen said waiting for her to set the tray down, then wrapped his arm around her waist and kissed her cheek.

"Hey, none of that stuff here. We're getting ready to eat." Alec guffawed.

"So, close your eyes," Pepper retorted good

naturedly. "How's it coming?"

"Really good. Got the seabird aviary finished. We'll have this one done in another hour or so. Then we'll program the cameras into the computer and see what we got."

"Wow."

"The cameras were really easy to install. Of course, I just hooked them into the wiring already in place. A little programming and they're talking to each other. Now I need them to talk to the computer."

"I'll leave you to it." She walked through the door and into her office. "I'm going to print out the labels we talked about last night and call the stationery store, see what the chances are of getting the invitations tomorrow. That way I have a day to get them addressed, stamped, and mailed before we leave."

"I love it when a plan falls together," Lathen called to her.

Chapter Six
All Packed, Crated, and Ready to Go

Before the sun crested the horizon, Lathen loaded Tonk and Ember's crates in the back of the LCWRRC van. He strapped the containers to the floor and commanded dog and wolf climb inside. Next was the crate with Kaylee inside; he picked it up and set her on the passenger's side of the backseat. Loading the dog food and ice chest for the osprey's fish on the other side of the seat seemed to him the safest way to make sure the dog food arrived intact.

Pepper carried out the last piece of luggage as Lathen loaded the rest.

"The animals have more stuff than we do. Only two suitcases for a week for both of us?"

"Yeah, I've always traveled light." She shrugged. "Besides, we can use Mom's washer and dryer while we're there." Pepper walked around to the back of the van and put her hand on Tonk's crate, opened the door, and stroked his soft muzzle looking into his warm brown eyes. "It's going to be fine. This will be a great adventure. New smells and territory to explore." The wolf groaned and licked her hand. She rubbed his ears and closed the gate to his crate. Next, she opened Ember's crate, ruffled the fur around her ears, and rubbed her muzzle. "I know you don't like being in the crate, but it's for your own protection. Soon we will be aboard an airplane, and your adventure will begin. Remember you are in charge of Tonk, so be brave."

Lathen peered over Pepper's shoulder as she soothed Ember and Tonk. "Are you sure they won't freak out on the flight?"

"Of course. Nervous…sure… But they'd rather be with us than left at home with Alec. They've made that quite clear to me. Kaylee included." Pepper made her way to the side of the van, opened the door, and put her hand on Kaylee's crate. "Well, this will be your first flight too. No loud whistling in the plane. Is that clear?" Opening the crate, Pepper stroked her wing reassuringly. "We are going to have a grand time." She closed the crate door and turned to find Lathen hovering behind her, again.

He enveloped her in his arms and brushed his lips over her cold ones, his warm breath caressing her face. Holding her close a moment more, he released her. "Better get in the van out of the frigid wind. I checked with Jay this morning, and he said according to the weather service, winds should die down before we take off. Should be a smooth flight to Denver. I've rented a large SUV for the duration of the Colorado visit."

"You think of everything." She planted a smacking kiss on his lips before climbing into the van. He closed her door and sprinted around to the driver's side and jumped inside.

The trip to Bar Harbor was uneventful. Upon arrival at the airport, Lathen pulled into a parking spot next to the sign for Jay's Charters and hopped out. "Wait here, I'll see if we can drive on out to the plane or if he has a dolly for loading the crates."

After a couple minutes, Lathen came back, another

man with dark hair streaked with silver in tow. He was stocky, wore blue jeans, and a black and silver parka. He was pointing to a sleek private jet across the tarmac. Lathen climbed back into the van. "We can drive out to the plane and load."

Jay and Lathen secured the crates next to the navy and silver leather seats where Pepper dropped her backpack. She was impressed with Jay's attention to detail inside the plane. There were crystal vases attached between the windows with fresh maroon carnations, white roses, and sprigs of greenery in each. As she passed the sparkling stainless steel galley, a pretty brunette smiled. The enticing aroma of freshly brewed coffee wafted through the cabin. Jay gestured toward the woman. "This is Patti. She handles the galley and customers' needs on the longer flights. Patti, you know my old friend, Lathen." Jay clapped Lathen on the shoulder. "And this is Pepper, his soon to be bride."

Patti smiled. "Nice to see you again Lathen. It's a pleasure to meet you, Pepper."

"Don't you have a co-pilot?" Pepper asked looking toward the cockpit.

"I've got one right here. Lathen's still got his license, even though he's bad about keeping his flight hours up. That reminds me, after the first of the year, you need a few more hours to keep current."

"Set me up right after the first, family will be gone by then."

Pepper's eyes rounded in surprise. "You didn't mention you're a pilot."

"Never came up. Learned to fly in Alaska with Dad, when I was a teenager. Haven't done a lot of flying since leaving the military. Just enough to keep my license current, though it was rough at times."

Jay hesitated a moment longer in the galley, giving Patti a wink then called out. "Who wants coffee before we take off?"

"I'll take a cup. Any chance you stock tea or hot chocolate?" Lathen asked.

"Sure." Jay turned to Pepper. "What's your preference?"

"Hot chocolate, please."

Opening the galley cabinet, he took three large, navy blue mugs bearing Jay's Charters logo in silver from the neat rows of dishes. Patti poured steaming coffee into two and hot water in one. Jay took a packet of hot chocolate, a spoon, and handed them to Pepper. "Better get buckled in, we'll be ready for takeoff shortly. Figure we'll be in Denver within seven hours."

Lathen and Pepper took their seats. She stirred in the hot cocoa mix, sprinkled a few mini marshmallows over the top, and took a sip. "Mmmm, this is good." She licked her top lip to make sure there wasn't a chocolate mustache. The plane taxied down the runway and was airborne in short order.

Pepper watched out the window as Bar Harbor Airport disappeared behind fluffy clouds that obscured the landscape with the occasional mountain peak protruding through the white layers. Lathen settled into his seat with a paperback novel about a sniper.

Jay called out it was safe to release the seat belts and move around a bit.

Tonk whimpered a couple times, a low warning growl came from Ember's throat in response. Tonk snarled and snapped at the air. Another loud rumble in

Ember's chest grew to a menacing bark. Pepper released her seat belt and got down on all fours staring directly into the crates. "Stop it you two, right now. If you don't behave on this trip, you'll be left home after this. Understood?" She got back to her feet and touched the crates.

Ember cocked her head and stuck her paw through the wire crate trying to reach Pepper's foot. Then Ember pulled it back inside the crate, snorted, and laid her head on front paws. Tonk woofed once and settled. Kaylee dozed through the flight. Pepper pulled out her tablet, checked off completed items on her wedding list, then pulled up a new release she'd been reading from her favorite romance author.

A few hours into the flight, Patti brought out sandwiches, chips, and soft drinks and served homemade chocolate cupcakes for dessert.

When Patti came back and sat down, with three bottles of water, she said, "We'll be landing soon, so buckle up. Light flurries at DIA, but otherwise perfect."

Kaylee blinked several times, stretched out one wing and leg then the other side. She fluffed, whistled quietly, and stared at Pepper. Then fluffed again, rearranged her feathers, and took an alert position on her perch.

"Yes, Kaylee, we are almost there," Pepper crooned to the osprey.

The private jet touched down. Lathen thanked Jay for the ride and confirmed a meeting time for the return flight early Sunday morning after Thanksgiving. Pepper sprinted toward the terminal when Lathen called out to her, "Jay arranged to have the rental SUV brought to the tarmac." He pointed to the large silver SUV waiting on the other side of the plane.

Pepper jogged back, leashed and released Ember and Tonk while Lathen carried Kaylee and her crate to the SUV, then went back to get her ice chest. Jay grabbed the crates and loaded them in the back of the vehicle. She walked the canines to the private terminal building where there was grass out front to do their business. After returning to the van, dog and wolf jumped into the SUV. Tails down, they entered the crates. Pepper locked the crate doors, and Jay closed the rear door. Lathen and Pepper said their goodbyes. Lathen started the SUV and followed the frontage road and navigation to I-70 toward Evergreen where her parents lived.

"It's about an hour drive, but we're going to hit rush hour. Traffic on I-70 will be a nightmare, count on a couple hours. Want to stop and grab a bite to eat before we descend on them?"

Lathen glanced over at her. "What time are they expecting us?"

"I didn't give them a specific time, just Sunday evening, in case we ran into problems." She shifted in her seat to check out the restaurant signs along the highway. "How about that one?" She pointed to a familiar sit-down eatery.

They went in and ordered. Pepper went back to the truck to feed Ember, Tonk, and Kaylee. By the time she returned, the food was served. They ate quickly, opted to take a piece of banana cream and coconut cream pie to go in case traffic was still snarled. Ninety minutes later, Lathen turned the SUV onto a gravel road in the foothills, slowed to a stop, and stared at a building resembling their original cabin in Maine.

"Told you it probably looked a lot like our cabin." Pepper smirked.

Lathen no sooner turned off the engine then the perimeter and driveway lights blinked on. Klaren, a petite woman with brown hair and bright green eyes like her daughter, came flying down the path toward them. She was dressed in jeans, a green and black plaid flannel shirt over a black turtleneck. Pepper stepped out of the SUV and gave her mother a warm hug.

Her father, Duncan, a tall, husky man with bright red hair and freckles that made him look younger than he was, sauntered up behind them and kissed her on the cheek. His worn jeans, a light blue sweater, denim jacket, and boots gave the retired Zoology professor the look of a seasoned rancher.

Klaren turned her attention to Lathen with a hug and kiss on the cheek while Duncan grasped Lathen's hand then pulled him into a quick hug.

"We're so glad you made it. Any trouble finding us?" Klaren asked.

"Nope, navigation system directed us right here. This is some kind of spread," Lathen said turning in a circle. The cabin with a two car attached garage was nestled in a valley with mountains surrounding it on three sides. The land adjacent to the cabin was fenced in with a white picket fence and iron gate across the road leading into the property. A huge red barn with a red roof stood beyond the fence to the left of the house.

Duncan ambled up the drive to the gate and swung the two sections closed threading a padlock through the latch.

Pepper laughed. "Now that we are here; you don't want us escaping?"

Her mother's lips twitched then kicked up in a wide smile. "Well…nooo, your dad figured Ember and Tonk had enough of being cooped up. You can let them out to run, can't get in any trouble around here. We normally keep the gate shut, pup here"—Klaren looked back to the whining husky puppy in the doorway—"doesn't seem to know how to stay in boundaries, yet."

"Aww what a cutie." Pepper started toward the door. "When did you get her?"

"The day after we got back from Maine," her father said. "Neighbor raises Siberian Huskies. They had a litter of puppies, and your mother fell in love with this one. Refused to come home without her. Good thing the pups were ready for new homes, or I would have had to leave your mother there." Duncan chuckled.

"She has the most beautiful blue eyes." Klaren sighed.

"What's her name?" Pepper squatted down eye level with the pup.

"Timber."

"Are you sure a wolf on the property won't make your neighbors nervous?" Lathen asked.

"We own twenty acres which are pretty mountainous, as you can see. The cabin sits right smack dab in the middle of it. Unless Tonk is going to sit next to the property line and howl, no one will know he's here. Besides, our closest neighbor down the road knows you're coming and bringing a menagerie with you. He and his wife may stop by to meet all of you. If that's all right?"

"Sure the more, the merrier," Pepper said.

Duncan followed Lathen around to the back of the vehicle. Lathen opened the back and flipped the latches on Ember and Tonk's crates. The canines leaped out of the vehicle, did a couple laps around the cabin, stopped to sniff the pup at the door, and returned, Ember beside Pepper and Tonk next to Lathen.

Klaren shivered. "Why don't we go in the house and warm up. Duncan built a heated aviary onto the back of the cabin, for Kaylee."

"Thanks." Lathen carried the osprey and her crate toward the aviary. Duncan grabbed the two suitcases. Pepper slung a little purple pack over her shoulder and picked up the bird's ice chest.

Pepper started around back following Lathen.

Her dad grabbed her arm, and Lathen skidded to a stop a couple of feet in front of Pepper. "You can go right through the house. The aviary is connected. Haven't quite got the doorway finished, but it works."

Pepper pushed through the door into the aviary and skidded to a stop. "Oh—wow. Pops this is just like Kaylee's at home." She flung her arms around her dad. "You didn't need to go to all this trouble for us."

"Once I got started—it made sense to finish it properly." He put his hands behind his back and surveyed the area nonchalantly.

Pepper's eyes narrowed. "Pops, I know that look. What are you up to?"

He flung his arms wide. "Nothing. Your mom and I are hoping for more visits?" Her dad sort of shrugged and smiled uncertainly. "Besides we can use it for other things, maybe a greenhouse in between your visits."

Pepper chewed on her bottom lip. "That's so sweet, Pops. Not sure how much free time we'll have with the rehab and all. But—yeah, we'll be here more often."

Looking from father to daughter, Lathen raised an

eyebrow as Pepper glanced at him schooling her expression from incredulous to normal in the blink of an eye. He shrugged it off and set the crate on the bench in the center of the room.

The thought passed silently between them: *Why else would her father build an aviary?*

Her dad smiled wide as Lathen opened the crate, and Pepper offered her arm to Kaylee, who promptly jumped on and swiveled her head taking in the new surroundings.

After a few minutes, Kaylee flapped over to the perch and looked expectantly at Pepper. She reached into the ice chest and tossed a fish to the osprey. Kaylee settled into her accommodations.

Pepper returned to the family room where Lathen grabbed Ember and Tonk's bowls and filled them with fresh water and kibble in the kitchen.

"Where do you want us to set up the feeding area?" Lathen asked. "I'm afraid we are still working on Tonk's manners. He's a messy eater." He waved a couple large place mats in the air.

"It's okay. Timber still plays in her water bowl with her front feet. That's a mess." Klaren grimaced. "So just put their bowls next to the back door."

Lathen looked at the dainty pink paw printed ceramic bowls on one side of the door. He put Tonk and Ember's stainless steel bowls on the opposite side of the door. "Will that work?"

Klaren nodded, followed Duncan and Pepper into the family room.

The interior of her parents' cabin resembled the McKay cabin in Maine, except there was wall-to-wall carpeting and the log cabin furniture in each room matched the rustic setting. Whereas the McKay cabin had hardwood floors, a hodge-podge of furnishings Pepper brought from Salem and stuff Lathen had moved from his cottage. The only new items were the TV, couches, and end tables Pepper purchased shortly after arriving. There were always other pressing issues to tend to, rather than worrying about interior design.

Lathen smiled to himself, pulling out his phone and tapping the alarm icon. He entered the user name and passcode, handed the phone to Pepper.

She grinned and swiped through the video feeds. "Looks like all is well at home." Holding up her phone, she went on to explain the last minute surveillance cameras Lathen had installed.

Seated around the roaring fire, Lathen wrapped his arm around Pepper's shoulder as she leaned into him on the buff-colored leather couch.

Pepper's mom brought in four crystal wine glasses, set them on the end tables, and returned to the kitchen. Her dad brought in a bottle of red wine and set it on the china cabinet. A large bowl of chips, salsa, and guacamole sat on the dining room table adjacent to the family room. Except for the bedrooms, the rest of the cabin's rooms ran together with only the furnishings to distinguishing where one room started and the other ended. A long breakfast bar with tall stools separated the kitchen from the dining area.

"Thought you might like a bite of something when you arrived," her mother said walking out of the kitchen with a plate piled high of Pepper's favorite peanut butter cookies. She set them in the center of the table. "Why don't you gather around the table and grab something to eat. You can take it into the family room and enjoy the fire."

Pepper, followed by Lathen, picked up plates, heaped them with the Mexican snacks and peanut butter cookies, then returned to the warmth of the fire.

Once everyone was seated, Duncan said, "Elijah and Amy, Kolby and Hayley will be here Tuesday afternoon." He paused as Lathen nodded. "But you already knew that, huh?"

"Yeah, talked to Dad this morning before we left, and Kolby last night. They're excited about meeting you and seeing Colorado."

"Your dad and I talked for quite a while the other night." Duncan leaned back in his chair.

Grimacing, Lathen said in an uneasy voice, "You did?"

"Yep, he told me a bit of the shenanigans you boys pulled growing up. I told him what a determined child Pepper was. We decided you two deserve each other." Duncan chuckled.

"You did?" Pepper turned to stare at her father.

He ignored her. "Weather permitting we'll take a drive to Rocky Mountain National Park, see what roads are open. It's really a wonderful place during the winter. Lots of interesting wildlife venture out when the tourists are all gone. Great snowshoeing and cross country skiing most times, especially around Bear Lake. Nothing like Denali, but…"

"That's a great idea," Lathen said popping a chip loaded with guacamole into his mouth.

"Supposed to have a fast moving storm blow through Thursday night into Friday. Figured we'd take the trip on Wednesday, hunker down with turkey and the trimmings on Thanksgiving. Maybe drive around a bit on Saturday." Duncan leaned back against the double recliner with a plate of chips, guacamole, and a peanut butter cookie.

"That sounds great, Dad. Thanks for doing all this. I'm really grateful for the break."

"Glad to do it." He took a bite of the cookie and chewed. "Klar these are the best cookies you've made this year!"

"Don't talk with your mouth full, dear." Klaren laughed. "Pep, how are the wedding plans coming?"

Pepper peered at her plate, chased a spot of salsa around with a chip, and stifled a yawn. "Good. Amy found a wonderful wedding dress. A woman in the pack is sewing it for me. Another is creating a tiara." She whipped out her tablet from her backpack, found the email and pictures, passed the tablet to her mom. "Amy said she'd bring everything with her."

"I didn't know you were having trouble finding a gown." Klaren took the tablet, swiped at the screen a couple times, browsing through the pictures. "I've never seen anything quite like that dress. Amy's right; it's you." She handed the tablet back to Pepper.

Lathen stretched his legs and raised an arm above his head as Pepper's eyes drooped. "It's been a long day. If you don't mind, can we continue this conversation in the morning?"

"Of course. What would you like to do tomorrow?"

Lathen pushed to his feet and extended a hand to Pepper. She grasped his hand and stood slipping her arm around Lathen's waist. "We'd like to see your property, catch up, and relax. Seem to remember Mom saying something about horses?"

"We took in a few horses that needed a good home.

Came with a sleigh and horse trailer too." Her dad grinned. "See you two in the morning."

Chapter Seven
Who Says You Can Never Go Home? An Adventure on Horseback and Four-Paw Bliss

Pepper's eyes blinked open. Golden rays of sunshine streamed through frozen snowflake patterns on the window, shimmering like diamonds. She rolled over to face Lathen, his strong arms wrapped around her, and peered up at the butterscotch stubble on his peaceful face. *How did I get so lucky?* He tightened his grip then opened his eyes sleepily.

"Morning sunshine." He lifted his hand and brushed the sleep tangled strands of hair out of her face. Buried his face in her neck, kissing the bite mark that sealed her as his mate a few months ago.

"Good morning to you. Did you sleep…"

A knock on their bedroom door was followed by her mom's voice. "You guys decent?" She pushed the door open.

Pepper squealed, and Lathen calmly looked toward the door, one bare leg thrown over her, various body parts naked poking out of the covers.

Her mom drew in a breath and backed out. "Oh, not quite. But that's okay. Breakfast is ready, and your dad's out in the barn saddling the horses. You did want to see the property via horseback?"

"Sure. We'll be there in a few." Pepper pushed at Lathen's chest in an effort to break his hold. He trailed kisses from her throat, along her jaw line. When he reached her mouth, the tip of his tongue teased open her soft lips then gently explored. The kiss sent the pit of her stomach into a wild swirl of desire.

"If we don't get up…" she murmured against his lips. "She'll be knocking on the door again."

Raising his mouth from hers, he gazed into her eyes. "I love you. But you're right." He released her. "But she might be embarrassed if she barges in here again."

"I love you more. You're incorrigible. You know that? And you don't know my mother." Pepper swatted his arm and swung her legs to the side of the bed. "She'd probably stand at the door and watch."

Lathen chuckled. "Oh, one of those." Throwing off the comforter, he got to his feet. "How about a quick shower, behind a locked bathroom door?" He crossed to her and tugged her out of bed, she fell against him. He swept her up in his arms and carried her into the bathroom.

She squealed. But loved it when he swept her off her feet. So romantic.

****

Dressed in several layers, warm socks, and boots, Pepper along with Lathen walked into the kitchen where the aroma of bacon, eggs, and coffee wafted through the air. "Sorry, we're late. Kinda slow getting started this morning." Pepper shifted her eyes to Lathen, who couldn't hide a little smirk.

"No need to apologize, we're just glad to have you here." Klaren raised an eyebrow and gave her daughter a knowing look.

"Thanks for the invitation." Pepper forked up eggs

and slipped them into her mouth followed by a gulp of hot tea. "Yoweee. That's hot."

Her mom laughed along with Lathen.

"Gee who would have thought." Lathen shoveled in the last bite of egg and toast then put a lid on his travel mug of coffee. "I better get out there and help Duncan with the horses." He shrugged into his coat just as Duncan pushed open the back door. Ember, Tonk, and Timber scrambled in behind him.

"We let them out of your room a couple hours ago, figured they were hungry and you needed to sleep." Duncan said by way of explanation since Pepper was switching her gaze from him to Ember and Tonk.

"Oh, and Kaylee's been fed too." Her mom grinned. "I remembered how you ran the frozen fish though hot water before tossing it to her. She gave me a sideways glance for a beat or two before she tore into the fish."

"Thanks, but you should have woken us up. They're our responsibility. It was great of you to allow us to bring them and"—she shifted her gaze to Duncan—"and build a place for Kaylee to stay."

"Oh, we don't mind. Enjoyed taking care of Ember and Kaylee when you two were in Alaska. In fact, that's one of the reasons we adopted the horses and Timber. Didn't know how much we missed the unconditional love and acceptance of animals until we worked around your Center."

"It does grow on you." Lathen smiled wide.

"By the way, talking about your wildlife rescue and Lobster Cove. We've purchased the cottage we leased last time we were there. Hope you wouldn't mind keeping an eye on the place when we aren't there."

"Wow, that's great. No problem, we're happy to keep an eye on your cottage."

"We were thinking about volunteering at your place during the summer, early fall. If you don't mind?"

"Mind? We'd love it. But what about your horses?"

"Oh, we have a hired hand that comes in daily to help with the chores. When we are gone for a longer period of time, Jack and his wife, Gale, will live in the apartment above the barn/stables and take care of the horses and property. We plan on taking Timber with us; she'll love Lobster Cove." Duncan filled his travel mug with steaming fresh coffee.

"Sounds great. We look forward to having you and Timber help out." Lathen smiled watching the pup bounce and tumble all over Tonk and Ember. Finally, she let out a sharp bark correcting Timber. "I was about to join you in the barn to ready the horses."

"Already done. Came back in to see how long before you two were ready to go."

"We'll kennel Tonk and Ember."

"You most certainly will not," Duncan said. "They can come with us. The horses are used to dogs, had several where they came from."

"But Tonk is a wolf…usually puts prey animals on edge. Though he wouldn't hurt them."

"He was in the barn with me and the others. The horses didn't pay him any mind."

"Okay."

Pepper helped her mom put the dishes in the dishwasher and clean up the kitchen. Klaren packed a few snacks, bottles of water and filled travel mugs with coffee and hot chocolate. "I think we're ready to go. I have a ham in the oven, so we'll need to cook yams when we get back and supper will be ready."

Coats, hats, and gloves on, the group walked toward the barn. Kaylee soared overhead whistling sharply to make sure her flock stayed together. Timber yipped and nipped at the heels of everyone, including Ember and Tonk who barked a correction, then chased each other on the way to the building.

"I think you might want to pick up Timber, she looks a bit worn out," Klaren said to her husband entering the corral where the horses were waiting.

He scooped the pup up and set her in the saddle in front of him. "She's used to riding on the horses with me. Even takes a snooze on occasion." Duncan peered adoringly at the pup and chuckled.

"See, and he claims it was me that wanted the pup. He's spoiling her rotten." Her lips twitched for a beat then curved into a wide smile.

"Oh, I can see that." Pepper snorted a laugh, checked her saddle's cinches and stirrups before swinging up into the saddle, reins held in her right hand. She twisted in the saddle to face Lathen as he swung into his saddle. "How much time have you spent on a horse?"

"Enough to know we'll be sore tonight," he shot back, settling in. "But that's all right, it's an exciting way to see the property."

"Oh we won't be out that long," Duncan assured them. "Got too late a start. It's dark in these parts by four o'clock." On Midnight, a sleek black gelding, Duncan led the way up a well-worn path into the hills on the property. Beside him, Klaren on Rita, a buckskin mare. Behind them, Pepper on Jasmine, a Blue Roan Gypsy, and Lathen on Scout, a large buff Palomino, who was in no hurry to leave the corral.

Her parents' property backed a national forest giving them a wide riding area. The couples made frequent stops to explore the countryside, hike, play with the canines, and eat the snacks prepared by her mom. By late afternoon, the group returned to the cabin. Kaylee perched on the leather gauntlet covering Pepper's arm after she dismounted.

"It was such a beautiful day, nearly sixty degrees in November, hard to believe a snowstorm is on the way for Thanksgiving." Pepper glanced at the cloudless deep blue sky.

"It'll be a cold one tonight," her mom predicted. "Clear skies. But we'll take the nice weather and hope it holds through Wednesday. Your family will love Rocky Mountain National Park." She nodded to Lathen. "It's a fun drive. Weather permitting, we should be able to hike around Bear Lake too."

Inside the house, her mom checked on the ham, Pepper peeled, cooked and candied sweet potatoes, then made deviled eggs from Aunt Ashling's family recipe. When she finished, she went to check on Kaylee and feed her.

Lathen and Duncan put the horses away with the help of Timber, Tonk, and Ember, then they all trudged into the house. Lathen cleaned the dog bowls and fed Ember and Tonk. Duncan fed Timber her puppy food, but she rushed over to see what the others were eating. Ember snarled a warning as Timber swiped a mouth full of food. Pepper's dad picked the pup up and returned her to her own bowl. "Better learn your manners, or you're going to be in a heap of trouble."

A cinnamony, citrusy aroma filled the cabin and

Pepper's mouth watered. Klaren stirred a mixture of honey, orange marmalade, cloves, and a few other ingredients in a sauce pan for a ham glaze and soon pronounced the meal ready.

As the couples sat around the dinner table, their conversation touched on wedding plans, the purchase of the cottage, Christmas, and New Year's. Pepper sighed, glad to spend Thanksgiving in Colorado.

"We'll probably close on the cottage while we are out there for your wedding." Her father cut his ham slice in pieces and popped one in his mouth. The sticky warm glaze dripped a bit onto his chin. He cut the deviled egg in half and slipped a piece in his mouth. Around the bite of egg, he said, "Klaren you have to get this recipe. Best damn egg I've ever tasted. The center isn't mushy but firm and the taste is tangy. I love it."

"I agree. Pepper, how come Ashling never shared the recipe with us?"

"Probably because you never asked. You were pretty busy with your careers when I spent summers with her. That's when I learned to make them." She scooped up a fork of candied sweet potato and put it into her mouth, stabbed the last quarter of deviled egg with her fork, finished chewing, and popped the morsel in her mouth.

Lathen finished the last bite of four deviled eggs on his plate, picked up his and Pepper's dishes and silverware, rinsed and arranged them in the dishwasher.

"My goodness—you have him trained well. I still can't get your father to do that with his own dishes, let alone mine." Klaren huffed.

"Not true," Duncan said indignantly.

Lathen and Pepper picked up the rest of the dishes

while Klaren put the ham and leftover yams in containers, storing the food in the fridge. The deviled eggs were all gone.

Her father picked up a bottle of wine, grabbed glasses, and walked into the family room. He settled into the couch beside the fireplace and picked up the remote, scrolling to an action adventure movie.

Lathen's gaze flicked to the screen as he joined her dad. "Wow. Pepper and I wanted to see that when it was in the theaters, but…we never have time. Hey, Pep, come in here."

Pepper and her mom sauntered in and settled next to their men, as the movie started. Lathen wrapped his arm around Pepper, and she snuggled against him sipping her glass of chardonnay. Midpoint of the movie, Duncan paused the show because Pepper wanted popcorn. She and her mom made a huge bowl of popcorn. Klaren set it in the middle of the coffee table. Pepper searched through the cupboards until she found the ranch and cheddar topping she knew her mom always kept handy.

After the movie, Duncan asked, "When should we expect your family tomorrow?"

"Early afternoon. Dad will have everyone on the plane long before dawn." Lathen ambled to the door, slipped into his coat, and let Tonk and Ember outside. Timber bounded after them. "We never let the dogs out alone after dark. Too much trouble for them to get into." He stepped outside and closed the door behind him.

Pepper stood and picked up the popcorn bowl and toppings. "I don't know why, but I'm exhausted. Think we'll call it an early night again, while we have a chance."

"It's the high altitude. You're not used to it. Make sure you drink plenty of water."

"Yes, Mom." Pepper grinned trying to stifle a jaw-popping yawn, with little success.

The handle on the door twisted. Lathen strode inside followed by Tonk, Ember, and Timber. "Nightly duties done." He yawned. "Hate to be a party pooper, but…"

"I already told them we'd call it an early night. Tomorrow your family arrives, and the Thanksgiving festivities begin," Pepper sing-songed.

"Do you need any help with the wedding plans?" her mother asked hopefully.

"Not at the moment. But we'll go over them in the morning. Oh, yeah, I have all the family's invitations in our suitcases. They turned out beautifully. I'll go get them really quick." Pepper sprinted down the hallway and was back in the blink of an eye. She laid three cream envelopes addressed in a calligraphy script with deep purple ink on the coffee table.

Lathen's eyes went wide. "Wow, decided not to go with the label option? When did you have time to…wait… I didn't know you were a calligrapher."

Waving her hands in a dismissive gesture, she peered up at him coyly. "I'm not. But I have other talents."

The light dawned slowly as his eyes took on a mischievous sparkle. "Oh, those talents. Not for personal gain?"

"It wasn't personal gain, the way I see it. It was a need. If I didn't get the invitations addressed, the people wouldn't know when or where the wedding or reception would be held, and they'd be terribly disappointed. So it was for their benefit," she said smugly checking her light lavender polished nails.

When Lathen attempted to cover a laugh with a contrived cough, her dad roared with laughter. "I see your talent to rationalize the use of magic as a child carried over into your adult life. Bravo."

Her mom narrowed her eyes and shot Pepper a speculative glance. "Well, it's your story, make it a good one."

"Yep, it's my story, and I'm sticking to it. But the ultimate gain was the people on the guest list." Pepper shrugged.

"Still, I don't see how you do it all. That's why I offered to host Thanksgiving. I knew you were running yourself ragged. Magic or not." Her mom smiled. "Besides, it's going to be so much fun having a houseful of people."

"Thank you. Night." Pepper walked up the hall hand in hand with Lathen, Ember and Tonk trotted along behind. "Don't worry about feeding everyone; we'll be up early."

Duncan and Klaren glanced at each other and grinned. "Bet not," Duncan whispered then cleared his throat. "Hey, Lathen before you hit the sack or whatever you plan to do, could I have a word?"

"Sure, maybe even two," he said on a laugh, tapped Pepper's rear and winked. "I'll be right back."

Chapter Eight
A Family Gathering, Fun, Food, and Chatter

Lathen looked at his watch as he and Pepper trotted Scout and Jasmine into the barn. Jack was waiting for them. Duncan and Klaren had returned earlier to get ready for company.

A sonar ping went off in his pocket. Lathen pulled his phone out of his jacket pocket and glanced at the screen. "Dad and the family just landed at DIA."

"Great, they'll be here in a couple hours, maybe earlier depending on traffic flow on I-70." Pepper dismounted, handing the reins to Jack. "Sure you don't want any help? I'm not in the habit of handing a sweaty horse over to someone else to be groomed and taken care of."

"If you aren't up at the cabin in the next few minutes, Mrs. McKay will have my hide." Jack grinned, the bronze leathery skin around his eyes crinkled as he took Jasmine's reins. "Now scoot. You too, Mr. Quartz."

"Got ya. But it's Lathen and Pepper. Mr. Quartz landed at DIA a few minutes ago." Lathen grinned at Jack and walked Scout to his stall. He drew a small carrot out of his pocket, offered it on the flat of his hand while rubbing the horse's neck.

"Lathen, ya coming?" Pepper called over her shoulder as Tonk and Ember stood midway between them looking from one to the other.

"Yep." He ambled out the barn door, caught Pepper's hand, and linked his gloved fingers through hers. Ember and Tonk raced to the house barking and yipping.

"Dad texted me. They touched down at DIA a few minutes ago." Lathen glanced around the room strewn with decorations. "Need any help?"

Klaren thrust a cardboard box full of Thanksgiving decorations into Pepper's hands. "Please set these around in the family room, the guest bathroom, and extra bathroom." She turned to Lathen. "Your family knows they are staying here? Right?"

Lathen shrugged. "Dad didn't mention anything about it." He gave Pepper a sideways glance, as if she would know. "Believe they have to leave on Saturday morning, rather than Sunday though, some pack business that can't wait."

Duncan nodded. "So I heard." He peeked over the top of the newspaper he was reading in the recliner. "Klar, I informed Elijah of that during our last conversation. Even though he claimed to have made reservations in town, I told him to cancel them. The family is staying here."

"Lathen, would your brother and his wife like the extra room or the apartment above the barn?"

"Dad and Amy would probably appreciate the apartment. They're newlyweds you know." He smirked. "Besides, Pepper and Hayley have become so close, it's best to have them in the same vicinity. They'll chatter all night, no matter where they are."

"As if you and your brother don't," Pepper retorted. "Not to mention the midnight runs."

Hey, we include Dad in those, and it's required. Duncan, you're welcome to come along too," Lathen said.

"Well...since I only am a biped, I couldn't keep up with you, but feel free, just stay well inside the property boundaries and careful in the national forest, if you go that far. Don't want any of you coming back with buckshot from the neighbors." Duncan set aside the paper and laid his half-spectacles on top. "Better go check the apartment, make sure it's ready for guests. Lathen, you want to join me?"

An eyebrow raised, Lathen nodded. "Sure."

"Great." Klaren shoved a box overflowing with stuffed turkeys, pilgrim figurines, and garland into Lathen's arms. "Put these on top the dresser, around the breakfast bar, and tiny coffee table, next to the loveseat. Please."

Lathen looked from Klaren to Duncan and Pepper. "I...uh...don't know anything about decorating. Pepper want to..."

"No...she needs to help Klar. I know what to put where." Duncan whisked the box out of Lathen's arms and strode toward the door.

Mouth open, about to answer, Pepper closed her mouth and shrugged, giving Lathen a look that said "you're on your own."

She continued setting out the tiny pilgrim statuettes in the middle of the coffee table and a colorful ceramic turkey on the fireplace mantel. Fresh flowers sat in the center of the massive log dining table with turkey shaped salt and pepper shakers on either side.

With four small beanie turkeys under her arm, she brought the empty box with bubble wrap back to her mom. "I take it these go in the bathrooms with the guest soap?" She indicated the turkeys stuffed under her arm.

"Yes. Thanks," her mom said.

He watched Pepper disappear down the hallway and scratched his chin. "Huh? Okaaay?" Lathen's forehead scrunched in puzzlement as he stood halfway between the family room and kitchen.

"Coming?" Duncan asked opening the back door.

"Right behind you."

****

By the time Lathen and Duncan headed back to the house, a large SUV was pulling to a stop in front of the gated driveway. Duncan picked up Timber, flicked his wrist, the gates unlatched and swung open. Lathen called Tonk and Ember to his side. The vehicle continued up the driveway.

Pepper threw open the front door, sprinting up the path, and skidded to a stop beside Lathen. Before the SUV came to a complete stop, Hayley had the car door open. Kolby had her by the arm and said something to her. His own door opened and with a blur of movement, he was at her door. When he reached for her hand, she grasped it and hopped out, her large baby bump leading the way.

Pepper met her half way around the vehicle. "My goodness, that baby is growing."

"Tell me about it. She's a holy terror. Gonna be just like her father!"

"It's a girl? How exciting." Pepper glanced over at Elijah as he helped Amy out of the car. "Boy oh boy is that little girl going to be spoiled." She patted Haley on the arm, kissed Kolby on the cheek, and went to hug Elijah and Amy.

Lathen stood beside his father trying to make introductions. Ember, Tonk, and Timber raced around the car, sniffing the air and the newcomers. Kaylee soared overhead, swooping down to get a better look. Finally, Lathen gave a shrill whistle and pointed to the house. "Ladies, join Pepper's mom, Klaren, standing on the porch and go on in the house. We'll grab the luggage and be right in. He whistled at Kaylee and motioned her to Pepper. She sheathed her arm in a leather gauntlet and held her arm high. After a couple of circles around the house, the osprey reluctantly landed on Pepper's arm, then the women laughing and giggling trooped into the house.

"Wow, quite a group we have here," Elijah said with a chuckle, reaching for a couple suitcases.

"Let me handle that," Duncan said. With a wave of his arm all the luggage disappeared. "You'll find the bags in your rooms." He glanced sideways at Elijah. "Your son thought you and Amy would be more comfortable in the apartment above the barn. Is that all right?"

"Yes, of course. But we don't want to put you out," Elijah said in his usual booming voice.

"Not at all, plenty of room. Kolby and Hayley are in the extra guest room."

Kolby gave two thumbs up and followed Lathen, with the rest of the group into the cabin. When Lathen walked in his eyes rounded, he blinked and glanced around. Somehow the family room and kitchen seemed to have expanded. He shook his head and looked at Pepper with one eyebrow raised, taking off his coat.

After clasping Lathen's shoulder, Duncan said quietly, "This cabin will meet the needs of our guests regardless of the number. An option you may want to discuss with Pepper before the wedding. I understand you were considering having the reception at a community center."

"Dad, the wedding invitations give the location of the reception; change is not an option," Pepper said in a warning tone.

He shrugged. "Just saying…more convenient."

"For who?" Pepper retorted.

Lathen rubbed his chin with thumb and forefinger. "Pep, I think we may want to discuss this later on."

"We can discuss it, but…I have my own reasons for having the reception off-site," Pepper said narrowing her eyes at him.

"What's the problem over here?" Hayley asked cheerfully. "My brother-in-law trying to run the show again?"

"Yes, but I have him under control." Pepper took Hayley's arm and tugged her toward the back door.

"Lathen, under control." Kolby shook his head and guffawed. "Never happen."

She shot him the stink eye and continued to drag Hayley toward the back door. "You have to see the horses that Mom and Dad took in. Beautiful creatures." Pepper turned to invite Amy to come along, but she was engrossed in conversation with Klaren looking over an ancient book open on the kitchen counter.

"Sounds good. I've sat long enough." She pointed to the hooks by the front door. "Let me grab my coat."

"We'll be right back," Pepper said over the din of conversation, giving a low whistle for Ember and Tonk to follow. Timber trotted behind them. She caught her father's glance and approval before allowing Timber to tag along.

Lathen gave her a thumbs up and strode across the floor to the knot of men standing by the fireplace. The Quartz men were tall and muscular with sculptured facial features. Kolby had coppery blond hair, his mother's green eyes, and Lathen's dad, light brown hair with streaks of gray and blue-green eyes he'd shared with Lathen. Then there was Duncan McKay, tall, but stocky with bright red hair graying slightly at the temples and a sprinkling of freckles across his nose and cheeks. As Lathen joined the group, he thought how different this holiday season would be compared to previous years, and smiled.

Klaren bustled around the rustic log dining table arranging chips, dip, veggie plate, meat and cheese platter including her famous peanut butter cookies, these with a chocolate kiss in the center. She reached in the matching china cabinet for plates and silverware. Amy took the mugs from her and carried them into the kitchen. The large capacity coffee maker sat on the kitchen counter with the smaller one filled with hot water. Tea bags and hot chocolate mix were arranged in a wicker basket decorated with red and green bows.

"I'm going to set the mugs between the coffee maker and the basket," Amy called from the kitchen.

"Great. All right everyone, come help yourselves." Klaren stood at the table surveying the spread. Lathen herded the men to the table. As he passed by Klaren, she caught his arm. "I'm going to show Amy the apartment and find the girls. We should be right back, provided I can pull Pepper from the horses."

"Good luck with that. If you aren't back shortly, I'll come with reinforcements." He chuckled and leaned in to hear the rest of the conversation regarding wildlife conservation between his brother and Duncan. Behind the others, Elijah filled his plate, then joined the little group and settled onto the couch at the far end of the stone fireplace. Lathen put his plate down and tossed a couple good sized logs in the fireplace. The fire crackled and popped sending orange sparks up the chimney as flames raced up all sides of the new wood.

"So Elijah, Pepper tells me you're a tour guide for Denali National Park? Must be an exciting job." Duncan took a drink from his steaming mug of coffee.

"It can be. But mostly it's rewarding, showing people that have never been to Alaska the breathtaking views, unusual wildlife, and secrets of Denali." Elijah scooped salsa on a chip and popped it in his mouth.

"Pepper raved about the park and the access you gave them during the trip last August." Duncan set his mug on the table.

"Your daughter did her research before arriving. She knew as much as I did about some things." He grinned and sipped his coffee.

"The trip was a dream come true for her. Klaren and I have been planning a trip to Alaska since we retired, but something always comes up."

"If you two can get up to my Alaska…say June of next year?" Elijah said decisively. "You can stay with us. I'll arrange a private tour for a week in the back country of Denali. How's that sound?"

Duncan raised his eyebrows and blew out a breath. "That would be my dream come true. As far as I know, we don't have any vacation plans for next year."

"Good, it's settled. After the wedding, we are spending Christmas and New Year's with the kids, as I assume you are. So we can work out the details between now and then. The first of the year the airlines may have some good deals on flights to Alaska, book 'em for early June." Elijah leaned back in the recliner and grinned at his son. "Lathen, you fell for the right woman, her family fits right in."

"Dad, really." Lathen raised a brow as he shifted his gaze to Duncan. "Pack mentality. We have one flaw that runs through the family, we don't seem to have filter on what we say." He shook his head.

"I take offense to that." Eli bristled.

"Kolby, Hayley looks great." Lathen ignored his father. "How's she feeling? I'd ask her myself, but Pepper is monopolizing her time so far."

"Doing good. I kinda keep my head ducked and out of her way. On any given evening, it's tears, rage, smiles, and then over again. Thankfully the morning sickness, she had all day, is past."

"She's big as a house. Sure she should be traveling to the wedding?"

"Just try to stop her. And if I were you, I'd keep the big as a house to yourself, if you value your life." Kolby laughed.

"Of course. I was just surprised what a difference three months made." Lathen did a purposeful eye roll.

"Dad, you and Amy…doing well?"

"Oh, she keeps him in line like nothing the pack's ever seen," Kolby interjected. "On Saturday…you know, his day off…Mic…"

"That's enough. Tales of the pack can wait. In answer to your question. I thought there'd never be another. Being a single parent all those years then baching it after you two left the nest, I didn't lack for female companionship, but…got set in my ways. Amy, she has…ideas…hell it's been an adjustment, but I wouldn't trade her or our life now for the world." He paused as if he was deciding to comment further but shook his head. "Are we going to be able to see Rocky Mountain National Park?"

Lathen grinned, his father still wasn't comfortable with discussing feelings, so he let it go and glanced at Pepper's dad.

Duncan came to Elijah's rescue. "Yep. Heck of a snowstorm is predicted to blow in Thanksgiving Day ending by Friday afternoon. Give me a chance to try out the new sleigh on Friday. If you're interested? But tomorrow, we'll head to RMNP bright and early. Spend the day. Do some hiking, maybe snowshoeing in the higher areas. Or just drive through. October and November have been really mild so far."

"How far from here?" Elijah asked.

"Couple hours' drive."

"Looking forward to it." Elijah shifted in his chair to face Duncan. "Pepper got her love of animals from you?"

"Partly, but mostly from her Aunt Ashling. She did wildlife rescue and rehab before the need for such things were known. Pepper was a natural."

Lathen pushed up from the couch. "I'm going to go find the girls. Don't think they are going to come back on their own."

Elijah snorted. "You really expected them to?"

"No." Lathen grimaced.

Duncan stood. "How about we join you." He glanced at Eli and Kolby.

"Sure. I'd like to take a look at the horses." Kolby

pushed up from the couch and stretched his legs.

"Eli you can check out the apartment you and Amy will be staying in. Take a look at the horses and the sleigh I got with them."

Lathen's dad raised his brow. "A sleigh came with the horses?"

"Yeah, hell of a deal. Apparently the man passed away, the wife couldn't care for the horses alone. Her kids couldn't afford to keep them."

"That's a terrible situation," Lathen said.

"We tried to help her out. After a month, she offered to give us the four horses, the sleigh, and horse trailer, if we promised to give them a good home for the rest of their lives. She cried when we loaded everything up. Felt really bad for her, but it was too much for her. She stops by to visit with the horses about once a week. Takes them for a ride sometimes."

"Too bad. But a nice opportunity for you." Elijah got to his feet. "Let's take a look at the horses."

Lathen shrugged into his coat and opened the back door. Ember and Tonk rushed in barking, but Timber was nowhere in sight.

Chapter Nine
Escape from the Testosterone—First Glimpse of the Wedding Dress

When Pepper pushed one side of the barn door, it creaked and groaned as it slid open. Jasmine nickered softly, Midnight pawed the ground with his hoof snorting loudly.

"It's okay... It's just me, and I've brought a friend."

Jasmine swung her head around and over the stall gate to stare at the newcomer. Her ears twitched forward and back.

"I brought you an apple," Pepper cooed, drawing her hand from her pocket, offering the small fruit to the horse on the flat palm of her hand. The horse took the apple gently with soft lips brushing Pepper's palm. "That's a good girl." She stroked the horse's forehead and gave her cheek a pat.

Scout snorted and pawed at the ground watching Pepper with soulful eyes.

"I've got an apple for each of you, just settle down."

Hayley sidled up beside Pepper. "Can I give him one?"

"Sure. Make sure you keep your hand flat and no sudden movements. They are gentle horses. I can't imagine how hard it was for the owner to part with them." Pepper relayed the story her mom had imparted when they'd been out for the first ride.

"How sad." Hayley held the apple out for Scout then giggled when the large palomino's lips tickled her hand as he took the fruit. "What a beautiful sleigh over there. Looks like Santa's sleigh with the red paint and silver trim. Look at that, bells on the harnesses too."

"Yeah, I can see Mom's touch on it. See the glittered holly garland and red/green bows on the silver rails." Pepper smiled. Before this visit she'd never known her mother to care for animals like her dad, Aunt Ashling, and herself. But her mom's love of the newly acquired horse, Rita, and pup, Timber, was another side she'd not seen...or maybe not taken the time to notice.

Lathen's reunification with first his brother last summer, then his pack and father in August before their wedding had given her a new perspective into her own relationship with her parents, especially her mom.

"What about the other two?" Hayley asked giving Pepper's shoulder a slight tap.

Midnight tossed his head back and forth, snorting several times. When he was done, Rita's soft whinny caught Pepper's attention. She handed another apple to Hayley and pointed to Rita.

"Hang on, there're apples for all." Pepper gave Jasmine one final rub on the neck and stepped over to where Midnight stood still shaking his head impatiently. "A bit spoiled are we?" She offered the apple to him. The horse eyed her sideways before he nudged her hand then carefully took the fruit. Almost as if he disagreed with her assessment. She laughed, scrubbing her hand over his neck under his mane. "Now that's much better. Huh?"

"So how are things going? You all ready for the baby?" Pepper eyed the growing baby bump beneath Hayley's coat.

"I hope so. The nursery is painted, bought the crib, changing table, and dresser the day before we left to come here. Baby shower is two weeks from now, just before we leave for your wedding."

"Oh, I wish I could be there." Pepper sighed. "Too many things happening all at once."

"We can video chat you in on the shower," she offered.

"Hey, that would be great."

"Plans for the wedding done?" Hayley asked with a smirk.

"Surprisingly enough, I'm close. About had a melt down over the wedding dress, but Amy saved my sanity."

"She told me. The dress is beautiful. It's in the black garment bag, along with the shoes and Gloria's rose tiara kinda thing. They're absolutely you! The bag is probably in the apartment"—she glanced overhead—"where Eli and Amy are staying."

"I was going to show you the living area anyway; let's take a peek?" Pepper said conspiratorially, walking across the barn floor to the stairs leading to the apartment.

She opened the door. The living room and kitchen were all one room with a small table dividing the areas. A door off the living area opened to a cozy bedroom and king sized bed with a wildlife motif comforter and curtains. The floor was polished hardwoods throughout with matching accent throw rugs. Sliding glass doors opened up to a balcony facing the cabin and the mountain range.

Hayley walked to the glass doors and peered out. "Bet the sunset is spectacular from here."

Pepper slid the door open and stepped out on the balcony with Hayley right behind her. "You're right. But I think your guest room faces the same direction only on ground level in the cabin. Didn't figure you'd appreciate climbing the stairs to here."

The girls returned to the room, Hayley shivered closing the balcony door. "Look there's the garment bag."

The barn door creaked open, a woman's voice called out. "Pepper, Hayley you two still in here?"

As soon as Pepper heard voices, she scooted to the other door and opened it. "Mom, Amy come on up, we were just admiring the view Eli and you will enjoy during your stay."

"Oh, I bet you are. Hayley couldn't wait to show you the wedding dress." Amy climbed the stairs ahead of Klaren. She breezed into the room where the garment bag remained untouched resting on the bed.

"Innocent." Pepper declared triumphantly but feeling a little like a kid caught with her hand in the candy jar.

"We were talking about it," Hayley said sheepishly.

"So what are we waiting for?" Amy padded to the bed, picked up the bag, and hung it in the open closet. She pulled the zipper down to display the shimmering cream dress designed to hug the curves of the woman who wore it. The matching ballet slipper flats with small purple bows tumbled out of their box onto the floor.

Pepper's breath caught in her throat, then the air whooshed out of her. "It's absolutely beautiful. Exactly what I envisioned." Pepper held it up in front of her and twirled.

Amy looked Pepper up and down. "I'm positive the dress will fit so you can try it on later. But if you could just slip the shoes on and make sure they fit, I'd feel better," Amy said, bending down to pick up the shoes, handing them to Pepper.

Sitting on the side of the bed, Pepper took off her boot and sock, slipped one foot into the shoe. She stood up on her feet. "It's a perfect fit. I don't want to mess up the inside with my sweaty feet, so I'll try them on together later. If that's okay?"

"No problem. When I made the purchase, the sales lady said they ran a bit wide."

Pepper removed the shoe and reached for the dress again. Holding it up, she swayed in front of the full-length mirror on the closet door. Hayley settled the purple rose tiara on Pepper's head. The greenery and tiny roses trailed down her wavy light red hair that cascaded to her waist.

"It's a perfect match to your shoes, with the purple scalloped edges around the bottom of the gown and side slit," Hayley said admiring the dress. "Try it on."

Pepper fingered the material and looked at Amy. "I'd like to make sure it fits."

"Sure, try it on. But I can guarantee it will fit you perfectly," Amy said, a touch of mystery in her voice.

Carefully, she removed the dress from the hanger and hugged it to her. "It feels so...I don't know...makes me feel so special." Pepper shrugged off the parka and wiggled out of her jeans and shirt.

Hayley untangled the tiara from Pepper's hair and helped her slip the dress over her head. It slid down her body in one smooth motion, hugging her curves, flowing to the floor. Amy lightly tugged Pepper's hair from under the dress and let it fall in waves down her back after zipping up the dress.

"You will be a beautiful bride," Amy murmured.

Pepper's mom clicked her tongue in approval and sighed. "My baby is getting married." Moisture glistened in her eyes, and she blinked rapidly.

"Aw, Mom, you knew this day would come." Pepper hugged her mom.

"I wasn't so sure. Dedication to your profession...kept you..." Her mom brightened and smiled wistfully. "Along came Lathen, swept you off your feet—and here we are." She spread her arms wide enveloping Pepper in a hug, kissed her cheek, then held her at arm's length before reluctantly letting go. Turning toward the window, Klaren wiped a lone tear from her cheek.

Amy reached out, took the rose tiara from Hayley, and placed it on Pepper's head, arranging the trailing greenery with tiny rose buds among the light red strands of hair. She nodded her head in approval.

With a swishing motion, Pepper twirled around the room, holding the edge of her dress. "This makes me feel so... I've never felt like..."

"It's woven with wolf magic and love," Amy grinned. "Eli said you are the first non-wolf...well...witch, Lillian has made a dress... I can't help but wonder... Oh, never mind. You won over the women in the pack so completely, you're one of their own now." She shook her head. "When Eli introduced me to the pack, it took months for them to accept me. You come waltzing in and have them eating out of your hand in one day."

"Ohhhh…not all," Pepper said, remembering Lathen's old girlfriend who had slapped him across the face when she'd seen him preparing the community center in Alaska for Eli's wedding. Pepper felt her cheeks blush as the scene unfolded in her mind. She'd used magic to nearly strangle the life out of that bitch.

Laughter bubbled from Hayley's throat. "But she didn't take the most eligible bachelor in the pack off the market. You did."

Before Amy could respond, the barn door scraped against the floor as Lathen pushed the door open. Pepper felt his presence and stilled. Her mind's eye opened, and she saw him standing inside the doorframe.

He scanned the interior for the women but looked up the stairs when he heard footsteps overhead. "What are you girls doing up there?"

Klaren scampered to the door. "We'll be right down."

Pepper hurriedly slipped out of the dress, kicked the shoes off, and carefully untangled the tiara from her hair. Hayley took the dress and tiara, put them on a hanger in the garment bag, and zipped it up, careful not to catch any material in the zipper. Amy dropped the shoes back in the box and closed the closet door.

"Whew," Hayley said. "That was a close one. Don't want the groom seeing the wedding dress before the wedding."

"I thought the groom wasn't supposed to see the bride in the wedding dress," Pepper said.

"Same thing." Hayley huffed.

A whine, growl, and loud thump came from the inside the closet. "Oh nooo." Klaren yanked the closet door open. Timber lay sprawled on her back, hind feet kicking in the air, needle sharp puppy teeth chewing on the bottom corner of Pepper's wedding shoe box. Her mom whisked the pup into her arms. "You naughty little creature." She held her up and kissed Timber's wiggling wet nose.

Pepper examined the shoes. "No harm done." She peeked further into the large walk-in closet. "Where are Tonk and Ember?"

"Is Timber up there with you?" Lathen called from the bottom of the stairs. "Ember and Tonk tore in and out of the house when I came looking for you, but no Timber."

Opening the apartment door, Pepper stepped out on the small wooden landing. "Apparently Tonk and Ember ditched Timber. She's up here trying to chew up my new shoes."

"What kind of trouble are you girls getting into without male supervision." He snickered.

Balling up a wad of tissue paper she still held from the shoe box, she hurled it at him. "Nothing to concern your testosteroned mind with."

"What? Never heard of such a thing. You made that adjective up." He roared with laughter.

"Maybe…" she conceded as she flounced down the stairs toward him, Hayley, Klaren, and Amy on her heels. At the bottom of the stairs, she flung her arms around his neck and planted a smacking kiss on his lips.

His large hands encircled her waist, and he smiled against her lips as he deepened the kiss. Leaning into him, she returned his kiss with reckless abandon. Klaren swatted Pepper's butt as she passed by, the other ladies giggled.

"Pepper, come along, time to release him and help fix dinner, you can finish what you started later." She chuckled, led the others toward the barn door, heard voices and turned. "Everyone convened out here?"

"Kolby and Elijah wanted to see the horses, check out the sleigh," Duncan said.

"Then Lathen got derailed." Kolby snickered glancing up the stairs.

"You heard your mom; we'll finish this tonight," Lathen whispered against her ear, his voice husky. Reluctantly he released her, turned his attention to his brother, gave him a middle finger salute.

Kolby snickered again as his dad chuckled. "Boys will be boys, regardless of their age."

Even with the rude interlude, desire zinged through Pepper's body as she and Lathen walked to the cabin hand in hand, his breath rapid as if he'd ran a long race. She smiled. He was as aroused as she.

After a dinner of chili and cornbread, the group sat around the fire sipping wine, exchanging tales of life in Alaska, and at the Lobster Cove Rescue and Rehab Center. In addition, Duncan and Klaren described retired life in the country as opposed to the daily grind of college professors in the city.

Pepper stifled a yawn and proposed an early night since they planned to leave before dawn for Rocky Mountain National Park.

Lathen suggested they take two vehicles. The couples agreed and decided that Pepper, Kolby, and Hayley could accompany Lathen in the rented SUV.

While Klaren, Elijah, and Amy would ride in Duncan's crew cab truck. Goodnights were said, and each couple retired to their rooms.

"Alone at last." Lathen closed the door to the bedroom quietly and crossed to Pepper. Taking her in his arms, she felt his heartbeat increase against her chest. She drew in a breath as her own heart thundered. The caress of his lips on her mouth, trailing along her jaw line and to the rise of her breast shot spirals of desire through her body. His hand slid under her sweater, releasing the front hook of a wispy lilac silk bra. Her breasts spilled into his hand as the other pulled the sweater over her head and tossed it aside. He fondled one firm breast, its pink nipple a ripe berry and lowered his head flicking his tongue across the tip, drawing it into his mouth. She shivered at his tantalizing touch.

"In a hurry are we?" she cooed. Curling her fingers into the bottom of his shirt, tugging it over his head, the shirt slid to the floor.

She slipped her fingers inside his waistband and flicked open the button, lowered the zipper. The jeans hung on the curve of his firm ass until she tugged them down, where they pooled on the floor.

He stepped out of them, swept her up in his arms, she kissed him, lingering as their tongues entwined in a sinuous dance. He eased her onto the bed.

When his fingers stroked between her breasts, along her ribcage, and across her belly, pleasant jolts of desire swirled where she was already hot. Unbuttoning her jeans, he slid the zipper down and peeled the jeans off her legs, leaving only her lilac silk panties.

With a dark and smoldering look, he stared at her

semi-naked body, his fingers teased lower, pulled her panties aside, and stroked her warm, wet flesh. He bent over and breathed a warm kiss through the silk of her panties, slipping a finger inside. A soft moan left her lips as she arched against his hand. Panties went flying when he crawled between her legs, running his hands up her thighs. Heat seared through her. He knew how to touch a woman.

Breath ragged with desire, he whispered, "You are absolutely beautiful."

She leaned forward, his impressive erection straining for release, Pepper pulled at his underwear, and his length sprang free. He wiggled out of the fabric, lowering himself onto her. His erection pressed against her opening. As he leaned on his elbow, she arched up, knocking him off balance. He rolled to his side, and she straddled him, pushing him onto his back.

"My turn." She giggled hovering over him. Slowly she eased around him. Painstakingly slow, she allowed him inside her an inch at a time. When he was buried to the hilt, he groaned and arched his hips finding a rhythm to please.

"No, no, no, not yet." She raised up.

"Tease." He grunted with a smirk, grasped her waist with both hands, and thrust into her until she covered her mouth to muffle the scream as an orgasm ripped through her.

When her pleasure subsided, he rolled her onto her back. Her breasts crushed against the hardness of his chest as they found the sequence that bound them together soaring higher and higher until she crashed over the edge of ecstasy again. This time, he followed her, his breath coming in long, shuddering moans. After a few minutes, he rolled to his side and gazed at her. "I love you," he murmured against her ear.

"I still love you more," she said sleepily.

"No way," he whispered, shifting so their legs entwined. She snuggled her head against his shoulder, enveloped in his arms, and drifted off to sleep.

Chapter Ten
An Exciting Sleigh Ride After a Thanksgiving Snowstorm

Wednesday morning a bright orange sliver of sun lay across the horizon. Breakfast consisted of muffins filled with egg, bacon, cheese, and various veggies depending on each person's preference. A recipe Pepper had found on the internet and tried at home. After the delicious muffins were gobbled down, plates put in the dishwasher, and table wiped off, everyone reached for their coat.

In layers of winter gear, Lathen, his brother, Hayley, and Pepper climbed into the SUV with steaming mugs of coffee and hot chocolate. Klaren, Amy, and Elijah clambered into Duncan's truck, their travel mugs filled with fresh coffee for the two-hour drive to explore Rocky Mountain National Park.

Upon arrival at the park, Lathen presented his annual park pass. The ranger told them Trail Ridge Road was closed due to a recent snow. However, Bear Lake Road was open and some of the hiking trails around it. "There's good snowshoeing farther up. Watch for weather change; we're expecting snow later this afternoon," Ranger Smith said with a smile, handing park brochures through the window.

"Kinda figured that. Thanks." Lathen pulled the SUV forward a couple of vehicle lengths and waited for

Duncan to clear the checkpoint. No other vehicles were behind them. Once the truck was even with the SUV, both men rolled down their windows.

"Bear Lake it is," Duncan called out cheerfully. "Glad we brought snowshoes."

"Yep, maybe another time. We'll follow you." Lathen rolled the window up and waited for Duncan to take the lead. "Girls are you going to hike round Bear Lake, or stay in the vehicle?"

"We're hiking of course," Hayley said indignantly. "I'm pregnant not incapacitated."

Lathen laughed, glancing at Kolby. "It's an easy hike and designated for the handicapped. Even have benches around the lake."

Hayley reached up and slapped Lathen lightly upside the head. "You knew that was coming."

"Hey, I'm just being thoughtful. I didn't mean…" He rubbed the side of his head, sent a sideways glance to Kolby. "Help me out here, bro."

Kolby raised his hands, palms up in a gesture of surrender and shook his head. "No way! You dug the hole; you figure out how to get out. Besides, I gotta live with her." He neatly dodged a swipe from his wife.

Pepper sat silent, her hands folded in her lap, smiling like a Cheshire cat.

Easing the SUV into the parking spot next to Duncan's truck, Lathen jumped out, skimmed the hood of the SUV as he vaulted over, and opened Pepper's door. "My lady?" He bowed deeply.

She flicked her hand with flourish, then took his and slipped out of the vehicle. "Who says chivalry is dead. But I'm not helping you either."

Lathen frowned at her, then snorted. "Figures."

Kolby assisted Hayley out of the vehicle. They joined the group standing behind the truck.

"This trail leads around Bear Lake Loop, up to Nymph Lake, Dream Lake, and on to Emerald Lake. Dream Lake is great for snowshoeing. Which I happen to have in the back of the truck. What's the plan?" Duncan glanced around the group unlocking the metal tool box in the back of the truck.

"I'd like to check out Dream Lake, get some pictures." Elijah held up his new camera. "It's one of the most photographed lakes in the park."

"I'll join you," Lathen and Kolby chorused.

"Me too, unless…" Amy said, peering over at the other women.

"No, go ahead," Klaren said. "I'm happy to walk Bear Lake Loop."

"Hayley and I will take the Bear Lake Loop too; if she wants to go farther, we will. Otherwise, we'll meet you guys back here," Pepper said, glancing at the snowshoes in the bed of the truck before pushing off the side of the truck.

"Hey, Pep, you don't have to stay here with me. Go ahead with them. Klaren and I'll have a good chat walking around the loop." Hayley zipped up her parka, pulled on her hat and gloves.

"That's exactly what I am afraid of." Pepper shifted from one foot to the other, her camera swinging from a strap around her neck. "But the trail to Dream Lake passes Nymph Lake and has breathtaking views of Glacier Gorge, Longs Peak, Hallett Peak, and Flattop Mountain."

"The girl does her homework," Eli said.

"We'll have plenty of time to gab later," Hayley

said giving Pepper a shove toward the others.

"I won't tell too many stories about your childhood... Promise," Klaren said smugly, crossing her arms across her chest.

"Yeah right. That's why your arms and ankles are crossed." Pepper huffed. "But I'm going to go with the guys and Amy anyway. Thanks." She hugged her mom and Hayley then took a pair of snowshoes Lathen handed her.

"Don't put your hands in the water. Bear Lake is the only lake in the park that has leeches," Duncan warned with a chuckle; he turned toward the lake. "It's completely frozen over anyway. I see people walking across it."

"You had to say that, didn't you Duncan." Klaren pursed her lips and frowned.

Duncan shrugged. "Well...it does." He tossed the truck keys to Klaren. "If you get back before us, just hop in the truck and wait."

His wife reached up and plucked the keys out of the air. "I put a set of truck keys in my backpack. Keep yours." She handed them back to him.

The group talked as they made their way around the Bear Lake loop. Evergreen trees and aspens grew close to the winding path around the lake's shore. A wooden bridge over the shallow narrow end allowed a glimpse of cutthroat trout during the summer, according to the posted sign. Hayley and Klaren stopped and sat on a bench before venturing on up to Nymph Lake, where beautiful yellow lilies make their home on the deep blue waters. Today, it was also frozen. Pepper waved as she loped up the hill to catch up where the guys and Amy headed toward Dream Lake.

Lathen let the others take the lead up the trail and caught Pepper by a gloved hand. "Your dad and I were talking last night. He said something about the use of magic at Christmas time held no consequences."

She tilted her head a bit and narrowed her eyes. "Depending on what it's used for. Yes, that's true. Christmas magic is different than the regular magic according to the McKay's folklore, which is what my dad is talking about. I have no idea why, except maybe when the witches married mortals Christmas magic spun from their beliefs. Why?"

"Maybe we could use the spell he talked about, then we wouldn't have to use the Lobster Cove Community Center for the reception. The ceremony and reception could all be held on the property."

"I've thought of that. But then we wouldn't be able to invoke the rights of a bride and groom to leave early…if we wanted to. Because everyone would be in our home. Which is where I want to spend our wedding night…alone."

"But Gwen will be there."

"Gwen's different than having the whole town, family, and friends at the cabin. Then trying to get everyone to leave at a reasonable time."

Lathen groaned and tapped himself in the forehead. "Oh…I see now."

"Along that line though… Maybe we could use magic to build a temporary large, heated structure for one night near the pond and hold the reception there. If we feel like leaving the reception early, we could escape to the cabin. Still, the reception location is on the invitations."

"True, but I like that option," Lathen said nodding.

"We can mull it over."

"We'll work on that with Aunt Ashling when we get back home. Since she's overseeing magic at the pond."

Lathen looked up ahead and noticed the other couples had stopped to put on their snowshoes. Pepper and Lathen did the same, and their little group continued to Dream Lake.

As Elijah and Pepper finished taking pictures, light snow swirled through the air. Pepper took the camera from around her neck and carefully handed it to Lathen.

He pushed the review button, scrolled through the pictures and nodded. "Awesome."

Duncan smiled peering over Lathen's shoulder. "During the summer, the lake reflects its surroundings like a mirror image. No matter which outlook you take a picture from, it looks different. That's why they call it Dream Lake." The snowflake size and intensity increased. "I don't think we want to go on to Emerald Lake."

"Agreed. Let's head back," Elijah said. When the group arrived at Nymph Lake, they took off the snowshoes.

By the time they reached the vehicles, the snowflakes were still on the increase; the ground was covered with a couple inches of snow. Duncan yanked open the door to the truck, and warm air whooshed out. Hayley and Klaren sat in the back seat warm and toasty.

"I'm riding home in this truck," Hayley said leaning over Klaren.

"Me too." Pepper climbed into the front passenger seat, closed and locked the door.

"I guess we are riding with Lathen," Elijah said on

a laugh, wrapping his arms around Amy. "I think you've been abandoned by your kind."

"No, I wasn't as fast as Pepper. Or I'd be in that seat and she'd be standing out here." Amy grimaced.

"It won't take long for the SUV to heat up," Lathen said glowering in Pepper's direction. She merely stuck her tongue out at him and turned her attention to the women in the back seat.

He fobbed the vehicle open, clambered inside, and started the engine. The drive home was treacherous, blowing and drifting snow caused the red tail lights on Duncan's truck to disappear and reappear several times during whiteout conditions as Lathen tried to keep the truck in sight. The two-hour drive took four. It was nearly eight o'clock when he pulled into the McKay driveway behind Duncan.

Klaren popped out of the truck first and hurried up the path to unlock the cabin. When she pushed the door open, Ember, Tonk, and Timber came bounding out, all wiggles and wagging tails. Just as quick they were off chasing each other, barking and rolling in the snow. Kaylee's loud whistle could be heard between wind gusts that nearly toppled Elijah and Amy as they trudged into the house. The group took off their boots. Lathen sniffed. "Something smells awfully good. Beef stew?"

"Yep, I put it on this morning before we left. I'll whip up cornbread, and we'll have dinner in two shakes of a peacock's tail." Klaren grinned and hurried off to the kitchen.

"Need any help?" Amy followed behind her. Hayley plopped onto the couch, hand over her belly. Kolby settled next to her. Duncan flicked his fingers at the fireplace, and it roared to life.

"That's more like it." Pepper's dad started to ease into the recliner farthest from the fire. "Hey Klar, do I need to make coffee?"

"Nope, it's handled, be a couple minutes."

Pepper sprinted to the aviary to sooth Kaylee. Within a few minutes, she walked into the room with the osprey on her gauntleted arm.

"She refuses to eat," Pepper announced straightening papers below the bird's portable perch in the family room. "I'll thaw a few fish cubes for her, throw them in her bowl a bit later."

Lathen whistled for Ember, Tonk, and Timber to come inside. "Don't want them wandering off in this storm."

The canines barreled into the house covered in snow and paused momentarily to shake. The wet, cold stuff flew everywhere. The fire sizzled as droplets steamed on the hearth. Lathen filled the empty bowls next to the door and got the dogs and wolf fresh water. Pepper brought out a towel and wiped them down, mopped up the floor. The furred creatures ate, drank, and settled down in front of the door, each vying for the premier place to look out the side glass window. After growls, snarls, a couple barks, and a yip, Ember laid her head on her paws and watched out the window.

"Come and get it," Klaren called from the kitchen. "Grab a bowl and ladle up the stew. Cornbread, plates, and butter are on the dining table along with the silverware and glasses. The coffee is done, mugs beside the coffee maker. Pepper, the tea bags or cocoa mix is in the basket. Make sure you drink lots of water. Otherwise, the altitude will mess you up."

"So that's your problem," Kolby teased his brother.

"Nope, I'm just fine. It's you we wonder about," Lathen shot back, punching Kolby in the arm as he rounded the table to take a seat next to Pepper, who had already scooped up a spoonful of stew, blowing on it.

Elijah smiled at his boys and sat next to Amy with his bowl and a heaping plate of cornbread. "Klaren, your cornbread is wonderful. What's your secret?"

"I already gave the recipe to Amy," she said smugly taking a chair next to her husband.

By the time dinner was over and the dishes stacked in the dishwasher, Lathen wasn't the only one with drooping eyelids; the others were ready to turn in for the night.

"Thanks for the tour of Rocky Mountain National Park. It is an amazing treasure. We'll make a point to visit during the summer and get the full experience."

"Glad to do it. Wish the storm had held off a bit longer. But we're back safe and sound." Duncan glanced out the front bay window. "It's really coming down out there."

"Didn't bother us. All and all, I'd say it was a successful outing. I've lots of pictures to show the folks back home. It's really a winter wonderland when the snow is falling, blanketing everything with a frosty cover."

"Looked like a storybook snow," Amy added with a yawn.

"Let us know when you decide to make a summertime visit to our fine state. We'll be happy to play tour guide," Klaren said.

"Will do." Eli nodded.

"Tomorrow, Elijah, I'd love to compare photos.

Maybe even swap a few, put them on a couple of thumb drives." Pepper glanced where she'd left her camera bag on the floor next to the door.

"Of course." Popping the last bit of cornbread in his mouth, Eli stood. "Amy, what you say we check out their wonderful apartment," he said in a smooth, deep voice, an eyebrow raised.

Amy's chair scraped the floor as she got to her feet. "Night everyone. See you in the morning." She turned to Klaren. "What time do you want me in here to help with Thanksgiving dinner?"

"Oh, whenever you get here is fine. Most of the prep is done. Turkey, gravy, stuffing, and pumpkin pie is all that's left."

"The pumpkin pie is my specialty," Pepper said.

"'Night." With Eli's arm around Amy's waist, they walked out the back door.

Lathen stood at the door and watched them laugh and toss snow at each other making their way to the apartment. A strange sense of contentment and belonging welled up inside him. This was truly going to be a holiday season to remember. Pepper's soft hand caressing his cheek brought him out of his thoughts. His head turned, he caught her hand and brushed his lips against the palm.

"You about ready to turn in?" Her eyes rounded at the yawn that caught her by surprise.

"Sure." He noted while he'd watched his dad and Amy, that Kolby and Hayley had disappeared.

****

Pepper peered out the window. Large, wet snowflakes floated through the crisp morning air adding a sparkling cover over the ground. Several inches of the white stuff covered the outside windowsill. The intensity of the flakes increased along with the wind howling around the cabin.

"Yeah, it's going to be a doozy of a storm," Lathen said standing at the front window watching Ember, Tonk, and Timber race, roll, and tumble in the snow. "I hope you have a good rug at the front door. Those dogs are going to be soaked and tracking it all over the house."

"On the flip side, all the heavy wet snow will make perfect conditions for sleigh rides tomorrow afternoon with the worst of the storm over. If the forecaster's predictions are correct," Duncan said with a wide smile as he ambled across the floor to stand beside Lathen.

The rich aroma of roasted turkey, candied yams, and pumpkin pie floated through the house. When everyone was seated, Pepper glanced around the dining table at their blended family and sighed. "I'd like to start a family tradition. How about we go around the table and state what we are thankful for this year. It's been such a year of transition for all of us."

She shrugged uncertainly but brightened when all heads nodded in agreement. "I'll start. Last year on Thanksgiving, Gwen and I sat in Salem with a microwave turkey dinner while trying to keep a tiny fawn alive. This year, I am thankful that fawn lived and for the love of a wonderful man, the acceptance of his family and pack, and the love and understanding of my family."

Lathen stroked her knee, nearly to the thigh and smiled. "I'm thankful for Pepper, my family, and the pack's forgiveness. To include the unconditional love her mom and dad have bestowed on me. No questions asked. Most importantly, thankful for all the men and women in the armed forces that are willing to make the ultimate sacrifice to protect our way of life and keep our nation free."

Pepper's mom's eyes misted, a wide smile curved the corners of her lips. "I am thankful for my husband of many years, and what a blessing my daughter found Lathen. That Elijah, Amy, Kolby, and Hayley have joined our family and are here to share our Thanksgiving holiday."

Kolby shifted uncomfortably in his chair. "I'm not good at things like this. But here it goes. I'm thankful my brother's back, my dad is happily married to Amy, God bless her. Thankful to be part of the McKay family and most of all my wife, Hayley and our soon to be born daughter."

Hayley grinned. "I'm thankful for everything everyone else has said and for my husband. He'll make a great father."

"Gee why didn't I think of saying that." Kolby chuckled.

Elijah paused then blew out a breath. "I'm thankful for the safety and anonymity of my pack, for Amy, my family, and the addition of the McKay's to our family."

Amy's gaze wandered over all the people at the table. "I'm going to take a page from Hayley. Thankful for everything everyone has said and for Eli's love, though he can be a big pain at times."

Duncan licked his lips. "I'm starved so ditto to everything said, thanks for my wife and this wonderful dinner. Pass those delicious candied yams."

Everyone laughed and began handing the food from one to another. Duncan offered the duty of carving the turkey to Elijah, but he declined. "It's your home; you do the honors."

The clatter of dishes being passed and ting of forks scraping plates replaced the conversation while the couples enjoyed the Thanksgiving bounty. Pepper thought about her friend, Gwen, at the Salem Wildlife Sanctuary and wondered if she was alone this Thanksgiving.

After dinner, Pepper excused herself and walked into the bedroom. She picked up her phone, touched the screen, and scrolled to Gwen's number. It only rang once, and she picked up. "Pepper, is everything all right? Aren't you with your family in Colorado?"

"Yes, but I was thinking about you and wanted to say Happy Thanksgiving. Wish you were here. Are you spending it at the Sanctuary again?"

"Yeah, we have an injured yearling that needs round the clock care. But I had the strangest sensation that things are changing. I hope for the good." She laughed. "Remember last Christmas, we were sitting around your apartment, and you had the feeling…more like a premonition that you wouldn't be here this Christmas."

"Yes, we laughed it off."

"But look where you'll be this Christmas. Married to a handsome guy, who loves you, with your own Rescue. It's kinda the same thing. But I can't see me going anywhere."

"Neither did I, but…"

The door creaked open, and Lathen poked his head inside, then started to back out. Pepper motioned him in. "I called Gwen to wish her Happy Thanksgiving."

He crossed the room and put his arm around her

shoulder. "Tell Gwen the same from me. Ask her to try to come a few days early for the wedding and spend at least Christmas with us, if not New Year," Lathen said quietly.

"Gwen, Lathen just came in and insists that you come a few days early to help me with the wedding preparations, then spend Christmas and New Year with us. He won't take no for an answer," Pepper said in a warning tone.

Gwen laughed. "That's funny, I told everyone since I worked Thanksgiving, I would be gone for a couple of weeks around Christmas. I've been able to hire a few new people, thanks to the generosity of a charitable donation from an estate in Lobster Cove, Maine."

"Oh, really…imagine that. So we'll see you in a few weeks. Happy Thanksgiving."

"Happy Thanksgiving to both you and your families." Gwen ended the call.

Pepper sighed and peered up at Lathen. "I wish she would find someone…"

"You never know," Lathen said mysteriously.

Chapter Eleven
Never a Dull Moment with Family, Friends, and a
Wolf Pack

The room was washed out in gray and white by the silver moonlight filtering through the window when Pepper's phone buzzed. She rolled over and picked up the phone. "Hello?" she mumbled in a sleep muzzy voice. "Alec, what's wrong." Instantly awake, she sat straight up in the bed. "When did it start?"

"This morning—I mean yesterday morning. The owl was lethargic, but the sounds she's making now aren't normal. Her breath is coming in rasps. She's leaning against the wall of the cube in the warmest part of the enclosure. I didn't want to stress her, but I'm sure her fever is up."

"Did you call Dylan?"

"Sure did. She's out of town on an emergency. Supposed to be back this morning, but…"

"Didn't they leave a vet on call?"

"Yes, but his knowledge of avian medicine is limited. Not comfortable around wild birds…at all. The owl tore open his hand with her talon when he tried to examine her. Got fluids in her and a mild sedative so he could examine her. She started to perk up, so I didn't want to bother you. Figured I wait for Dr. Foster. I left her a message…but… It doesn't look good."

"First of all, you should never sedate a sick bird

until you know...mask the real problem. Oh, sorry Alec...I know you are doing your best, but you should have called. Don't worry about bothering me, ever." Her tone sharper than she intended.

Half asleep, Lathen reached over, rubbed her arm, and shook his head slowly. Pepper's voice calmed. "Sorry. Let me think." Pepper hopped out of bed, grabbed the green and black plaid flannel robe from the bottom of the bed, wrapped it around her naked body, and paced across the floor. "Okay, there's a broad spectrum antibiotic in the locked cabinet in my office, top shelf in the right back corner. The key is in the middle left drawer in the little pink metal box. Go get it and call me back."

"You got it."

"What's going on?" Lathen flicked on the bedside light, pulled himself up, and leaned against the headboard.

Pepper glanced at the clock, the blue digital readout said two-thirty a.m. "The owl is running a fever, lethargic, and tore open the vet on call. One of the wounds must have gotten infected." She blew out a breath, looked at her phone. "I'm going to try Dylan again."

"Wait, if Alec left a message, she's otherwise tied up, or she would have called him. Can you use magic to carry you back to Maine?"

"Yes and no... I never honed that ability and..."

"Given your state of mind, you'd better not try tonight. What about Gwen? Maybe her vet is on call. At least you could talk to..."

The phone Pepper held tight to her chest chimed. She glanced at the screen, accepted the call. "Dylan."

"I just talked to Alec, got his message, and started back as soon as I got things wrapped up with the emergency. Especially after I got the message from the on-call vet. He's new. I'm fifteen minutes away."

"Thinking infection?"

"Probably, I've drugs with me, in addition to what you have, so…we'll do the best we can. I'll be in touch as soon as I've had a look at the bird. Sit tight, there's nothing you can do from there." Dylan ended the call.

Pepper relayed the conversation to Lathen, even though with his preternatural hearing, he'd probably heard most the conversation. It made her feel better to talk the situation over with him; she glanced at the clock again. *Shit, I hate waiting.* She started pacing again.

He stood up and pulled on sweat pants, intercepted her mid pace, wrapped his arms around her, held her tight as he murmured against her ear, "Wearing a path in the carpet isn't going to help anyone. Let's go to the kitchen and get some tea."

"But it's a little after three in the morning. We don't need to wake up the household."

"Then keep your voice down. It'll be fine." Lathen opened the door and peeked out. "Coast is clear." He smiled wearily.

Seated at the kitchen table, she watched Lathen put two mugs of water in the microwave, sort through the basket of tea bags, and pluck out two. He waved them in the air in triumph. "Chamomile and honey. That should do the trick." The microwave dinged quietly at the same time Pepper's phone chimed.

"Dylan. How's the owl."

"She's doing better. The wound on her head is hot

and infected. Cleaned the wound out, applied a topical antibiotic as well as gave her an injection. Turned up the humidity in her cube, so she'd breathe easier. Stress caused her rasping, it's subsided now. Added an oral sedative, most of which I am wearing, but got enough inside to relax her. Sure miss your calming ability in working with these creatures. She's resting comfortably now, she'll be fine. No need for you to rush home." Dylan yawned into the phone.

"Are you sure?"

"Yes. I'm going to go home and go to bed, but my cousin, Brock is visiting. He's a vet, works in a practice in Salem, and has agreed to stay here until the owl is out of the woods. So to speak." Dylan giggled at her pun.

"That's bad," Pepper said wearily, taking a sip of her luke warm tea, frowning. She passed her hand over the cup and steam rose from the mug; she took another sip. The corners of her mouth turned up in a half smile.

"Hey, I've been up for nearly forty-eight hours straight. I'm entitled. Talk to you this evening."

Pepper disconnected the call, pushed up from the chair. "Shall we go back to bed?"

Getting to his feet, Lathen shuffled to her. "Yep, sounds like the owl is going to be fine." He rubbed her shoulders, let his hand slide to the small of her back, guiding her through the hall and into the bedroom. "Sleigh rides today."

"You're really looking forward to that. Huh?"

"Yup."

"Me too. A sleigh ride is so romantic. Two people cuddled up under a blanket. Mugs of their favorite warm beverage. The horses and sleigh all decorated for the holidays." Pepper sighed and raised her hand to cover a yawn.

"I didn't know you were such a romantic," Lathen said, lifting the covers for her then crawling in next to her.

"Every woman is a romantic," Pepper mumbled snuggling against him, her head on his shoulder.

"You've watched too many Christmas movies." He chuckled. "On that channel that starts them right after Halloween."

"Hmm?"

When Pepper opened her eyes again, the sunlight filtered through the curtains and warmed her face. "Is the storm over?"

Lathen blinked. "It appears so."

Pepper listened for a moment. Cheerful voices came from the direction of the kitchen, along with the aroma for freshly brewed coffee. "I believe we are the last to wake up."

"I imagine. It's eleven-thirty. Almost missed the morning entirely." He rolled over and brushed his lips leisurely over hers. "We better get up. Breakfast and sleigh rides await."

Her stomach growled loudly as if in agreement. She laughed along with Lathen. Pepper bounced out of the bed. "Last one in the shower has to wash the other." She turned to see Lathen's mesmerizing aquamarine eyes sparkle with mischief as he sauntered across the bedroom floor to join her. "I like that challenge."

Pepper towel dried her hair, then dressed in flannel lined jeans, thermal shirt under a favorite brightly colored flannel shirt, warm socks, and insulated boots.

"You're going to be too warm while eating

breakfast." Lathen stood, top button on his lined jeans undone, one arm in his fleece flannel shirt, bare chest and back muscles rippled as he slipped the other arm into the shirt and buttoned it.

Pepper licked her lips stopping to watch Lathen get dressed. *He is one sexy package.* She stepped to him and unbuttoned the top three buttons of his shirt, her fingertips caressing the skin left bare by her actions. Leaning into him she nuzzled his neck, drawing in his fresh, clean scent, a mixture of pine, cloves, and spice.

"You want me to freeze to death out there?" A chuckle rumbled from his throat.

"Nope, just eye candy for breakfast." She smirked.

"Others may not be appreciative."

"That's their problem," Pepper shot back opening the bedroom door. "Mmmm something smells good. Mom's scrambled egg casserole."

He pulled on his socks and shoved his feet into the boots. "Breakfast will be a fast affair anyway. Bet we're the only ones that haven't eaten."

She stifled a giggle. "Everyone else is probably ready for lunch."

They walked into the kitchen, and Pepper shot him a sideways glance. Hayley was making a peanut butter sandwich on a plate with chips.

"It's about time, sleepy heads. Rough night?" her father asked.

"Yeah, the owl we told you about took a turn for the worse, vet was out of town, and Alec was worried. But it's all good for now." Pepper grabbed a spoon, scooped a couple big spoons of casserole, and plopped them on the plate. She took a cup, poured hot water over a spiced orange tea bag, and settled into a chair beside Hayley.

"Never a dull moment. Huh?" Hayley asked.

Pepper glanced over at Hayley noticing dark circles under her eyes. "You look a bit rough around the edges this morning yourself."

"Baby kicked all night."

"Yeah, she even got me in the back." The corner of Kolby's mouth kicked up in a lopsided grin as he reached over to touch his wife's belly. "She's going to be a handful. I can tell."

"She comes by it naturally," Eli said with a chuckle.

"So what's the plan for today?" Lathen asked taking a bite of toast before washing it down with a gulp of coffee.

"Thought we'd hitch Scout to the sleigh and take turns riding around the property. I've also saddled the other horses so the rest of us could follow the trails through the acreage on horseback."

"I'm going to stay here. Cinnamon rolls are in the oven, and I'll keep the hot drinks fresh and ready," Klaren said.

"I want to go for one sleigh ride, then I'll come in and help you." Hayley shifted in her chair rubbing her back.

"Are you sure that's a good idea?" Kolby asked his forehead creased, brows knitted together. "After last night…"

"I'm fine. The baby was just excited about the sleigh ride," Hayley said with a dismissive wave of her hand.

Kolby glanced from her to his dad and Amy. "Okay. But only one."

"Amy and I'll follow Duncan on horseback, then come in and warm up by the fire," Eli said, pushing up from the chair.

"Works for me." Duncan grabbed his coat as the rest followed suit.

When Kolby and Hayley returned from their sleigh ride, Pepper and Lathen filled up mugs with coffee and hot chocolate then charged out the cabin door. Tonk and Ember raced beside them barking excitedly. Kaylee soared overhead. Pepper shaded her eyes to check on the bird and whistled to get her attention, letting her know not to leave their sight.

Klaren held Timber's leash. "You can't go every time, little girl." Klaren cooed to the wiggling, whining puppy straining to follow the others.

"Mom, we'll take her in the sleigh with us," Pepper said reaching for the leash. "It's not fair for her to have to stay behind because she can't keep up with the other two." She climbed into the sleigh, sat the dog on the seat beside her, and tucked half the blanket around her. Lathen jumped in and eased into the seat. Pepper covered his lap with the rest of the blanket.

"Cozy. Huh?" He scooted next to her and wrapped an arm around her shoulders.

As the horse tugged at the sleigh, Duncan, Eli, and Amy returned. Amy climbed off the horse and handed the reins to Kolby. "You go on with your dad and Duncan. I hear the fire calling my name." She shivered. "Somehow nineteen degrees seems colder here than at home." She stomped the snow off her boots and hurried into the cabin.

Lathen slapped the reins; Scout started out in a walk. Pepper watched the steam rise from the little hole in the top of her travel mug; she took a sip. "Mmmm. Good stuff."

He followed a trail the sleigh had traveled before. The sun glinting off the newly fallen snow, piles of the white stuff clinging to the pine boughs made for a beautiful scene. Pepper pulled out the camera from her backpack. "Could we stop here for a moment? I'd like to get a picture of Scout, you, Ember, Tonk, and Timber in the sleigh."

Pulling up on the reins, he called out, "Whoa, up there, Scout." Pepper unwrapped the blanket and stepped out of the sleigh, nearly falling head first into the snow when her foot caught in the corner of the blanket. She turned to see Lathen's hand over his mouth she suspected covered a grin and frowned at him, but was unable to keep a straight face.

Pepper called Tonk and Ember to stand by the side of the sleigh, had Kaylee land on the edge, backed away, focused, and took the picture. Checking the digital screen, she smiled wide. "Perfect." She clambered into the sleigh just as Lathen's phone rang.

He yanked the phone out of his pocket and glanced at the screen, took off his gloves, and accepted the call.

"What's up Mike? Oh, hi Lynette." There was a short pause. Lathen's forehead creased and his jaw muscle twitched. "I'm in Colorado."

Another pause. "No, Jay is out of state too. Slow down Lynette, we'll get this handled. Put Mike on the phone. But first, do you have another phone? That's good. I want you to call Alec, a friend of mine. He's in Lobster Cove and can be in Bar Harbor in a few. Tell him Mike needs help; he'll understand. He's been there just like Jay and I have."

A longer pause. "Like hell he won't. Tell him I'm on the phone. Does he know you called? Then tell him I called." Lathen waited, his knuckles turned white from his grip on the phone. "Mike, settle down. Tell me what happened." Lathen listened for a long time.

"Dude, when did you take your medication last?" He handed the reins to Pepper and hopped out of the sleigh, pacing. "You need help. Mike… Mike…wait…"

Lathen blew out a breath; it circled his head like smoke in the frosty air. "Mike, okay…relax, we aren't going to make you do anything you don't want. But you can't scare your wife like this. Babies cry. It's a fact of life. Now take it easy. Remember my buddy Alec? He's on his way to you. We'll get this worked out."

He put his hand on the side of the sleigh, put his head on his hand. "You gotta pull it together. You want to see your little girl grow up? She needs you. Lynette needs you. It's just a rough patch; we'll get through it. How long have you been out of medication?"

Lathen nodded. "I understand…first let's get your… Hey…listen to me. Don't worry about the funds. It's covered." Lathen kicked at the snow and paced some more.

Tonk and Ember came to his side and walked along beside him. "Can you send Lynette and the baby to the pharmacy as soon as Alec arrives? The car ride will calm the baby. Okay, tell her to call me when she gets there. I'll handle payment. Don't worry about it. No handouts, you'll have to work it out at the Lobster Cove Wildlife Rescue & Rehab Center." He looked up at Pepper patiently waiting in the sleigh.

She nodded. *What the hell is going on?*

"No, Pepper won't mind. You know Alec works

there too. He's the manager." Listening a long time, Lathen blew out a breath. "Okay…Alec should be there within a few minutes…have Lynette get the baby ready to go… Good." He climbed back into the sleigh and took the reins.

Duncan, Eli, and Kolby cantered by, stopped. Lathen waved them on. "Tell me what you know about wildlife, construction, or maintenance."

Several minutes passed as Lathen guided the sleigh across the trails listening. He handed the reins to Pepper. She slowed Scout to a walk while Lathen continued the conversation.

With relief in his voice, Lathen said, "Alec's there. Good. Let me talk to him a minute. It's going to be fine, Mike. Jay and I'll be back this weekend." Lathen waited for Mike to hand Alec the phone, explained to Pepper what was going on.

Pepper shifted in the seat, relieved to see the cabin come into view.

"Alec, Lynette's going to go pick up medication. Take Mike for a long walk; make sure when she gets back she clears out all the guns in the house. The pharmacy is only a few blocks away. Mike's in a bad place right now… What, she's leaving…good." He paused.

"Okay, you'll need to stay with him for a while, maybe the night 'til the medicine kicks in. Mike won't go to the hospital. No use trying to force him. We don't want him more agitated than necessary. Did you get someone to cover for you at the Center?"

Lathen slumped in the seat. "Good, we're on the downside of this, I think. Mike's going to need… Yeah, I know… He's going to be working with us at the

126

LCWRR for a while. Okay, I'll see if I can get a hold of Jay. Call me if you need me. Let me talk to Mike again." Lathen switched the phone to his other ear. "Mike, Alec's going to stay with you for a while. You need to walk off some of that tension. Tomorrow, I want you to report to the Center in Lobster Cove at eight a.m. Alec can give you the address and directions. Have Lynette drive you, so she'll have the car if she needs it. Okay. Call me if you need me. I'll see you soon." Lathen touched the screen and ended the call. He looked over at Pepper, rested his head on her shoulder.

She reached up and stroked his hair. "Intense...have you got a handle on it?"

"Yes, for now, but... We may need to leave tomorrow, if I can get a hold of Jay. I'm sorry."

"Not a problem, I'd like to get back too. I feel so helpless...being clear out here...when I'm needed at the LCWRRC."

"The owl is in good hands, and you know it. Dylan's cousin is staying at the Center while Alec is with Mike. We're going to owe Dylan's cousin a fortune."

"Couldn't be helped. Besides that's what the emergency fund is for." Pepper rubbed Timber's ears. "Dad and Mom will understand. Your family is leaving tomorrow anyway. Right?" She paused for a couple beats. "You ready to tell me what's going on and who is Mike?"

Lathen sighed heavily. "Yeah. He's one of the veterans on my radar, kinda like a support tree. Mostly, Jay handles it, since you and I got together, but...well...things happen. Mike's been out of work for a while, trouble holding down a job because of his combat PTSD. Didn't stay on his meds, no money, couldn't get into the VA…just a series of things sent him into a downward spiral."

"I see… You never mentioned this part of your life before. Don't you think…"

"Yeah, probably should have, but knew it wouldn't make a difference to you. You don't mind that I offered him a job, only for a little while?"

"If we take time to train him and he works out, he can stay as long as he wants. Look how well Alec's done."

Lathen nodded, raised a brow. "But Alec had less baggage than Mike, like me he was single. Injured physically and psychologically, but no one depended on him…but Mike. It makes a difference."

"Isn't his wife…I mean he's got support…"

"No what he has is a young wife trying to cope with a colicky baby, who cries for hours, day and night. On top of the baby, she's got a husband who is more of a weight than a help, and they're struggling financially. He couldn't get his meds and was ready to end it all. I think we brought him back from the brink. That's why Alec will probably stay the night. A job will help in a lot of ways." Lathen scrolled through the numbers on his phone.

"Financially, but shouldn't the VA help with his medical care, prescription costs?"

"In an ideal world, but the VA system is broken; it's getting better—but not fast enough for people like Mike. So guys like Jay and I step in to fill the gaps as best we can. Speaking of Jay, I need to make that call." Lathen winced. "At least Jay got a few days with family." He tapped the screen and put the phone to his ear. The phone rang only once. "Jay, Lathen, we got a situation with Mike."

Tonk and Ember chased after the sleigh as they pulled in behind the cabin. Kolby, Duncan, and Elijah were waiting for them. Pepper jumped out of the sleigh. Lathen climbed out, held an index finger up, then walked away from the group talking with Jay.

"Is there a problem?" Duncan asked reaching to take a wriggling Timber from Pepper. "Are we finished with the sleigh for today?"

"Yeah. I think Lathen and I are going to have to head back to Lobster Cove tomorrow." She explained the situation to the group and the fact if Jay wanted to leave tomorrow morning, they'd have to leave too.

"Oh…your mom is going to be disappointed. She had tomorrow all planned." He shrugged. "She'll understand. We'll be in the Cove in a couple weeks anyway."

Pepper hugged her dad. "Thanks for understanding. It's just the nature of our business. Wildlife and apparently mankind too."

Lathen trudged over to where everyone stood and glanced at Pepper.

Lathen's warm breath formed a wreath around his head. "I talked with Jay. He wants to fly back to the Cove tomorrow. Mike's been unstable for a while. Jay thought he'd reached a good place. But…apparently not. Didn't know he was off his meds."

"Figured." Pepper wrapped her arm through Lathen's. "Bet Mom has the leftover chili warming on the stove and a new batch of cornbread." She sipped from her travel mug, wrinkled her nose, and popped the top, looked glumly at the contents. "My hot chocolate is

129

cold, what's left of it. My toes would love being next to a roaring fire."

"Duncan, need some help with the horses?" Lathen asked.

"I'd appreciate it. Jack has today and the weekend off."

Kolby and Eli took horses to the barn while Lathen helped Duncan unhitch the horse and put the sleigh away.

Pepper walked toward the cabin then stopped at the sound of her father's hushed voice.

"Lathen, I need to make a decision before Klar and I leave for the wedding. What do you think…?" Duncan glanced around and lowered his voice another notch.

Chapter Twelve
Back to the Cove and Wedding Plans

Well before the sun was up, the vehicles were packed and goodbyes said. Lathen turned the rented SUV toward DIA to meet up with Jay. The air was cold and ice crystals sparkled in front of the vehicle's headlights as he drove I-70 toward Denver. Jay was supposed to meet them in front of the rental car building with a van. But when he pulled up to the area, Jay waved him to the side of the building.

He walked up to the driver's side of the SUV. "Just drive to the plane. We'll unload the animals. Pepper can stay with the plane while we take the SUV back to rental, then return to the plane via shuttle. I can't see stressing the animals out any more than necessary."

"Where's the plane?"

"If you unlock the back passenger's side door, I'll get in and show you," Jay said.

Lathen and Pepper flicked the lock button at the same time, it unlocked then locked again making him laugh. Pepper held her hand up. "Go ahead."

Jay shook his head and pulled on the door handle, pointing to where the plane was parked.

"We don't have to go through security?"

"Nope, all taken care of." Jay buckled his seat belt. "Now drive. Want to get airborne before the commercial flights start taking off."

Lathen pulled up behind the private jet, cut the engine, hopped out, and opened the back. When he released the latches to the kennels and hooked leashes to Tonk and Ember, Pepper took the leads.

"I'll be right back to help you with the crates. I want to start the engine and get us cleared for takeoff." Jay sprinted up the steps to the plane.

Donning gloves, Lathen picked up Kaylee's crate and carried it up the stairs into the plane. He returned to the door of the plane in time to see Pepper take a quick look around and snap her fingers, the crates, and cooler with Kaylee's fish disappeared along with their luggage.

She walked the wolf and dog outside. The warm breath from their muzzles formed a foggy cloud in the cold air when they sniffed. Finally, the canines found a place and took care of business. Leading them up the stairs to the inside of the plane, Tonk balked, she gave him a sharp command. He stood braced for a second then trotted up the remaining stairs, ears plastered to his head. Lathen had secured their crates to the floor and stashed the suitcases in designated compartments.

"Nice trick. Thanks, but you could've…"

"Nope—knew exactly where Jay was, and no one else was nearby," Pepper said smugly commanding Ember and Tonk into their crates. Reluctantly with tails down they complied. Tonk barked, Ember growled, and Pepper gave them both a stern look. Silence reigned as they lay down.

"Wow you guys are quick." Jay glanced from the tied down crates and flipped open the luggage compartments.

"I'll take the SUV…"

"No need. One of the clerks was heading back to the building, so he offered to take it back. Toss me the keys." Jay stepped out the door and waited.

When Lathen tossed the keys, Jay reached up, snagged them, moved to the first stair, and threw the keys to a man with a car rental logo on his jacket. "Thanks, Josh, appreciate it." Jay pushed a button inside; the stairs pulled up and the door closed. "Patti, how about some coffee and hot chocolate?" He raised an eyebrow and glanced at Pepper.

"Sounds great." Pepper nodded.

"Patti brought some pastries, help yourselves." Jay grabbed a mug of steaming coffee and scooped up a pastry on his way to the cockpit.

When everyone was seated and belted in, Jay taxied the jet down the runway. Once they were airborne, Lathen released his seatbelt. "I'm going to go talk to Jay for a few minutes." He leaned over and released Pepper's seatbelt. Caressing her cheek with his fingers, he kissed her firmly on the lips. "Be right back."

"No problem." Pepper twisted in her seat checking on Tonk and Ember. "Kaylee, doing okay?" Pepper cooed. The osprey whistled softly in response. Pepper leaned her head against the seat, blew out a breath.

"You're not afraid of flying, are you?" Patti asked making her way to the galley. "It's cold but great flying weather."

"No, just thinking about all the things I have to do when I get back."

"Wedding jitters already?" Patti raised one brow and glanced at Lathen who stopped beside the galley to grab another pastry.

"Not at all, just got this nagging feeling..."

Pepper's voice faded out when Lathen reached the cockpit.

"Hey, Jay, heard anything more from Mike or his wife, Lynette?"

"No, Alec said he left around midnight. All was calm. Mike reported for work early this morning. Lynette dropped him off. A job is what Mike needed. That was great of you."

"Pepper believes in paying it forward."

"That's quite a gal you got there. Lucky man. Now don't screw it up. Get the ring on her finger."

"You know if I hear that phrase one more time...first my brother, then my dad, and even Amy, my dad's new wife. I'm not going to screw it up."

"We all just want the best for you...we know you."

"Maybe, but things have changed more than you'll ever know." Lathen thought back to the summer when Ashling had suggested psychological problems kept him from phasing, not physical. And how angry he'd been at her and even Pepper when she suggested the same thing only calling it survivor's guilt. He hadn't even thought about phasing when he came to Klaren's rescue that Halloween night.

Jay waved his hand in front of Lathen's face. "Hey dude, where'd you go?"

"Nowhere...I'm right here. So...how was the visit with your sister?"

"Great, but I was ready to leave when you called. Her kids are great, but four kids under the age of eight is too much for me. The twins are only six months old. Family likes Patti...so..."

"And you lecture me on relationships. Maybe you

better take a closer look at yours."

"Patti's okay... She doesn't put up with my shit and calls me out when I'm out of line. But...not like what I see going on between you and Pepper... Even I can see you've got something special."

"I am well aware of that. About Mike, are you going to insist that he check in with his doctor? Or you want me to?" Lathen shifted uncomfortably in his seat. Too many people giving him relationship advice...he was doing just fine.

"See if the job and meds stabilize him. Lynette has a doctor's appointment for the baby to see if there is anything to do for her colic. If everyone in that household gets some sleep, it will help. My sister had some ideas. Her oldest was a colicky baby. She called and talked to Lynette."

"Sounds like you have things handled. I'll talk to Alec and see how Mike worked out today. I'll let you know."

Pepper stepped quietly into the cockpit, reached over and put her hands on his shoulders, leaned over and kissed his neck. "Hungry?" You have your choice of hot turkey or a ruben sandwich, chips and a soft drink. Patti's already munching on the egg salad one."

"A ruben will work for me. How about you, Jay?"

"Same, unless you want it, then turkey is fine." Jay waved his hand as if it didn't matter. "Sorry for the lack of variety. It was kinda short notice to get food together for the trip. Should have a few wine coolers left." He turned to look over his shoulder, searching for Patti.

"Mom packed homemade cinnamon rolls for us to reheat. We can eat those for dessert," Pepper said.

Patti entered the cockpit area and gave Jay a crusty

look. "The coolers we have are…"

"Don't worry about it; soft drinks are fine. In fact bottled water would be perfect," Lathen said picking up on Patti's sharp tone.

Pepper followed Patti into the galley. "Yeah, we can't seem to get enough water since visiting my parents' place." Pepper came back with plates of sandwiches and chips.

Patti returned with four bottles of water. "Probably a good idea we all drink H2O. Last night I had a couple glasses of wine with dinner and felt like I'd drank a whole bottle by myself—this morning—well, I've felt better." She shuffled back to the seating area, eased down.

Jay snorted. "She was a bit tipsy last night, had to put her to bed, even before you called. Sis said it was because Pat didn't drink enough water at high altitude in Denver."

"I'm going to check on Tonk; he's digging at his left ear and whining. Might have an ear infection. Didn't think to bring ear drops with us." Pepper sighed.

"I think there are some in the first aid kit strapped to his crate," Lathen offered. "Figured the change in altitude and airplane flight might cause a problem, since he's prone to ear problems on that one side."

****

"Look at you. Gonna make a wildlife specialist out of you yet." Pepper laughed, scooted past Patti and squatted in front of Tonk's crate, jerking open the Velcro flap on the kit. She felt around inside until her fingers closed around a small bottle; she pulled it out. "Sure enough." When she unlatched his crate, Patti straightened in her seat.

"You're not going to let that wolf out in here. Are you?" She rose and sidestepped to the other side of the plane, eyes big as saucers.

"Oh, he's harmless, and his ear is bothering him bad. Huh boy." She glanced up at Patti, whose face turned ghostly white. "Are you afraid of…"

"No—Sort of—Yes, I don't care for dogs, especially wild wolves."

"He's…"

Lathen sauntered into the passenger area. "Patti, Jay wants to talk to you." Then he leaned over Pepper whispering. "Jay said she's deathly afraid of dogs. Thought I'd better come help you. Get her out of here."

"Good call." She let Tonk out, caught him by the harness, he grumbled. "Okay, boy, let's see what's going on here."

Lathen caught the sixty-pound wolf pup between his legs and rubbed Tonk's jaw and right ear, holding him steady while Pepper used a small flashlight from her backpack to look into his left ear. "It's inflamed, but not bad. The minor changes in air pressure are probably adding to his discomfort." She walked to the galley and ran hot water over the bottle while filling a cup, letting the bottle float in the cup of warm liquid as she made her way back. After putting a couple drops in his ear, she wrapped a pain pill in a piece of cheese left from her sandwich, fed it to Tonk, and returned him to the crate. Ember eyed her hopefully. "Okay, okay. Pepper tossed a bread crust in Ember's crate and hoped Kaylee couldn't see.

****

A couple hours later, they were at Jay's Aviation hangar in Bar Harbor. The LCWRRC van was right where they left it, with the addition of several inches of crusted snow on the vehicle. Lathen started the engine and let it warm up while he loaded the animals in the back.

As he headed for Lobster Cove, a thick fog rolled in. It wouldn't be long before visibility would be less than a few yards. He hoped to be off the road by then; dusk and fog were a dangerous combination. The roads were clear, but snow had fallen recently in Lobster Cove if the foot or so of snow pushed to the side of the road was any indication. With the storm from Colorado headed eastward, things were only going to get worse.

"I'll be glad to get home." Pepper reached over and rubbed Lathen's shoulders. "It was a nice visit with everyone," she said wistfully.

"It was, but I don't mind having you all to myself again." He glanced over at her and winked. "Family is great, but going to take a little getting used too, after..."

"Yeah, I know what you mean, but still, I wouldn't trade spending the holidays with family for anything. After the last ten years of spending them alone or with Gwen."

"I didn't mean... Only that I'm not used to..." He thought for a few beats. "Yeah, I agree with you." He turned up the driveway to the cabin. Ember and Tonk whined while Kaylee whistled enthusiastically before he stopped the van. "Guess they're glad to be home too." He pulled in behind a silver SUV parked beside Alec's pickup.

"Must be Dylan's cousin's vehicle." Pepper shoved open the van door and jumped out of the seat, stretching her legs before opening the back passenger door, reaching for Kaylee and crate.

Lathen sniffed and whirled around in alarm until he saw the smoke curling out of the stone chimney. The cabin was ablaze with lights. Lathen glanced over at the visiting veterinarian's cottage attached to the seabird aviary. The windows were dark. "Looks like everyone took advantage of the fireplace in the cabin."

He took the crate from Pepper as they walked toward the cabin. "So much for having you all to myself.

When she pushed the door open, warmth and the mouthwatering aroma of pizza greeted them. Ember and Tonk rushed inside, noses in the air as they circled the kitchen table.

"Welcome home," chorused Alec and another young man with shaggy black hair and brown eyes. Alec put a large pizza in the middle of the table set with four plates and silverware. The coffee maker hissed as steam wafted from a pot on the warmer.

"Mmm…This is a nice homecoming." Lathen carried Kaylee into the aviary and released the latch on her crate. She whistled and glided to her perch eyeing the holding tank.

"We stocked the tank this morning," Alec called from the other room.

Pepper took a fish out, tossed it high in the air for Kaylee. The bird gracefully took flight, whistled loud, caught the fish in her talon, and returned to the perch, tearing into its flesh.

"Glad to be home, huh girl?" Pepper watched the bird for a beat then scooted through the door Lathen held open.

Returning to the kitchen, he swiped the pot and poured the dark liquid into a mug, inhaling deeply.

"Learned to use the coffee bean grinder, I see." He gave Alec a dour sideways glance then grinned.

"I didn't think you'd mind. This is the first time I've used it, so no guarantees." Alec jerked his chin toward the young man entering the kitchen. "Oh, nearly forgot. This is Brock Scutter; he's Dylan's cousin. Works in Salem for a small animal practice. Speaking of that." Alec grimaced. "The rescue is just about full. The nor'easter that blew in here shortly after you left created havoc for the wildlife in Arcadia National Park. Several injured birds, some endangered, and you're the only licensed center allowed to accept 'em. At least, that's what we were told when the wildlife officers brought 'em here."

"Why didn't you call us?" Pepper padded into the kitchen.

"There wasn't much you could do from Colorado. That's what you pay me for, to handle things when you're gone. Granted there was a bit more than usual, but... It's all good," Alec said glancing from Pepper to Lathen. "Good thing you planned on using the community center for your reception, the buildings around here are full."

"Looks like most will be able to return to the wild this spring, but...until then..." Brock shrugged, hand extended.

Lathen stepped forward and grasped his outstretched hand. "Nice to meet you. Thanks for jumping in to help. Sounds like it's been crazy around here."

"Sorta. But I didn't mind. There's also a harbor seal in the marine habitat, boat propeller sliced and diced it pretty good. Along with a river otter found somewhere and brought in by who?" He turned and looked at Alec.

"Not really sure. An older man from town, I think. He brought it in during the middle of the storm and chaos."

"Wow, and we expected it to be a quiet December." Pepper stood for a moment hands on hips, before raising one to stifle a yawn. "I think we'll wait until tomorrow to meet them face to face." She walked to the computer banks and checked the screens. Flipping from one enclosure to the next. "Good thing we...uh...you installed the cameras before we left," she said with a tired laugh.

Lathen nodded and joined Pepper at the bank of monitors to peruse the newly acquired guests.

"It's quite a place you have here," Brock said peering over her shoulder. "State of the art."

Pepper shrugged. "Couldn't have done it without him." She glanced affectionately at Lathen. "Guys, let's eat before the pizza gets cold, or Tonk or Ember serve themselves."

"Oh...I almost forgot." Alec hit the heel of his hand to his forehead. "Jody in the bakery wants Lathen to call her. Something about the big oven went on the fritz, can't get a part for three weeks."

"What? She's making the wedding cakes in less than three weeks." Pepper jumped up nearly upending the table.

"Now don't get your knickers in a knot." Lathen loved saying that if for no other reason than the looks he got. Great tension breaker at times.

Pepper stared wide-eyed at him. "Don't what?"

He chuckled getting the desired reaction. "I'll see

Jody tomorrow morning." He caressed his hand up and down Pepper's arm. "It'll be fine. Trust me."

With a raised brow, Brock looked over at Alec, who gave him a sideways glance. They simultaneously grabbed pieces of pizza and took large bites.

"Geesh...It's starting already," she groaned. "And I haven't been..."

"You're exhausted and over reacting. What you need is a good night's sleep. See how things look in the morning." Lathen scooped up a piece of pizza and dropped it on a plate, the warm cheese stringing from pizza pan to plate, handed it to Pepper. Then he picked up another piece and took a bite, chewing thoughtfully. He'd felt the strange aura when he drove up the driveway but chalked it up to being tired and new people on the property...now he wasn't so sure.

"It was nice meeting you. Now that you're back, I'm going to spend time with my cousin. If you need me." He reached into his shirt pocket and pulled out a card. "Cell number is on the card. Give me a call." Brock strode toward the door. "I'll be helping Dylan out for a few days."

"Thanks for everything." Pepper followed behind him.

The door squeaked loudly when Lathen pulled it open. He narrowed his eyes at the offending item. "What is it with all the doors in this place. Hey Alec before you leave, help me get the rest of the luggage out of the van."

Lathen watched Brock get in his truck and drive away. "So how did Mike really work out?"

"Good. He has a way with animals. Didn't say much, but got the feeling he was trying to...I don't know…settle, maybe?"

Lathen nodded his head. "I understand. With all the new animals, we'll put him on full-time for a probationary ninety-day period."

"He has a doctor's appointment tomorrow, so he'll be late coming in. I told him no problem."

"That's fine." Lathen handed Alec a couple suitcases and took a small flashlight out of his pocket, shined it around inside the van. "Huh?" He picked up Kaylee's cooler and travel perch, slung a small duffle over his shoulder, then shut the van door with his foot.

Pepper shivered and moved out of the doorway as the men brought in the suitcases and closed the door.

"Pepper, did you bring in the garment bag? I didn't see it in the van." Lathen pointed to the floor beside the stairway. "Just put the luggage there."

"Yes, I ran out and grabbed it earlier."

After dropping the suitcases, Alec zipped up his coat. "I'm out of here. See ya in the morning."

"Night. Thanks for everything. Appreciate it." Lathen clapped Alec on the shoulder.

"Yes, thanks so much." Pepper followed the guys to the door and patted Alec on the back. With an arm wrapped around Lathen's waist, she leaned into him, her cheek against his warm back.

He shifted, put an arm around her shoulder, bent to nuzzle her neck, and inhaled deeply. *God he loved her warm citrus scent.* "Alone at last."

Chapter Thirteen
Lobster Cove Christmas Traditions—Arrangements to be Made

Pepper tossed and turned for most of the night. Finally, at four a.m., she slipped out of bed, wiggled her toes into her slippers and pulled on her robe, then padded downstairs to the kitchen.

While she filled the coffee pot, she tried to shake off the last tingle from the shiver that ran up her spine. It was just wedding jitters she told herself filling the teakettle. A microwave would warm the water for her tea, but she liked the familiar whistle of the kettle. Reminded of the countless hours as a young woman she discussed wildlife conservation, rehab, and rescue with Ashling in this kitchen, before life became so complicated.

Restless she wandered into the living room, checked the monitors. With an empty mug in hand, she returned to the kitchen and pulled out several boxes of tea bags. She sorted through them, decided on a black cherry berry blend to start her morning. A shadow fell over the kitchen table; she froze, hands balled into fists.

"Rough night?" The soothing voice of her fiancé broke the silence followed by a shrill insistent whistle.

"Shit! You scared the bejeebers out of me." She whirled around to face him.

Dressed in worn jeans, no shirt and only thick

socks on his feet, Lathen laughed holding his hands up in a surrender gesture. "You love that word." He yawned, raised a hand, raked his fingers through his sleep-tousled hair, then rubbed at his eyes.

"No, that's not it. You enjoy sneaking up behind me." Pepper huffed out a breath and tried to calm her ragged nerves. She pulled the robe tight around her and tied the belt.

"Something bothering you?" He sauntered over and took a mug out of the cupboard. After pouring the coffee, he held the large mug out watching the steam rise as he wrapped his hands around the cup, fingers overlapping.

"No... Not really. Waiting for the other shoe to drop." She eased into the wooden chair adjusting the seat cushion tied to the back.

He raised an eyebrow and searched her face. "When did the first one drop?" Lips twitched as one corner of his sexy as hell mouth curved up in a devilish grin.

"Bastar...Brat, you're baiting me. Not biting." Pushing up from the chair, she walked toward the sink, washed the mug, set it in the drainer to dry.

"Can I?" He brushed her hair aside and nibbled on her neck.

She pushed him away and narrowed her eyes. "No." Regardless of her attempts to ignore her reaction to him, sexual awareness zinged through her.

"You know what you need?"

"Yes, to put this all behind me and get back to running the Center," she said testily.

He reached out and brushed a wayward strand of hair from her face. "A nice walk around town, take in the Christmas decorations. Why don't you come with me to the bakery? Shouldn't take long to troubleshoot and come up with a temporary fix. Then we'll stroll Main Street. Lobster Cove does Christmas up right."

"Can't. Gotta play catch up after being gone for a week." She stuck her lower lip out in a pout.

He leaned over and kissed her bottom lip, pulled back with a grin. "Okay, let's check out the new occupants. I'll feed and water them while you deal with the urgent matters, then we'll ride into town. You can finish up the rest of the paperwork when we return."

She looked at him dubiously. "I know you. We'll be gone all day."

"Too much excitement, too little sleep has left you on edge. The creatures will sense it. You need to relax." He frowned, paused for a beat. "Not having second thoughts?"

"No…well…yes, but not about marrying you," she said quickly. "About this whole big wedding thing. The town, your pack, my parents, Aunt Ashling, the ghosts and arrangements—so many things to go wrong."

"Okay, want to run off and get married?" he offered, taking two bowls from the cupboard and spoons from the silverware drawer.

She paused for a couple beats, shoulders slumped. "I guess not. Already sent out the invitations." When she pulled the too-full pitcher of orange juice out of the fridge, it splashed on her robe and slopped on the floor. "Great, now we have a sticky mess."

He grabbed a roll of paper towels, patted the front of her robe, a little longer than necessary, then knelt down to mop up the floor. "Hey, as long as my pack gets a big dinner, they are fine with anything else we do. That's the big deal in my world. The ceremony…" He stood, waved his hand dismissively, holding a wet paper towel. "It's merely a…"

"What about the townspeople that have been so supportive of the Center? Mom and Dad would be…Mom would be upset. What about my generations of see through relatives?" She glanced at her white robe with orange stains down the front, made a sour face.

Lathen roared with laughter. "That's my girl. We'll make it through this just fine." Tossing the soiled towels in the trash, he turned to her. "Gwen will be here next week, Hayley the next. With Mike, we have an extra hand to help out around here, so I can help you."

"I've so much to do. And Hayley…" She paused and tilted her head up to watch Lathen's expression. "How is Mike doing? Are you sure he can handle…"

"Alec believes so, thinks he has an aptitude for working with animals. Mike will be late due to a doctor's appointment this morning, which bodes well for him. But only time will tell." Lathen leaned down and brushed her lips with his, then trailed his tongue along her neck, nibbled at her ear.

She giggled, put her hand on his chest and pushed. "We are never going to get anything done…"

Eyebrow raised, he licked his lips. "Oh I disagree." He took her hand in his and put it around his neck, pulling her close.

"Let me rephrase. No work is going to get done— so we can leave—if you don't get your libido under control."

"Spoil sport." When he released her, she sprinted up the stairs with him in hot pursuit.

A few minutes later, Pepper descended the stairs

dressed in snug purple jeans, a matching plaid shirt, and black ankle boots. On the landing, she turned and sucked in a breath when Lathen bounced down the stairs his flannel shirt flapping open, the tight black t-shirt underneath showing the contures of his chest.

In her mind, the well-known magazine's sexiest man alive didn't hold a candle to Lathen. She smiled, her gaze wandered over his fit body.

He winked at her, struck a pose, and swiveled his hips. "Now who's checking who out."

They sat down at the table and rushed through a breakfast of cereal, toast, and orange juice. Lathen rinsed the dishes and stacked them in the dishwasher as Pepper filled his travel mug with coffee, hers with tea.

Lathen shrugged into his coat and pulled hers off the peg by the door, nodding in the direction of Tonk and Ember lounging below the front window.

Lathen opened the door, a blast of cold wind blew through the room. Ember raised her muzzle, sniffed and growled, ears back, her hackles raised. Mike was sauntering across the path toward where Alec stood down by the barn.

"Stay," Pepper commanded to both canines. "We need to bring Mike in here to meet Ember and Tonk, so they don't corner and pin him."

Whistling to catch Mike's attention, Lathen motioned him into the cabin. Introductions were made, while he held out her coat and slipped it over her shoulders. "Want me to zip it up?"

She batted his hand away. "I am perfectly capable of zipping my own coat. Let's go check on the new additions." The group trooped down the path toward the marine habitat.

****

Finished with the rounds, Pepper settled into her chair and flipped through the invoices and correspondence on her desk. Bless his heart, Alec had date stamped each envelope. Sorting them into two piles, she started on the immediate attention required pile, after listing the new residents and their condition on a spreadsheet.

An hour later she filed the paid invoices, noted the action taken on required correspondence, and prioritized the rest of the items. Snapping her fingers, she pulled out a new employee packet and made sure all the relevant forms were in place. Then she wrote Alec's name on a bright orange sticky, stuck it to the packet with instructions. The office phone rang. Pepper picked it up as Lathen strode through the door, Tonk and Ember at his heels covered in snow. She frowned at the three of them as the dog and wolf shook snow all over the floor. Holding up her index finger, she pointed to the paper towel roll. For the second time that morning, Lathen knelt and mopped up the floor.

A breathless Jodie said, "Oh, I'm so glad you're back. Is Lathen coming over this morning?

"Jodie, he just walked into the office, and we were heading your way. Need to talk with him?"

"Just a quickie," Jodie replied.

"He's taken, you know." Pepper snickered before handing the phone to Lathen, who'd heard Jodie's last comment and shook his head.

"No, Jodie, her mind went straight into the gutter. But I know what you meant. What can I do for you?" He paused and looked thoughtful for a moment. "I'll stop by the hardware store on our way there. Hopefully,

I can get you a temporary fix until the part comes in. You did order the part?"

Pepper signed out of the computer, stood, and put on her parka. She flicked the overhead lights off.

"Be there within fifteen or twenty minutes." Lathen hung up the phone and blew out a breath. "A smaller oven went out this morning. I wonder if she has a power surge problem."

"But didn't someone tell her she needed a part that was three weeks out?"

"Yeah, but a surge couldn't have…better take my voltage tester and… I'll be right back." He jogged through the door into the supply area and returned holding a black plastic case and hand full of wires with clips on the end. "All set." He strode past Pepper who was tying a brightly colored scarf around her neck and whistled for the dog and wolf.

They walked up to the cabin and let Ember and Tonk inside.

"You two stay here and keep an eye on things while we're gone," Lathen instructed the canines. Ember trotted to the front window, plopped down, and groaned as her tail swiped the ground once.

"She doesn't think much of your command." Pepper leaned down, ruffled the fur around Ember's ears, then Tonks. "Won't be gone long." Tonk stretched out, gave Lathen a sideways glance, and put his head on his paws.

"They played hard in the snow when we checked on the animals, probably sleep until we get back," Lathen commented.

"I know they'd rather be outside, but I like the added security with them inside the cabin, when we are gone. That way we know no one will mess around inside."

"Yes, this is such a high crime area. Not," Lathen teased, lifting her into the pickup, leaning across her to fasten the seat belt.

Smiling to herself, she settled into the seat, tingles ran up and down her body from the heat of him pressed against her when he lifted her into the truck. She enjoyed the rise he got after such activities.

Ice crystals danced on the breeze when Lathen parked behind the bakery. Lobster Cove was teaming with activity. Shoppers with bags of brightly colored packages scurried down the sidewalk on their lunch hour. Pepper hopped out of the truck and drew in a breath. The town had transformed into a winter wonderland. Evergreen garland and bright red bows adorned the street lamps.

Inside the bakery window was a whole town made of gingerbread. When Lathen pulled the door open, the most delicious aromas wafted out making her mouth water. Regardless of the cold cereal she'd wolfed down a couple hours ago, her stomach gurgled and growled. Snowflakes hung from the ceiling, sparkling in the sunlight. Jodie grinned from behind pastry cases, a green elf hat with pointed ears and bells at the tip askew atop her head.

Pepper waved at the woman. "I'll take one of everything."

"Shouldn't come to the bakery hungry." Jodie chuckled and turned her attention to Lathen. "I am so glad you are here. The small ovens are working again, but the big one still won't heat."

Before Jodie could follow Lathen into the back,

Pepper called out. "If you would be so kind as to get me one of those oooey gooey cinnamon rolls, I'd be forever grateful."

"Of course, want a hot chocolate with that?"

"Sure." Pepper bobbed her head.

"Yeah, I want what she's having, as soon as I troubleshoot your appliances," Lathen said. "Only I'll take a coffee. Please."

Pepper took the plate Jodie handed her and sat at one of two small tables near the front window. Jodie brought over a steaming mug of hot chocolate with a large swirl of whip cream on top. She pulled out a chair and sat on the edge. "Bet your parents were glad to have you home for Thanksgiving."

"They were."

"You ok?"

"Uh, oh—yeah, just got a lot on my mind. Didn't expect to have a full house this winter. Don't get me wrong, I love it and all the creatures are responding well to treatment and causing no problems. But I got behind being gone..." She waved a hand in dismissal, blew out a breath. "I'm fine, really."

"Are you trying to do it all by yourself? You type A's are your own worst enemy. Why don't you call Kelly at Wedded Bliss? She'd be happy to help out. Take over what you haven't completed yet."

Pepper chewed on her bottom lip for a beat. "I guess I could do that. I can't decide whether to have the reception at the community center, which I've already reserved, or bring in temporary accommodations at the Center. The ceremony will be held by the pond, we've special arrangements for heat there. But..."

Jodie raised an eyebrow. "Couldn't you use the

same—uh—special arrangements for additional space for the reception on site?"

"Could be there is a limit to…well…what I'm comfortable with…even Christmas magic has its limits."

"I don't pretend to know how that all works, but if you want to use the community center, give Kelly a call. She'll take care of the decorations and whatever else you need. You can take care of things at the Center and relax, enjoy your wedding. It's one of the most important days in your life; you'll remember it always."

"Family and friends are coming in early to help."

"No… Family and friends are here to share your day, talk about plans, be with you… Do you have the decorations for the reception?"

"No… I have my dress, someone very special made it for me, and it's perfect. The rehearsal dinner and reception food are all arranged, Love Caters All has it under control. I wanted the rehearsal dinner at my cabin, so need decorations there too. But maybe The Cliffside would be a better idea.

"My mom is a decorating fiend, but if I turn her loose—we don't necessarily see eye to eye. So I'll just avoid the whole situation, by doing it myself." Pepper sipped at her drink and nibbled on the outer edge of the cinnamon roll.

The bells above the bakery door rang as another customer rushed in. Jodie pushed up from her chair. "Good morning Ms. Rose, what can I do for you."

Lathen poked his head around the corner. "I've got another hour or so here, and I'll have everything working. Good thing I brought an extra surge protector. If you want to take the truck and go back to the center,

I'll call you when I'm done."

"No, I'm going to do a little shopping, check out the rest of the decorations in town, by then the Christmas lights should be on."

"Sounds like a plan." He winked at her and disappeared into the back.

Several customers filled the bakery. Pepper stopped and visited with them on her way out the door. She zipped her parka and wrapped the scarf around her neck, pulled her knit cap out of her pocket, slipped it on. The air had a bite to it but sparkled with moisture adding to the Christmas ambiance.

The white fluffy clouds from this morning had joined forces, sunlight streamed through only a few breaks in the now ominous storm clouds as a few snowflakes fell. Several inches of snow were forecast for the coming days. It would be a white Christmas, which somehow lifted her spirits.

At the gazebo in town square she fingered the white lights on the strings around the structure. Huge red bows adorned the edge of the roof every couple of feet with streamers and pine boughs at the supports. Across the square the smaller trees were strung with multicolored light strands. Red, blue, and silver balls decorated the main tree in the center of town square. A fiber optic star sat atop the majestic pine. Christmas carols filled the air from speakers positioned throughout the square.

Protected from the elements inside the gazebo, a cheerful flier pinned to the bulletin board announced the Christmas festivities for December. A huge celebration was planned for the tree lighting ceremony next week, a potluck in the church basement would follow. Caroling would take place the Wednesday before Christmas in the town square. "Everyone was welcome," another notice stated with a number to call to coordinate main dishes.

She pulled out her phone, typed in the number for the potluck coordinator, it went to voice mail and she left a message. Then she scrolled to the Wedded Bliss' number and touched the green icon.

Kelly's cheerful voice answered on the second ring. "Hello."

"Hi Kelly, it's Pepper McKay."

"Oh, hi. How was your Thanksgiving in Colorado and your parents?"

How did the whole town...a small town, of course... "Great!"

"Glad to hear it. Now what can I do for you?"

"I need a little help with the wedding decorations. Thought I could pull it off by myself, but with the storm and injured animals at the Center—well...I can't do it all."

"Thought you might be calling after I heard. Tell me what you have in mind, and I'll make it happen."

"I'm not really sure. Simple but fun...make sense?" Pepper described the decorations at Amy and Elijah's wedding and atmosphere she wanted to create at the rehearsal dinner and reception. Evergreens and purple roses, small lanterns that kind of thing.

"Got it... I'll put something together and give you a call to review them," Kelly said.

"Thanks." Pepper felt as if a huge weight lifted from her shoulders.

"No problem. It's what I do."

After she disconnected the call, Pepper walked

over to the main tree and saw slips of paper rolled up and tucked into several of the odd shaped ornaments. *What was that all about?*

A man strode by her, stopped, gave her a once over glance, and moved on. A shiver shot up her spine that had nothing to do with the cold. The magic signature was undefined. He looked a lot like Benjamin Bonchard only his hair was much lighter, build taller and thin. Mr. Bonchard had tried to steal the McKay magic last Halloween. Aunt Ashling's coven had spell bound him for his efforts with threats of worse if he continued on his dark path.

A strong arm whipped around her waist, the air whooshed out as she squealed. She balled up her gloved fist as a large warm hand wrapped around her wrist. "I've seen you defend yourself. Not going to chance it." A deep voice chuckled behind her.

"Lathen—I'm going to…"

He spun her around and covered her cold lips with his warm ones. Werewolves run several degrees warmer than most of the population, one of the things she loved about him. She relaxed into him. Their parkas making a *wisping* sound as the material rubbed against each other. "That's better," he murmured against her lips.

All at once the lights in the square blinked on. Low positioned red and green laser light decorations sparkled over the snow-covered ground and onto the gazebo, complementing the white lights. From the other direction, a blue laser sprinkled tiny snowflakes across the building. Evening fell quickly in December.

"This is absolutely beautiful." She breathed against his chilled cheek and whirled out of his hold taking in all the lighted decorations not visible earlier then pointed toward the bulletin board. "I've been reading the town's holiday events. Lobster Cove really embraces Christmas."

"Told you," Lathen said smugly. "Even some of the boats docked in the harbor are decked out with colored lights."

"Christmas was just another day, too much to do and no funds to do it with at Salem's Sanctuary. This year will be soooo different." Pepper reached for his hand and twined her fingers through his.

"Did your folks celebrate Christmas—Oh, witches don't believe?" A brown paper bag in hand, he reached in and handed her a lobster burger. "There's fries in the bag."

She took her glove off and held the warm burger in her hand, took a bite then peered into the bag, and snatched a couple french fries. "Irish witches do—we have enough mortals in our family that Christmas is a tradition, even if beliefs are different. It's just that I wasn't in a position to have reason to celebrate after becoming an adult. Made bad choices in men. Loved my work, but the pay was—lacking though the rewards made up for it."

"I see." Lathen scrubbed a hand over his chin. "So things are going be a lot different for you, as well as Gwen this year."

The warmth in his voice made her smile. *Yes indeed, things would be different.* "Yep."

He set the bag on a picnic table, reached in, grabbed several fries, and stuffed them in his mouth. "Mmmmm...I love warm fries. Not so good when they get cold." Shifting his eyes to hers, he frowned and swallowed. "I overheard you talking with Jodie. Everything okay? Or is there something you need me to do? We'll get this wedding worked out and enjoy our time with family."

She took a couple more fries from the bag and popped them in her mouth, chewed for a beat. "I called Kelly from Wedded Bliss. She's going to handle the decorations." Pepper shook the bag toward him and filled him in on her ideas and the arrangements. Her forehead creased thinking back to the man who'd crossed her path. "What do you know about Bonchard's family?"

Lathen took the final few fries and scrunched the bag up, walked over, tossed it into the trash can not far from the gazebo, scanned the area and turned back to Pepper.

"Why?" He raised an eyebrow.

Chapter Fourteen
Unexpected Visitors and the Past Comes Knocking

After a long pause, Lathen shrugged. "Not a lot. Rumor has it Ben's family kept to themselves. I heard he was an only child then someone else said he had a brother, but they never got along. His parents are dead and I haven't seen a brother around, so... Why? He isn't causing problems again... Is he?" Lathen asked pulling her closer.

"No reason...wait..." She blew out a warm breath; the air fogged in front of her. "A man that looked an awful lot like Ben cut through the square as I was admiring the decorations. Only his hair was shaggy and much lighter, he's taller than Ben, thin, but their faces...same sharp bone structure, dark beady eyes. When he stopped and stared at me"—she shivered—"but he went on his way... Spooked me, I guess. He didn't say anything. I couldn't get a bead on his magic signature. It was as if he disguised it."

"That's strange. Everyone has Merry Christmas or Happy Holidays on their lips this time of year." He paused for a moment. "We need to head home. How about cruising through town first and enjoy the light displays."

She nodded, slipped her glove on, and took his hand. "Maybe I should call Mom and in passing ask about him."

He cocked an eyebrow. "I'm not sure that's a good idea. Let me make some calls. Then we'll decide if anything needs to be done." He kissed the tip of her nose. "Don't worry...nothing is going to go wrong."

They strolled down the sidewalk toward the parking lot and admired the holiday decorations in the shop windows. He helped her into the truck and closed the door, scooting over to the driver's door in a blink of an eye he climbed inside. He rubbed his hands together and started the engine, turned the defroster on as the windows began to fog.

Half an hour later, Lathen turned the truck onto the gravel drive to the cabin, slowed, and stared at the dark SUV parked in front of the cabin. Slowly he guided the truck behind the vehicle, noticing that the plates were government issue. *What the hell is this?*

Pepper leaned forward in her seat. "What's a government SUV doing sitting in front of our home?"

"Maybe it's the DIFW," Lathen said hopefully. He turned off the headlights and cut the engine. The doors opened on the SUV, and four men in suits stepped out and waited.

Oh shit, this doesn't bode well. He recognized one of the men, Lt. Commander Raymond Sale. Lathen jumped out of the truck as Pepper opened her door. "Pepper, why don't you go on inside, let Tonk and Ember out, but keep them close. I'll just be a minute."

Pepper glanced from the men and back to Lathen. She opened her mouth to protest, but he shook his head and glanced toward the cabin where he could hear Tonk and Ember barking. For a beat he watched Pepper turn and walk the path to the cabin. He turned his attention to the men standing in the driveway.

"Good evening, gentlemen, to what do I owe the pleasure?"

Lt. Commander Sale stepped forward. "Long time Lathen. You look a helluva lot better than you did last time we spoke."

"Yeah, when you told me my injuries were career ending, gave me a medical discharge. Patted me on the back and said I was lucky to be alive. Has something changed?" He looked pointedly at the other men.

"Obviously." Raymond cleared his throat, shifted from one foot to the other, motioned to each man in turn. "Lt. Wade Johnson, Staff Sargent Tom Heller, Lt. Joseph Renner. This is Lathen Quartz, the best multi-talented computer-hack-programmer in the business. Not to mention his reconnaissance skills are… We need your expertise." He brought his gaze up to meet the former SEAL's dark look.

Lathen paused, bit his lip to keep from spouting a nasty retort. *Where were you when I needed help? Couldn't even get an appointment with the VA before I had to move on to keep my sanity. Now you come to me?* He blew out a breath knowing once you're out of the SEALs that's it. This kind of thinking would get him nowhere. He met the man's gaze with a frosty look. "Want to come in for a cup of coffee?" He swept a glance to the other men who nodded, hands in their pockets, collars pulled up against the cold.

"That would be great. Then we can discuss the situation."

"Understand, I have no intention of returning to active service of any kind or being at your beck and call. I won't jeopardize what I have here. Hell, I'm getting married in a couple of weeks. This LCWRRC is my life now. And I am helping other veterans that your system couldn't or wouldn't."

"So we've heard. You're doing a good thing here." Ray glanced around the area and shivered. "I'd like to discuss this over that coffee you offered."

Suddenly, the cabin door flew open. Ember and Tonk burst onto the porch, sniffed the air, and growled low in their throats. Lathen smiled at the expressions of shock on the men's faces. "You might want to stay close, Ember and Tonk don't think much of strangers."

Wolf and dog rushed toward the group, before they reached the men, Lathen put a hand up. "Leave it." He waved the canines into the yard and led the procession to the cabin. As he passed Pepper who held the door open, he whispered, "Nice timing."

She smirked. "They had to take care of business." Pepper shifted her gaze to Kaylee who sat staunchly on her perch inside the main room, feathers held tight, ready for a fight.

He brushed by the osprey, stroked a wing. "Relax. They mean no harm"—he cocked an eyebrow—"at present."

Pepper winked at the bird, who ruffled her feathers and took a relaxed stance on the perch, still watching.

Raymond and the men gave Kaylee a wide berth, as they stood uneasily in the center of the room.

Pepper snickered behind her hand. "Take a seat anywhere. I've already put the coffee on; it'll only be a couple of minutes." She gave Lathen a backward glance and walked into the kitchen, picked up a tray with a white china cream pitcher and a matching sugar bowl. Six spoons lay between the serving dishes and clattered against the china as she set the tray on the coffee table in front of the sofa where three of the men sat. "Lathen, would you mind helping me with the coffee?"

"Sure…no problem." He nodded to the men and took two mugs from Pepper after which she returned to the kitchen for the other mugs of steaming coffee.

"Mmm this smells great." Raymond took a mug from Lathen, sipped, then wrapped his cold hands around the warm cup. "Sorry for the intrusion. You're a hard man to locate. We tried the cell number we had for you several times over the last week. There was no answer."

"That's because Pepper and I were visiting her parents for Thanksgiving. We just returned last night."

Raymond shifted uncomfortably in the recliner. "You don't answer your phone when on vacation?"

"Not when the unfamiliar number is from a government agency," Lathen said nonchalantly.

"We should get down to business." Raymond slid his cup onto the tray and leaned back in the chair.

Pepper brought the other mugs and handed them out to the men. Lathen made the introductions, then settled into the double rocking recliner. He patted the seat beside him as an indication for her to sit.

"This op is classified," Raymond began with a pointed look at Pepper.

"Then my security clearance must still be intact." Lathen smirked. "But whatever you have to say, Pepper remains where she is. If that's a problem, I guess you should finish your coffee and be on your way."

Raymond frowned. "You know the rules."

"Yep, I do, so I believe our conversation is at an end. Now, did you guys have a good Thanksgiving?"

The men smiled and nodded as a group. Wade said,

"It was nice to have some time off. Had family in, that kind of thing."

Raymond frowned, let out a heavy sigh. "You're a hard one to deal with. Let me make a couple phone calls, and I'll get back to you." He shoved up from the sofa and strode outside, closed the door behind him.

Lathen chuckled and held up three fingers, then two, one and Raymond rushed in the door, phone to his ear, Tonk and Ember right behind him. "Lathen, call off your dogs."

Pepper motioned to the canines and pointed to the floor where they both settled beside her, low growls still in their throats. Raymond stepped out onto the porch.

"Anyone want a refill?" She returned to the kitchen and opened the oven, pulled out a sheet of lemon sugar cookies. A warm, sweet lemony aroma filled the kitchen and wafted into the living room.

"Is that sugar cookies I smell?" Lathen pushed up from his seat, turned, raised a brow at the guys. "You want a cookie? Pepper makes the best lemon sugar cookies I've ever tasted. Her grandmother's recipe." He grinned when two of the men licked their lips and nodded, with a quick glance at the door. "Don't worry, he'll come around."

Lathen made his way to the kitchen. "When did you have time to whip up a batch of cookies?"

"I always have different types of cookie dough in the freezer. Figured this might take a while, so I heated the oven and popped the cookies in before I let Tonk and Ember out."

"Nice job."

"You know; I don't have to sit in on your

conference." Pepper shrugged.

"What they want me to do, could have a wide reaching detrimental effect on our lives, our family, friends, and the townspeople of Lobster Cove. I have no intention of jeopardizing what we have." He winced. "But if they can find a way for me to assist them without a trace being made to the Center or myself... I'll consider it." He wrapped his arms around her waist and snuggled into her neck to trail kisses up to her jawline, ending at the corner of her mouth. "I love the way you smell—and taste."

Pepper giggled, turning her face to kiss him full on the lips. She nearly dropped a cookie as she finished layering the rows of cookies on the crystal plate given her as a house warming for her first apartment by Aunt Ashling. The platter had never been used.

Lathen kissed her softly, winked, and returned to the living room with a plate piled high with lemon yellow cookies, piped with white frosting.

The door banged open as a blast of frigid air blew though the room, napkins from the table swirled to the floor. Raymond's expression was pinched when he crossed the room. "You win, but we'll have to vet her before any further discussions." He looked around the room and handed the phone to Pepper as she entered the room.

She stared at him, then at the phone. "What?" Her gaze shifted to Lathen.

He peered questioningly at Raymond. "What's going on?"

"Need to get some information."

Lathen took the phone, ended the call. "Her information is available from federal applications she's completed. I know you checked her out before you arrived.

"Let me tell you how this is going to go. No communication to my home or the LCWRRC. I can review what you have going on at the naval bases near here, but no official word on what I'm doing or set schedule. The private sector is still light years ahead of the military in cyber ops and security. Not going to get caught in that situation, again." He gave the Lt. Commander a meaningful look.

"You can't dictate what you are and aren't going to do." Raymond paced the floor, his body rigid, his forehead creased.

"That's where you're wrong. I'm a civilian now. Remember? So we need to call it a night." Lathen snaked his arm around Pepper, rubbed his cheek on the top of her head.

Raymond stood, face red, hands flexing at his side, eyes bulging, and his lips set in a thin line. Still he said nothing.

"We've a lot to do between now and the wedding, not to mention the Center is at capacity from recent incidents. Think about my offer, it's the only one you'll get." He walked to the door with Pepper. "Thanks for stopping by." Cold misty air swirled into the room when he opened the door and the men left. After he closed the door, Pepper stared at him.

"You've got some balls, telling the government what you will and won't do."

"If it's that important, they'll meet my terms." Shaking his head slowly, scenes from the ambush and explosion flooded his mind. He blinked, scrubbed his hand over his face. He really didn't want any part of this. But…service to his country had defined his life…until… "Come on, let's go to bed."

Pepper leaned against him, rubbing her hand in circles across the tight muscles of his back, watched his jaw muscle twitch in time with the pulsing at his temple. "A nice warm shower is just what the rehab specialist orders." Her full lips turned up in a seductive smile.

He licked his lips, felt his crotch tighten. "Who am I to argue with the professional." He padded upstairs to the loft behind her and watched as her jeans slid to the floor, followed by her sweater and lingerie; he followed suit. All unpleasant thoughts faded away, leaving desire raging through his body when he swept her into his arms and carried her into the shower.

****

Lathen's eyes blinked open, and he rolled over to snuggle against Pepper. His phone rang, he cursed quietly, grabbed the phone, checked the ID and touched the green icon before the second ring. "Dad, what's up?"

"Is everything all right with you and Pepper?"

Lathen crawled out of bed, careful not to wake Pepper. "Sure. As far as I know, why?"

This morning we had a couple feds nosing around Half Moon Valley. Asking questions about you, Pepper, your relationship. You're not in trouble are you?"

"Of course not. Saw an old government acquaintance last night. Didn't like his message and sent him on his way. Are you and the family on schedule for the plans we discussed?"

Silent for a couple beats, his dad finally sighed into the phone. "I believe so. Could be earlier depending on the weather forecast. Storms will bring us in earlier, if need be."

"Nope, I've checked, and it's nothing you need to worry about, unless Amy is spooked about another encounter."

Pepper opened her eyes and squinted at the slice of sunlight spreading across her face. "Storm's over." She sat up and noticed Lathen standing at the window, the phone to his ear. She eased out of bed and wrapped her arms around his waist from the back, laid her head on his shoulder.

He tilted the phone slightly away from his ear and mouthed the word dad to her.

"Oh, how's Hayley doing?" she whispered.

"Pepper's awake and wants to know how Hayley is doing. No early arrivals, right?"

His dad chuckled. "Not yet, but she is big. Kolby tried to talk her out of the trip, but it was a no go. She is looking forward to the wedding."

"Well, Dad, we have to grab breakfast and make rounds. The Center is fuller than anticipated. A nor'easter came through while we were gone. Had a devastating effect on the wildlife. Give our love to Amy. See ya soon." Lathen disconnected the call and raged. "Son of a bitch." He paced the floor, scrolled through the numbers on his phone, took a tattered business card from his wallet on the dresser, and flipped the edge.

"What...your dad?" Pepper asked perplexed.

"No. Lt. Commander Raymond Sale. The bastard that was here with the three other guys last night. He's trying to force my hand—there were feds at the pack lands this morning."

"Oh...So what are you going to do?"

"Nothing. Dad understands how to shut them down; he'll inform the rest of the pack. Ray will be in contact sooner than later, and I'll tell him the deal is off. Now how about breakfast. I'm starved." He put the business card back in his wallet.

Pepper pulled on her worn jeans, a pink and purple striped sweatshirt layered over a black t-shirt, and ran a brush though her hair. She drew it back in a ponytail. "Sour cream waffles, bacon or sausage, hash browns okay with you?" She didn't wait for an answer. "Coffee will be ready in a few." She hurried down the steps to the kitchen.

Lathen clenched and unclenched his hand—wanted so badly to punch something, but instead he shook out his hand. *This was exactly what Ray hoped for—and it's not going to happen. I've nothing to hide, so Ray has no bargaining chips.* He smiled and dressed in jeans, blue plaid flannel shirt over a black tee, pulled on thermal socks, and looked for his boots. *Must have left them downstairs.* He sprinted down the stairs and slid into the kitchen, laying a loud smacking kiss on her lips. "Sorry about that, just got a little..."

"I understand. Ray doesn't know you very well."

"Not anymore." Lathen got out syrup, set plates and glasses on the table, along with a pitcher of orange juice.

She filled a mug with coffee, inhaled. "Mmm. I'll never understand how fresh ground coffee can smell so good and taste so terrible." Pepper screwed up her face, plopped a French vanilla tea bag in her mug, poured hot water over it, swirled the bag in the water. She breathed in the aroma, added milk and sugar, took a taste, and grinned. "Now that's more like it."

Laughing at her expression, Lathen scooped up the coffee mug and walked to the window. "Bet they're staying in a local hotel. How about a ride after breakfast and checking on the boarders?"

"Sure, I have a meeting with Kelly this afternoon. Going to drop off the decorations I purchased and let her handle the rest. Need to do a little administration work this morning."

"That'll work. Got a few things to handle before we leave."

They finished breakfast. Pepper put the plates and glasses in the dishwasher. Poured fresh coffee and tea in travel mugs, handed one to Lathen. After shrugging into his coat, he helped Pepper on with hers. On their way to check on the animals and birds, Pepper met Mike's wife in passing when she dropped him off. Pepper continued up the path toward her office. Lathen stayed behind to go over assignments for the week with Alec and Mike, and brief them on last evening's events, leaving out the reason for Ray's visit.

"If we have any strangers come around asking questions, refer them to Pepper or me. If we're not here, you have no comment about our whereabouts. Ask for their card or contact information, then escort them off the property indicating I'll be in touch."

"Got it boss," Mike said nodding his head vigorously. "I'll start in the seabird aviary." He strode off toward the old barn.

"So now that you are stable, Commander looking for favors?" Alec pursed his lips, staring straight into Lathen's eyes.

"Something like that. Made him aware, this is

where I belong now. But I will be checking in with the VA for more candidates to help out around here."

"Great idea. Mike and I are stretched pretty thin." Alec headed for the marine mammal habitat. "You coming?"

"I'll be right behind you. Pepper said the seal is healing nicely. Vet will be around this afternoon to check on it." Once Alec was out of ear shot, Lathen pulled the cell phone out of his pocket, scrolled through numbers on the screen, held the phone to his ear, as he meandered toward the cabin. "Hey, I need some information."

Chapter Fifteen
When It Comes Right Down to It—You Really Can't Trust the Government

Pepper signed off the computer, finished playing catchup from being gone, looked up to see the door handle twist. Lathen shoved through the door, Tonk at his heels.

"You about ready to go?" He watched Tonk slink over to join Ember on the blanket behind Pepper's desk.

"I am. Ember's been here with me all morning. Guess she thought I needed guarding after last night." Pepper eased up from the desk, stepped over Tonk and Ember. "Come guys, you need to patrol the ground while we are gone. The dog door is open in the mammal habitat?"

"Yep. Checked it." He held the door open for her and locked it behind them.

A few clouds obscured the sun as they drove into town. Pepper chatted about the decorations for the community center and the additional ideas Kelly wanted to add. At this point whatever Kelly came up with, she was on board. Lathen was unusually quiet on the drive. He slowed the truck to a crawl as they passed by Sea Crest Inn. Parked in the lot was the SUV with government plates from last night. He pulled in and stopped the truck on the other side of the parking lot.

****

"Come on this won't take long." Lathen jumped out of the truck then bolted across the parking lot. Pepper broke into a run to keep up with him, until he paused waiting for her to catch up near the entrance to the Inn.

"Are you sure this is a good idea? Maybe you should mull over the situation before taking action." She caught hold of his arm.

He shook his head, yanked open the door, and strode across the lobby to the front desk.

"Hey, Lathen. Matt call you?" Sammy, the front desk clerk glanced around. "I thought he was going to give the new guy a chance before calling you."

"No, Matt didn't call. You have a couple government types, one named Raymond Sales staying here. I have a meeting with them but forgot which room they are in."

"Oh, they're in the upstairs corner suite. Want me to call you up?"

"No that won't be necessary, but thanks."

Sammy nodded about to say something, when the phone rang. He waved to Lathen and Pepper and picked up the receiver.

Pepper closed her mouth and studied Lathen. "That was…"

"Ingenious," Lathen completed for her, taking the stairs two at a time. He knocked on the door, as Pepper caught up with him.

She took in a deep breath, but said nothing.

Lt. Commander Sale opened the door, his eyes rounded but a smirk quickly spread over his face when he saw Lathen. "So you made a decision already, son?"

Lathen took a step forward, his hands fisted at his

side. Slowly he unclenched them flexing his fingers. "First of all, I'm not your son. Second, if you ever pull shit like this again…" He paused as if considering what to say next or trying to keep his temper in check.

She wasn't quite sure which, as she stood off to the side and slightly behind him, out of sight of Ray. But she could see the muscle in Lathen's jaw working overtime. Pepper wondered if it wouldn't be better to walk away. But apparently he had a point to make.

Still standing outside the room, she said, "This is no place to discuss—whatever." Pepper spread her arms wide.

"I couldn't agree more." Raymond opened the door wide in a gesture of inviting them into the suite.

Lathen strode inside pulling Pepper along, but only far enough for Ray to close the door. "No. I'm declining your request." He paused. "I don't know what the hell you expected to find in Alaska, but I strongly suggest you call off your men, immediately."

Raymond scrubbed his hand over his face, rubbed his chin. "I'm sorry, I don't know what you are talking…"

"Cut the crap—or I walk right now." Lathen stood stock straight, as Pepper eased out from behind him, her hand on his arm.

Ray frowned as he locked eyes with Lathen then shifted his gaze to Pepper. "Why did you bring her?" Ray jerked his chin toward Pepper.

"Because my life is with her and the Center now. If you expect my help in any capacity, you need to be aware of my priorities."

"You know the requirements of being a SEAL."

"Only too well. The Navy decided I was not

mentally or physically fit for duty a few short years ago. Gave me a medical discharge. Need I remind you? Any requirements ended at that time." Lathen tilted his head. "What's changed?"

"At that time, medical officers deemed that you would never fully recover the abilities to pass... We thought your career was over. We had no way of knowing...it seems you are more than one hundred percent. Which is kinda..."

"You still can't be sure I'm one hundred percent as you put it. I have no intention of submitting to tests or rigors of—duty." He pointed thumbs at his chest. "Civilian and loving it. I can do more for the vets in need of a hand up from here, than the bullshit run around you give them. But that's a topic for another time."

"Okay. So your point?"

"For now, my sources tell me you are looking to hack a foreign government's security. Retrieve sensitive information, maps, plans, and get out without a trace."

Lt. Commander stood there, his mouth opening and closing without a word. His men's faces reflected shock, then disbelief as Lathen continued.

It was Lathen's turn to smirk. "What you're asking is—skirting legal boundaries. It would require a worm that is undetectable until you unleash it to corrupt their system, covering your tracks after the hack. Can I write code for such a purpose? Of course. But let me ask you this: if I can get this kind of intel, who else can?"

"Where the hell did you get... That's top secret..."

"Exactly my point."

"I'm not going to confirm or deny..." Lt

Commander blustered then schooled his face into a blank expression.

"And you want me at your beck and call. Not going to happen."

The flurry of voices faded away as Pepper watched the ebb and flow of the negotiations between the two men, while the others in the room looked on. Was Lathen torn between his commitment to the Center and life as a SEAL? She needed him there—Until a few years ago, most of his adult life was spent in service to his country, a commitment he'd given freely until he'd sustained life altering injuries.

Was it possible to return to the SEALs? From what she'd heard and read, that wasn't likely. So what did they want him to do? Or were they willing to make an exception? She couldn't…wouldn't think about that, she was overreacting. Despite her resolve, her thoughts kept swirling. Would taking this assignment require long absences from her—the Center? That would never work. She needed him—the Center needed him. Alec and Mike depended on him in more ways…

"Pepper…Pepper…" Lathen's voice penetrated her thoughts. "What do you think?"

She blinked and peered up at him. "About what?" When she took a minute to clear her head, she glanced from his steeled expression to the Lt. Commander's thunderous demeanor. There was really no other way to describe it. A storm raged beneath his attempt at a calm facade. Her lips twitched, he hadn't expected this. Or had he?

In a dangerously low voice, rocking back on his heels, Lathen said, "My family, Alaska, Pepper, and the Center are off limits. If you can abide by that, you'll have the opportunity to spread all your cards on the table, at a time and place of my choosing."

Raymond tented his fingers and shook his head. "Time is of the essence. And I'll need to know where you got the intel."

Lathen's eyebrow winged up, he shrugged. "You should have thought about that before you went nosing into my private life. Searching for leverage, where there is none, to force me to do what you wanted."

"We can't afford the whispers to be true."

"What the hell are you talking about?" Lathen stared incredulously at Ray.

"We both know what I mean. Your team's success rate was far and above the rates of other SEAL teams with the same characteristics. Rumors that something… or someone…well that…it wasn't humanly possible to pull off what your team did consistently. We suspect that your team was targeted by insurgents, for that reason. Any idea what made your team so successful?" Ray crossed the floor to the little fridge, took out a bottle of water, then offered one to Lathen, who politely declined. Pepper took a step forward and reached for the bottle of water. Unscrewed the cap and took a long drink. Thankful the testosterone and posturing in the room was dissipating.

"Guts, strength, cunning, intelligence?" Lathen shrugged again, the smirk returning to his lips.

"All the teams have those attributes. Nope—we think yours had something special."

"It doesn't matter. That something special died with our SEAL team's four deceased members and the three disabled."

"Two. You seem to have made an amazing

recovery."

Lathen waved a hand dismissively. "Good genes." When he lowered his hand, he took Pepper's, entwined their fingers, and turned toward the door. Over his shoulder he said, "I'll be in touch." He yanked the door open.

Sunlight flooded through the door, as the couple made their way down the stairs and out into the parking lot. The morning mist burned off making it a clear but cold day. Ice crystals shimmered in the air against the sun's rays. A truck equipped with a plow cleared the remaining ice and piles of snow to a far corner of the lot. The driver shouted a greeting to Lathen, who waved back then shoved a hand in his pocket.

Pepper waited for an explanation of what happened back there. Lathen was silent as he drove the short distance to Wedded Bliss and stopped the truck in front of the store.

"Don't you want to come in and see what additional decorations Kelly has picked out for the reception? I told her to keep it simple, no fru-fru stuff."

Lathen blew out a breath. "Sure." He shoved open the truck door and met Pepper in front of the truck.

"You don't have to come if you've something more pressing."

"Got a lot of things on my mind." He held the door open to Kelly's shop; she sidled through giving him a sideways glance.

Kelly greeted them with a wide smile. "I got this dynamite idea for your reception." She danced from one foot to the other. Then held up a corkboard with snippets of pictures pinned to it. "We'll make your reception a *céilídh*. You know a…"

"We know a *céilídh* is an Irish social gathering with music, folk tales, and dancing. We based our successful rescue/grand opening for The Lobster Cove Rescue and Rehabilitation Center on that type of celebration. Didn't have time for many stories and folk tales. The music was CDs, but it was fun."

"This time, you could have it all. I know this great Irish folk band. You'll love 'em. Allow time for the folktales and family stories." She flipped a knowing look from Pepper to Lathen. "We could use your miniature purple silk rosebuds entwined with green ivy for garland and centerpieces. All very simple, yet unique and…fun. What do you think?" She hung the corkboard on the wall, pointed out the white ribbons wound through the ivy and accented with the tiny purple rosebuds. A sketch of the McKay Crest, next to the word Quartz and the logo of the LCRRC centered below the two hung below the flowers. Pictures of ivy looped from the ceiling in each corner, along with several other ideas ripped from magazines filled the rest of the board. "We could use the McKay family crest on the back wall, with… Lathen do you have a family crest?"

"Not one that we could hang on the wall without questions being raised. How about a picture of the State of Alaska next to the crest instead? You said you wanted unique."

"Hmm… That might just work, with bears, wolves, and moose lightly morphed into the picture. Yes… Leave it to me. Oh…and the logo for the Center, since that's what brought you two together." She pointed to the board again.

Lathen looked skeptical, but Pepper nodded

chewing on her bottom lip. "I'd like to see an example of what you are talking about before I agree."

"Fair enough. I'll have it done and emailed to you this evening." Kelly picked up a pen and scribbled notes on her planner spread open on the counter.

"One more thing, you need to get a permit for Tonk, Ember, and Kaylee to attend the reception at the community center. They are ambassadors for the Center, so the council shouldn't balk."

Kelly fisted one hand on her hip, eyes bright with amusement.

"Honey, you and your Center won over the town long before your grand opening. They'll give you whatever you want, within reason." Kelly laughed. "It's a private party. We've had a lot worse than Tonk, Ember, and Kaylee in that community center and will again."

Rubbing his chin with thumb and forefinger, Lathen cleared his throat. "Not sure we should bring both Tonk and Ember." He stepped out of Kelly's earshot, pulling Pepper along with him, and lowered his voice. "Who will watch the property?"

A bit puzzled at his concern, she tilted her head and peered up at him. "Duh. Your state of the art surveillance system?" Pepper raised a brow in question while trying to figure out what exactly Lathen was getting at. "We'll apply for the permit but don't have to use it. If that makes you feel better."

He paused for a couple seconds and nodded. "Yeah, it does. Just a feeling…you know."

"I do." Pepper returned to where Kelly stood poring over pictures of tree decorations.

She flipped a page and pointed to medium size

purple bows on a flocked Christmas tree. "That's exactly what I had in mind. Will that work for you? We'll add a few color-coordinated balls with designs to highlight the decorations."

"Looks great." Pepper glanced at Lathen, who nodded.

"Good. Now all I need is a description or picture of what your wedding venue will look like, to make sure your reception's theme is consistent." Kelly pulled the pen from her hair and made notes as Pepper described the setting and decorations for the wedding. They discussed the set up in the community center, Pepper nixed the seating charts and agreed on the final prep.

"That's an awful lot of food." Kelly flipped the pages of the menu.

"Trust me on this. I attended a Quartz wedding last summer. Those people can put away the food."

"No one will go hungry from our wedding feast." Lathen shrugged. "It's kind of a tradition." He winked at Kelly.

"Thanks, Kelly, I think we are all set." Pepper sighed. "Sure glad I turned the reception over to you. The more I think about your Christmas *Céilídh*, the more I like it."

"No problem. It's what I do." Kelly grinned. "Lathen, it was nice to have a man's input…most stay clear of the wedding preparations."

"I tried, but promised Pepper I'd help." He grinned, slipping his arm around Pepper's waist nudging her toward the door.

"Any questions, call me. I'll have the photo emailed to you this evening," Kelly called out just before the door banged shut.

Once they were inside the truck, Lathen started the engine and eased back against the seat, waiting for the truck to warm up. He turned to Pepper. "I like Kelly's idea. It will fit with the traditional celebration my family does for weddings too." Lathen paused and blew out a breath. "I made some inquiries about the Bonchard family. It turns out that Ben has a younger brother, Brent. He fits the description of the man you saw in the park, lighter hair, and taller build."

Pepper sucked in a breath, her heart raced. "That's all I need."

He squeezed her shoulder. "Relax. Apparently the brothers didn't get along. Brent left town years ago. One of the older maids at The Sea Cliff said the boys never got along even as children. When Ben started dabbling in dark magic after high school, the animosity grew. Brent left town. Abruptly. Rumor has it that Ben was always the favorite son. As far as anyone knows, the only times Brent returned was to attend his mother's and then father's funeral a few years ago. Until you saw him the other day."

"So why do you think he's back—especially now?" Pepper chewed on her bottom lip, a nervous habit she'd had since childhood. "Looking to cause more problems?"

"Doubt it. If they weren't close growing up, why would Brent aid his brother in any way now? Doesn't fit."

"I guess you're right," Pepper said slowly. "Just can't shake the feeling something more is at play here than we see." Pepper wrapped her arms around herself.

Lathen flipped on the heater. Warm air circulated through the vehicle. "The coven was quite clear on the consequences Ben would face if he meddled in McKay affairs again. He's not the brightest bulb in the pack, but I don't think he has a death wish. If dark magic was the wedge that finally drove Brent away, why would he come back? It doesn't make sense."

"You're probably right." She twisted her hands in her lap. "I just want our wedding to be perfect."

"As does every bride, and it will be." He took her face in his hands, tipped her chin up and smiled. "Nothing is going to spoil our wedding. I promise." Lathen kissed the tip of her nose, her cheek, and finally brought his mouth over hers.

Giving into the passion of his kiss, her stomach spun in a wild swirl. *Would it always be this way?* She hoped so. The morning's concern melted away as he slipped his arm around her back pulling her closer to him, deepening the kiss. Lathen jerked up straight when there was a light tap on his window. With a sheepish grin, he rolled down the window. Matt, the maintenance supervisor for the hotel, stood, his hands shoved in his pockets.

"I guess we are going to have to get you two your own covered parking space," Matt said with a laugh. "Wouldn't know you have a lovely cabin of your own."

Lathen shrugged. "Hey, this hasn't happened since my brother was here last summer. Give a guy a break," he shot back grinning. "What's up?" He shifted in the seat still keeping his arm around a red-faced Pepper.

"Wanted to let you know the guys you met with have been asking a lot of questions around here. We're not telling them anything. Frustrating the hell out of them." Matt snickered. "But thought you should know."

"I'm aware. We had a discussion about their

methods, and they should be leaving shortly, or, at least knock off the questions."

"You're not in any trouble? Or leaving?" Concern furrowed Matt's brow.

"No, not at all. Looking for a way to bring me around to their thinking. That's all. Not going to happen. You and Patti coming to the wedding?"

"Wouldn't miss it. I gotta get back inside. New guy's taking way too long on repairs." Matt shook his head, gave Lathen a meaningful look, and hurried away.

"Well, that was embarrassing." Pepper giggled. "We're not horny teenagers."

"Hey—speak for yourself. The risk of getting caught is half the fun." A low chuckle bubbled up from Lathen's throat as he put the truck in gear and wheeled it around toward home.

A muted version of a popular song, dealing with the devil and Georgia caught her attention. She dug through her purse and pulled out her cell phone. "Hi Gwen. Don't you dare tell me something came up." Pepper smiled at Lathen knowing with his preternatural hearing he could hear every word Gwen said. It helped not having to repeat conversations. But a real pain, when she didn't want him privy to a conversation.

"Not at all. In fact, I'm able to get out of Salem a few days earlier than expected. Mind if I come on up?" Gwen asked in a cheerful voice. "Thanks to the charity of someone we both know," she added.

"Excellent, looking forward to seeing you. When will you be here?"

"End of the week," Gwen said excitedly.

"Great. Can't wait." Pepper disconnected the call

with a squeal, a wide smile spread across her face.

"See I told you it would all work out," Lathen said smugly, palming the steering wheel to turn the truck onto the cabin's gravel road. At the sight of only Alec's vehicle in the driveway, he breathed a sigh of relief and smiled. Tonk and Ember raced up the path, trying to beat the other in greeting the vehicle.

"You got that right." Pepper glanced toward him feeling his relief. "So what about Ray and the mission?"

"Leave it to me. It won't interfere with the wedding or our lives." Lathen hopped out of the vehicle, gave the wolf and dog a good ear scratch. He took a moment to survey the land while Tonk and Ember circled him. "Have you talked to Ashling recently?"

Pepper stepped out of the truck into the jumble of fur excitedly yipping at her feet. She paused and scratched Tonk's ear, patted Ember's shoulder, then joined Lathen, arm in arm watching the ominous dark clouds move over the bright blue sky. Ocean waves crashed against the rocky shore as seabirds searched for dinner. Wind gusts brought with it the scent of fresh brine. She cut her gaze toward the pond. "No, I haven't seen or heard from Ashling since I agreed to let her handle the arrangements at the pond. Come to think of it, she mentioned something about me having to release the wedding arbor from the trees."

Scanning the forest area, he squinted drawing his black parka around him, zipping it up. "We might want to do that sooner than later."

Pepper shivered, pulling her gloves on. "Hopefully, this squall will be short lived, and we can coax the arch out in the morning."

Hand in hand they trekked the path for final evening rounds to check on the creatures in their care. Everyone were fed and had fresh water, so she and Lathen trudged through the sloppy melting snow to the warmth of their cabin, followed by Ember and Tonk.

Inside, Pepper flicked her wrist at the fireplace, long fingers of orange and yellow flame shot up around the wood. Lathen grinned tossing a few more logs on the fire.

"What a useful talent." He shrugged out of his coat, then helped Pepper out of hers, hung them on the pegs by the door. "How about we spend a nice cozy evening in front of the fire, munching on warmed up meat pies and sipping fine wine? Later…"

She giggled. "Sounds good to me. I'll put the pies in the oven." She padded to the kitchen, opened the refrigerator. "As for wine, I don't know how fine it is, but all we have is the Chardonnay we bought before leaving for Colorado."

"It's a pretty fine wine," Lathen said in his finest English accent. Which really sucked. He joined her into the kitchen.

Pepper collapsed into gales of laughter. Bent over at the waist, she gasped for air. It felt good to laugh, she'd been so keyed up since their return.

Lathen raised a brow and chuckled. "Someone's still tired."

"Stressed. Maybe we should have let my parents have the wedding at their house." She clamped her hand over her mouth and shuddered. "I didn't really say that. Did I?"

Lathen couldn't help but laugh. "How much longer on those meat pies? Calling it an early night sounds really good to me."

"I just popped them in the oven, so it'll be at least fifteen minutes." She poured the wine in glasses and handed one to him, carried the wine bottle into the living room, and set it on the table farthest from the fire. "We can sip wine and enjoy the fire until the pies are done." Pepper plopped on the couch, the amber liquid sloshed in her glass. She held it up and steadied it, watching the firelight glint through the crystal.

"That was close. You nearly spilled it." Lathen eased down next to her, his arm resting on the back of the couch. He swirled the liquid, sniffed and took a drink. "Mmm... Good stuff."

A cool chill settled in the room as mist floated across the floor and settled in the corner away from the fireplace. Lathen exchanged glances with Pepper.

Chapter Sixteen
Turns Out Things Are Not Always as They Appear

The old rocking chair in the corner of the living room filled with mist and took on the shape of a tall man dressed in knee-length black breeches with a long dark vest over his peasant shirt and black shoes. He brought his right foot up to cross onto his left knee and shook his head.

"Aidan McKay, I thought you and Dusty left this world after telling your tale last Halloween?" Pepper said, barely able to believe her eyes.

The ghost made a sighing sound, then the rich bass of his voice wafted through the room. "That was me intention. But Ashling convinced Dusty all the McKay ghosts should stay for the wedding, then Christmas and welcome in the new year as a unified McKay Clan."

The chair rocked back and forth. Tonk and Ember sniffed around the chair, finally settling on either side of it never taking their eyes off the moving rocker. Kaylee's low whistle could be heard from her aviary, where Pepper had fed her a while ago.

Slowly Lathen leaned forward. "So to what do we owe the honor of your visit?"

"'Tis no honor. I be merely the messenger." He shrugged his shoulders and put his filmy hands palm up. "I am to remind you the wedding arbor is needed. Ashling wants to know if the wedding guests are aware ghosts will be at the ceremony."

"And why didn't she come herself? Rather than impose on the head of the clan?" Pepper held her finger up. "Hold that thought. I need more wine. Lathen?"

"I'll take some."

Pepper walked to the table in the opposite corner of the room and grabbed the bottle of wine. After pouring the liquid into their glasses that sat on the table in front of the fireplace, she plopped back on the couch. Reaching for her glass, she took several sips. "Okay, spill."

"Spill what?" Aidan looked perplexed, or at least as much as a ghost can express. "'Tis you two that have wine."

Pepper rolled her eyes. "Why is Ashling ordering you about?"

"I'm told, everyone else is too busy working on the arrangements. She also wants to know how many mortals you expect? Where you want the seating arranged."

"Oh for goodness sakes, where is she? I'll go talk to her."

"She is spending the evening with Ms. Denton. Said she couldn't think with all the ruckus the ghosts were making. Too many people trying to run things, if ye asked me."

Holding her head in her hands, Pepper moaned. "I don't need this. How will I explain this to Gwen?"

"Oh babe, Gwen knows everything there is to know about the McKay Land. Ashling was looking for you when she scared the shit out of Gwen as she was cleaning up the office following the grand opening. After Gwen had calmed down, your aunt felt it necessary to explain. Everything. I guess. I thought you knew."

Eyes narrowed, Pepper stared at Lathen for a couple of beats, her lips twitched and she threw her head back and gales of laughter filled the room.

Lathen watched her, then peered at Aidan, who calmly rocked in the chair and said, "Women be such puzzles."

"Especially the McKay women." Lathen continued to watch Pepper with a bemused expression. Which added to her mirth.

After Pepper composed herself, wiped the tears of laughter streaming down her face, she said, "Now it all makes sense when Gwen left, she mentioned...never mind... I'll take this up with Gwen and Ashling." Pepper took a couple more sips of wine. "Let's see..."

After she set her glass down, Lathen brushed a couple strands of hair out of her eyes and searched her face. "Are you all right?"

"I'm tired, my wedding is in a couple weeks, I have ghosts fighting over who is going to do what. Guests that have no idea the place is haunted and... Your family and pack, my parents, Gwen... To top it all off, the head of my clan, who is a ghost, is sitting in front of me wanting to know who is coming to the wedding and whether the ghosts will be outed. How could I possibly be all right?"

"When you put it that way." Lathen chuckled. "It sounds just a bit... I don't know...crazy?" His right eyebrow winged up. She saw mischief sparkle in his eyes. "We could still elope," he offered.

"No sir. Not after all the trouble—Not on me watch." Aidan shook his head so vehemently his upper torso blurred.

Pepper smiled, glanced at Lathen. "What do you think—about twenty-five to fifty close friends and family at the ceremony?"

"I doubt the pack will be there, they'll be more interested in the food and tall-tale telling at the reception. Not to mention questioning why the dinner wasn't before the ceremony. So you are close on that count." He snatched the wine glass from the table and took a gulp.

"The seating area should be at the end of the pond by the benches. Ashling mentioned purple rose bushes around the pond. Lathen and I are going to get the arbor first thing in the morning, weather permitting."

Lathen's stomach gurgled. "You know the timer for the meat pies went off a while ago." He glanced toward the kitchen. "Want me to go get them?"

"Oh crap, I forgot. They'll be ruined, all dried out." She thought for a moment then waved her hand toward the kitchen. "They'll be fine."

"I've got what's needed." Aidan rose from the chair, lifted his hand in a wave and faded away, the mist crawling along the floor disappeared entirely.

"Never a dull moment around here." Lathen took the tray of pies from Pepper and set it on the coffee table. The silverware clattered as he slipped the napkins out from under them, inhaling deeply. "I'm starved."

"Marrying a McKay witch may be more than you bargained for," she teased. "Too late to change your mind."

"Don't intend to." He forked up a bite of meat pie, blew on it for a minute as the steam rose, and popped it in his mouth. "Mmmmm. Delicious! Life with a witch can be quite satisfying. If you know what I mean." He wiggled his eyebrows.

"Always with the sexual innuendos. You're such a male." She took another sip of wine before setting the glass down and reaching for the meat pie. Scooped up a spoonful, and she let it sit in the dish for a couple beats then slipped it into her mouth, closed her eyes savoring the flavor.

"Gee thanks for noticing. I can demonstrate more fully tonight. If you don't fall asleep on me. Heck...maybe if you do." He forked up a couple more bites of meat pie, shoved them into his mouth.

"Lathen—you're incorrigible." She finished half her pie and raised her hand above her head and stretched.

"But you love me anyway." He scraped the remaining crumbs from the dish, licked them off his fork, and slid a sideways glance in Pepper's direction. She'd finished the last bite when he stood, turned, and swept her into his arms amid her giggling protests. "Time for bed."

She wrapped her arms around his neck, breathing kisses from his jawline to the pulsing hollow of his throat. Bounding up the stairs, he angled his body through the doorway and tossed her onto the bed.

Pepper's eyes grew wide as he shrugged out of the plaid flannel shirt and pulled the t-shirt over his head. When he unbuckled his belt, he shot her a smoldering look. Kicked off his boots, unbuttoned his jeans, slid the zipper down slowly all the while keeping his gaze locked on hers. He slipped the jeans off his undulating hips, peeled the denim off one leg at a time while perfectly balanced on the other foot.

She gave a low seductive whistle. "Take it all off."

"Your wish is my command." Stepping out of his jeans, he reached over and pulled off her shoes, letting them clatter to the floor. "Your turn."

Leaning over, he unbuttoned her jeans, lowered the zipper, and tugged them off. Slowly and seductively his gaze wandered over her, lingered on her lips as her tongue traced their outline, then his gaze slid down. He took one leap and landed lightly beside her.

"My favorite part," he whispered, lips against the soft shell of her ear, sliding his hand under her sweater, calloused fingertips rough against the silkiness of her bra and he released the front clasp.

"Oooh, you play favorites?" She arched toward him as he cupped her firm breasts, his mouth covered hers hungrily, parting her lips, his tongue thrust inside exploring, caressing.

Pepper moaned quietly. He kissed the corner of her mouth, trailed kisses across her jaw down her neck; his tongue teased the swell of her breast. He paused to tug the sweater over her head without missing a beat; his tongue circled her nipple drawing it into his warm mouth. His teeth scraped lightly as the berry hardened, and he sucked gently while his hand kneaded the other breast. Her thoughts shattered as his hands and lips continued their hungry, intimate exploration of her body.

The hardness of his desire rested against her hip. She slipped her fingers under the waistband of his briefs, thumb catching the band and pulling his underwear over his hips, freeing him. "My favorite part," she cooed, wrapping her fingers around his thick shaft.

"Good to know." His breath coming in gasps as she worked her magic on his naked body. Unable to stand anymore, he grasped her hands and held them over her head, pinned against the bed. "No more. My turn." He knelt to the side of her legs and pulled her panties off, teased a long finger inside her for a moment, she arched against his hand, then he slipped between her legs, spreading them wide baring her center to his gaze. "Absolutely beautiful." Lathen kissed his way across her belly to the joining point of hip and inside her thigh, his breath warm against her skin.

She writhed beneath his mouth and cried out as the first orgasm ripped through her. Before she'd come down from that crest, he brought her to the edge again with his finger curled tightly inside her working that magical spot, she spread wider.

Her hands curved around his shoulders and pushed him back. "I want you inside now."

"I love it when you take command." He snickered and flicked his tongue once more. She arched her body and knocked him to his back, then scrambled up to straddle him.

"I'll show you command." Slowly easing him into her inch by painstaking inch until she took all of him. He withdrew and thrust into her, a raw act of possession. She smiled down at him.

Things had changed since his wolf returned, he felt the change as she did, but it seemed to him she wasn't about to relinquish control tonight… Teetering on one knee, her balance wavered, and he flipped her onto her back, buried himself deep inside her. *Got ya.*

"Turnabout's fair play." He grinned. Together they found the rhythm of passion, surrender, and in the end ecstasy. Still moist from lovemaking, he rolled off of her and leaned up on his elbow snaking the other arm around her waist. "See sharing control isn't so bad." He shot her a cheeky grin, brushed several strands of damp red wavy hair from her eyes, and caressed his lips over hers.

"Hmmmm." She buried her head in his shoulder and drifted off to sleep. Sometime during the wee hours of the morning, he slid out of bed. Barely awake, she yawned and drifted back to sleep.

Chapter Seventeen
Oh, My God, Only Two Weeks Before the
Wedding—Panic Sets in—Decisions to be Made

Unable to sleep, Lathen slipped out of bed, grabbed
a pair of jeans, and padded into the hallway. Motioning
Tonk and Ember to follow, he led the way to the back
door, laid his jeans on a chair, opened the door, closed
it silently, and phased into wolf form. Three sets of
paws pounded the ground across the meadow and into
the forest under the pale moonlight. Twigs cracked
under his paws, an owl hooted its displeasure of having
its hunting ground disturbed by interloping predators.
Small creatures scurried away as he tore through the
trails. At last, exhaustion slowed his pace. Tonk and
Ember caught up to him, tongues lolling out of their
mouths, breathing hard. Ember nudged him at the
shoulders, he butted her with his head, and they trotted
back to the cabin. On the porch, he phased to human
before opening the door.

Inside he pulled on jeans and silently padded
across the kitchen. He raked his fingers through his
hair, rubbing the tension knot at the back of his neck.
The run had eased the stress, but he still had no idea
what to do about Raymond and his request. Sure, he
could unravel the encryption codes, write the code for a
worm or virus to act as they needed, depending on its
execution requirements. But did he really want to get

involved or bring Pepper into… In his mind, he knew he wasn't at fault for what happened to his team, but his heart—that was another thing entirely.

Searching through the cupboard, he found the last bag of his favorite coffee beans and poured some into the grinder. Before he flipped the switch, he paused. *This will wake Pepper up, and I still need to sort things out.* Was he willing to risk what he'd built with her, to help his country, again? If things went south, could he protect… What exactly did they need from him?

He had lots of questions but no answers in sight. Like it or not, he needed to have a conversation with Ray, before making any decisions. He should have let the man lay it out before stalking out, letting his temper control him, yet again. Lathen's intel was correct, the Commander's face and men's reactions confirmed it.

Lathen pulled out the tub of ground coffee, added a scoop, water, and turned the machine on. The enticing aroma filled his nostrils, as he watched the stream of steaming dark liquid fill the pot. The minute gurgling sounds stopped and the stream turned to drops, he filled his mug and sat at the table. With both hands wrapped around the large mug, he stroked his thumb over the handle of the smooth ceramic, trying to figure out what to do next.

Pepper appeared standing behind him dressed in her robe, hands resting on his shoulders, thumbs caressing small circles at the back of his neck. "What are you beating yourself up about now?" she asked quietly.

He'd felt her presence before she touched him, so he merely leaned into her. "Nothing."

She made a clicking sound with her tongue. "You

can't make a rational decision without finding out exactly what they need you to do."

"But anything I do could eventually be traced—to me—then to here. If there was a leak."

"You can't tell me a computer programmer—uh—hacker of your caliber couldn't cover your tracks."

Lathen shook his head. "Not that…"

"Oh, cut the crap. If you weren't that good, they wouldn't have been on our doorstep shortly after we arrived home. Hell, they have a whole military to choose from. Who do they call?" She leaned over and pointed a slender finger in his face. "Not the ghost bust…" she snorted recalling the old movie.

He snapped at her digit, she giggled, jerked her hand away and patted his shoulder. "Go talk with them. See what exactly they want entails. You're not bound to the military or SEALs anymore. If you don't like the risk, walk away." Pepper wandered over to the cupboard, took out a mug, heated water for tea. Kaylee's soft whistle reverberated through the quiet house as the yellow rays of sun peeked over the horizon.

"It's not that easy—I spent nearly fifteen years—dedicated my life to this country." He paused. "How do I walk away—when they need my skills—and live with myself? Part of the reason I had such a hard time pulling myself together after the physical wounds healed was because it was my fault four of my SEAL team died and three of us were badly injured. I'm the one with the preternatural abilities. I should have been able to save them. At least sensed what was coming. But I didn't." His voice rose to a loud growl. "They shouldn't have died on my watch."

"Ohhh...so you're a precog now, in addition to a werewolf?" She arched a well-shaped red brow, taking her mug out of the microwave and swishing an orange spice tea bag through the water viciously.

"Noo...but you know."

She pulled out a chair and flopped down, waving her free arm in the air. "No. I don't. We hashed all this out before I agreed to marry you. Healed your shattered psyche.

"You help others heal as well. One visit from some damn spook and you run right back to...to what? Playing the blame game? Not going to happen on my watch," she said vehemently.

His eyes went wide at her tirade.

"If you want to help. Fine. But as the man I agreed to marry. The man reunited with his family, and pack. Not the man so racked by guilt, he was unable to function. Clear?" She added milk and a dash of sugar to her tea, took a gulp, set the mug on the table harder than necessary.

Lathen's gaze met and held Pepper's fiery stare for a couple of beats. "I love it when you get fired up." One corner of his mouth curved up into a half grin. "If someone tied your arms, you wouldn't be able to talk at all," he teased, hoping to lighten the mood.

The thin line of her mouth relaxed into a smirk, Pepper reached across the table and swiped at him.

Dodging the blow, Lathen grinned wide. "I don't plan to be anything but the man you agreed to marry. So...on that note. I'll contact Lt. Commander Raymond Sale, get the details, and we can make a decision."

"Whatever you decide is all right with me. I trust you," she said quietly. "I know you wouldn't put our lives, Mike, Alec, or the Center at risk. You've made that quite clear, and I appreciate it."

Kaylee's whistling grew louder while Tonk and Ember nosed their bowls across the kitchen floor.

"Probably better feed the critters before we have a mutiny on our hands." Lathen stood and took Pepper in his arms, kissing her soundly. "I'll feed them, if you want to get breakfast started."

"Sounds like a plan. I'm going to run up and get dressed first."

"Toss me down a shirt, would you?"

"Nope, I like you half naked." She ran her fingertips over his bare chest, tracing the muscles. "But if you're going to whine—I'll do it—under protest."

"Thanks. I'll make it up to you tonight," he said in a low seductive rumble, then tossed three logs in the fireplace. "Your turn."

She whipped around, flicked her hand toward the logs, instantly flames raced up the wood. "Good enough?"

He nodded, poured kibble in the dog and wolf's bowls, then jogged down the hallway to Kaylee's aviary. After tossing fish to the osprey, Lathen started back to the kitchen when his phone rang. Pulling it out of his pocket, he checked the screen and rolled his eyes, let it go to voice mail.

After breakfast, they trudged through the slushy snow to make sure all the animals and birds were fed and watered, while Tonk and Ember raced circles around them barking and yipping. Alec and Mike had the day off. Pepper stopped, talked, and cooed at each animal. He was always in awe of her ability to make even the most cantankerous creature docile. The moose was healing nicely. It would be returning to the wild in early spring, as would most of the birds in the seabird aviary. Next stop was to make sure the vet quarters were neat and tidy since his dad and Amy would be occupying the space until the New Year.

"Brock must be a neat freak. Looks like it did when we left." Pepper ran her finger along the countertop next to the sink, turned, and crossed the floor, stepped outside. She stopped to put her sunglasses on and glanced into the forest. "We need to find the arbor. Do you remember exactly where you found the anomaly?"

"Sure do. The wood to make your bench was offered from an adjacent tree." Lathen tromped through the snow and ice until he came to a twisted tree trunk leaning against an upright tree. "This is it."

****

The closer Pepper moved to the tree, the bark seemed to shimmer in the golden sunlight. When her fingertips caressed the wood, it vibrated warm under her touch, rough edges blurred like a trick of light. The trees creaked and groaned as they blended into a wedding arch with intricately carved moon phases on one side and star alignments on the other. She stood in awe running her fingers over the lettering carved across the top of the arch, *síorghrá* separated by a Celtic knot then more letters *go síoraí.*

Lathen reached up to support and tip the arch so they could better study the lettering. "What do the words mean?"

"My Gaelic is rusty, but I think it's Eternal Love separated by the Celtic Trinity Knot then the word Forever." She closed her eyes feeling the heat, then suddenly it was gone. Her eyes flew open. "Where did it go?"

His head tilted to the side, one eyebrow raised in question. "I'm not sure. It shimmered and faded away. Did you inadvertently send it somewhere?"

"No, I was trying to visualize how it would look standing between the two benches at the pond."

Alarmed, Pepper followed by Lathen sprinted, slipping and sliding over the snow into the clearing and down the path to the pond. Between the two benches, a few yards from the pond's edge stood the arch. It appeared to be settling into the soil, sending roots deep into the dirt.

****

"What the heck?" Lathen pushed his parka hood from his head and stared wide-eyed. Suddenly, he had an epiphany, watching the base of the arch dig its roots into the rocky ground. An idea formed in his mind for a special wedding gift for his bride.

"It's relocating." Ashling appeared out of the swirling mist beside her favorite pine. "Thanks for bringing it down. We needed the arch situated so we could plan the rose bushes, seating, and walkway for the ceremony."

As Ashling explained about the arch being a living thing, like the bench he'd built last summer for Pepper, his concept grew. Magic would be required. He scrubbed his hand over his face and peered at Ashling. *That was it, I'll enlist her help, maybe Aidan's as well.* Lathen smiled to himself when her voice penetrated his thoughts.

Ashling sidled closer to him, eyes narrowed. Her frosty breath in his ear, she whispered, "What are you up to wolf?"

"Something we'll discuss at a later date, Auntie." He knew she didn't like it when he called her auntie, which in all honesty was exactly why he did it.

She huffed, raised her arm in a threatening gesture then dropped it, and floated toward her niece.

Eyes rounded, Pepper stared at her aunt transfixed, oblivious to the conversation around her. "I—uh—didn't move it." She walked beneath the arch staring at each side where roots were disappearing into the soil.

"Sure you did. Thought about how it would look and here it is. Nice." Lathen pumped a fist in the air.

"Well…not intentionally," Pepper retorted. "What's it doing?" She pointed to the ground.

"Permanently settling into its new location. It is a living thing and needs nourishment from the earth," Ashling said nonchalantly. "Now that you're here. Who is performing the ceremony? The McKay spirits would like to attend. But if that is going to be a problem, we'll just disappear into the mist and float across the pond during the nuptials."

"I…we…haven't talked about that."

"You haven't made arrangements for someone to perform the ceremony?" Ashling blurted. "You've only a couple weeks left. Better get a wiggle on, girl. Winter Solstice, Christmas is a busy time… Laws of the land prevail, especially when you are a business owner, profit or not. Gotta be married by an official."

"Listen to the woman of unconventionality, spouting advice on the law of the land. Your relationship with Colleen was anything but conventional."

"Not my—our fault. Now days, we would have been married. Be that as it may, we remained true to ourselves and each other." The usual gray misty aura around Ashling changed to slightly red.

Though Lathen enjoyed watching Ashling get riled, he considered a solution to the problem, rubbing his chin thoughtfully. "My dad is ordained to perform marriages. Performs wedding ceremonies for pack members all the time. The marriage license is issued locally." He narrowed his eyes at Ashling. "Yes, we've already gotten the license. I don't see a problem with having him perform the ceremony."

"I love that idea. We better ask him," Pepper said excitedly.

"No, I'd rather it be a surprise when he arrives." Lathen's lips curved into a wicked grin.

"Won't he need to bring…"

"Just himself, a pen to sign the license, and we'll have plenty of witnesses." He reached over and kissed the tip of her nose. "Our vows are already written."

"True. Okay that's one more thing taken care of." She reached her arm through Lathen's. "We'd better be getting back. I'd like to stop by the office and finish up any paperwork. Then try to clear the schedule for a couple weeks before the wedding, since Gwen is coming in early. We can start decorating the cabin, get the tree up, and maybe add a touch of festive garland to each of the animal habitats."

"I'll leave you to it, then." The mist thickened, Ashling's form faded and disappeared right through the window glass.

Lathen chuckled. "The creatures don't care whether or not their area is decorated."

"How would you know?" she asked indignantly over her shoulder. "I only have the wedding decorations and a few Christmas ones I picked up recently in town. But Mom is bringing her extras, and Amy said your dad had a box of tree ornaments for each of you boys. He's bringing yours with them."

"Okay, so where are the decorations you have?"

"In the supply room in a box marked decorations," she said flippantly tugging him up the path.

After they arrived at the office, Pepper disappeared behind the computer, and Ember relaxed at her feet. Lathen walked through the office into the supply room. He picked up the boxes and carried them up to the cabin, Tonk on his heels. In addition to the boxes he brought to the cabin, sat several small boxes marked "decorations" and one big one marked "tree." They were stacked in the middle of the living room floor. He took off his parka and scratched his head. He'd slit the top of the first box open when Tonk raised his head, ears flat and growled menacingly. A knock sounded on the door. Tonk jumped up and let out a sharp bark.

"That's enough boy. Sit." Lathen opened the door.

Lt. Commander Sale stood on the porch, dressed in casual attire, shifting from one foot to the other. "May I come in?"

Lathen paused for a long moment, his forehead creased, then pushed the door wide open and motioned the man in. "What brings you out this way?"

"We need your expertise and are willing to work with your terms," he said stiffly.

"Have a seat." Lathen motioned to the couch. "I'll put the coffee on. Then you can fill me in." He strolled into the kitchen, got mugs from the cupboard, and poured water in the coffee maker. A few minutes later, Lathen emerged with two mugs of steaming coffee on a tray along with a plate of warmed peanut butter cookies, fresh from the microwave.

Ray accepted the coffee. "Thanks." He took a sip, pulled a file out of his briefcase, and spread the contents across the coffee table.

Lathen sat down, grabbed a cookie, took a bite, and chewed while he looked over the paperwork. He shook the cookie crumbs over the plate. The men were deep in conversation, bent over the table when Pepper and Ember swept through the back door.

"It's freezing out there," she called from the kitchen. "And…"

Lathen glanced up from the paperwork.

Pepper shrugged out of her coat, unwrapped the scarf from her neck, tossed them at the peg on the wall and raised an arm toward the living room fireplace.

Before he could utter a word, she twisted toward him. "Why didn't you…" She stopped mid-sentence, dropped her arm and blew out a breath. "Didn't know we had company."

Lathen breathed a sigh of relief. "Ray stopped by to discuss the situation he needs my assistance on."

"Oh." Pepper arched a brow and fisted one hand on her hip.

"Yeah, seems the problem has escalated, and he needs me to report to the navel base approximately an hour away from here tomorrow morning. Should only be there a few hours and be home by supper. Can we make that work? Alec and Mike will be here tomorrow."

"I guess so." She nibbled on her bottom lip.

"The Lt. Commander is well aware of our schedule. At worst, I'll need to check in a couple more times between now and the wedding. At best tomorrow will be it. I'll be directing the operation. There are plenty of skilled computer programmers available. Once we get what we need, I've written code for a worm that will activate once the intended person signs in. It will crash their system making the files unrecoverable. Our penetration will be undetectable, if everything goes as planned. Ray's put the safety measures we discussed in place. So no worries there."

Pepper hesitated for a couple beats as Lathen's calm washed over her. "It's your decision."

Ray looked from Lathen to Pepper, cleared his throat, glanced at his watch and stood. "I have to be going. See you at five a.m. tomorrow?"

"I'll be there. And I'll be gone by fourteen hundred hours."

"Fair enough. If the guys can't handle things on their own by then, we have little hope of completing the mission."

Lathen shrugged. "If they are as good as you say, no problem. If not, I've a backup plan." Lathen shoved up from the couch, grabbed Pepper around the waist, and walked to the door. He let Ray out and closed the door behind him.

"So did you get what you wanted," Pepper asked flicking her fingers in the direction of the fireplace.

"Yep." He smiled as the fire roared to life. "Ray almost got more than he expected." He raised an eyebrow, his lips twitched. "Might want to make sure we are alone, before…"

"I did. Sorta." She grimaced. "I'm glad things worked out. Gwen will be here on Friday. So I have a couple of days to tie up any loose ends." Pepper stared at the pile of boxes in the center of the room. "Where'd these come from?"

He shrugged. "Don't know. They were here when I arrived with your boxes."

She examined the boxes and opened a couple. "They must be Ashling's. She and Colleen loved to decorate at Christmas time."

"Great. So where do you want the tree?"

"In front of the big picture window facing the ocean."

Lathen opened the box, set up the tree, and tested the light strands before hanging them. "This tree smells like real pine."

Pepper snapped her fingers. "Of course. It's Ashling's. I remember now. It's enchanted. Colleen was slightly allergic to pine, so bringing one in the house was out of the question. Ashling created that one. Which is the best of both worlds. Looks and smells like a real tree, but doesn't shed needles or bother Colleen."

Lathen nodded, rummaging through the boxes. "The lights were hers too?"

"Yep. Colleen liked colorful lights. Bubble lights were her favorite."

"That explains the several strands of bubble lights. Boxes and boxes of spares that seem to all be empty. Unfortunately, there's a couple lights out on each strand."

"I can fix that." She waved her arm over the tangle of bubble lights. "They'll work now."

Pepper helped Lathen untangle the strands and arranged them on the tree. After locating a power strip and plugging all the lights in, he asked, "Wouldn't it be easier to use magic to light the tree?"

"That would be frivolous, not celebratory and not something I'm willing to do," she said primly. "There is a difference."

Lathen's eyebrow shot up nearly to his hairline. "But I thought Christmas magic could be used at will, with no repercussions. Your mom said…"

"My mother and I don't always see eye to eye. Dad and Ashling believed that Christmas magic should be used conservatively even though we don't pay the physical price during the holidays. I share their feelings."

"Got it." He shrugged.

They worked well into the night decorating the cabin. Lathen wound multi-colored lights along the porch railing while Pepper hung lights in the windows. The big pine beside the driveway was the only outdoor tree they decorated, and that took a multitude of light strands to accomplish. At Lathen's insistence, they had to have a tree topper for the big tree. She used a bit of magic to create a brightly lit blue star atop the pine.

"All done," Lathen declared, rubbing the back of his neck. He needed to wolf out, as Pepper liked to say, and go for a run. Could he wait until his dad and brother arrived? He scrubbed his hand over his face and sighed. "Pepper, I'm going for a run, need to work out the nervous energy before reporting to the naval base tomorrow."

Concern wrinkled her brow as she studied him. "Okay, a good night's sleep might be a good idea too."

He caught her in his arms and kissed her. "I won't be gone long."

The grandfather clock in the living room chimed the last notes of midnight as Lathen strode through the door. He ascended the stairs silently so as not to wake Pepper and slipped between the sheets.

"Better?" she asked sleepily.

"Yes. Go back to sleep." He wrapped an arm around her, curved his body around hers.

It was still dark when Lathen rose and showered. Walking out of the bathroom toweling off, he noticed Pepper was not in bed where he'd left her. The aroma of freshly brewed coffee wafted up from the kitchen.

He padded downstairs to find a warm bowl of oatmeal on the table beside a plate of buttered toast. Pepper sat at the table, her hands wrapped around the mug of hot chocolate. A half-eaten bowl of hot cereal in front of her.

She smiled up at him. "Can't send you off to save the world on an empty stomach."

"I appreciate that. One stomach growl and the whole mission could be compromised." He shot her a cheeky grin. "Nothing to worry about. I'll be home before you have a chance to miss me."

She rolled her eyes then met his gaze with a saucy smile. "I'll be too busy to miss you."

"Okay then." He sat down, shoveled in the oatmeal, and chewed through three pieces of toast. Taking the last swig of his coffee, he glanced at the empty travel mug setting next to the coffee maker.

"Didn't want to fill it until you were on your way out. Are you ready to go then?" Pepper stood up from the table, filled the mug with steaming liquid, and handed it to Lathen. "Play nice with the other kids." She grinned.

"Not possible." He paused for a beat. "But I'll try." Taking her into his arms, he kissed her thoroughly.

"There, that should hold you 'til I get back." He shrugged into his parka and took the mug she handed him.

With a smile, she drew his face to hers in a renewed embrace, kissed his lips softly. "Good luck."

"Luck has nothing to do with it when you are as good as I am." A cold burst of air rushed in as he opened the door, turned and winked at her, then closed it behind him.

It had been several years since he'd darkened the entrance of a military installation. Mixed emotions swirled through him as he took out the security badge and ID Raymond had given him. Would this be the only assignment required of him, or would there be more? He started up the truck and turned out of the gravel driveway.

Chapter Eighteen
A Week Before the Wedding and All Seems Deceptively Quiet—Never a Good Sign

As golden rays crept beneath the curtains and spread across the bed, Pepper stretched, yawned, and rolled over to cuddle with Lathen only to find a huge copper wolf sharing her bed. She shrieked and jumped out of bed. Tonk and Ember rushed into the room and looked around eventually pinning their gaze on Pepper.

The wolf's aquamarine eyes blinked open and stared at Pepper for a second. The edges of his fur blurred as he returned to human form curled up naked on the bed, looking confused.

"You nearly scared ten years off my life." Air whooshed out of her as she plopped on the edge of the bed. Pepper's heart thundered in her chest. "Well what do you have to say for yourself?"

Finding nothing out of the ordinary, Tonk and Ember made a whiffling noise and trotted out of the room.

"That's never happened before." Lathen raised his hands, palms up in a gesture of surrender. "Hazards of living with a werewolf?" he offered, a sly smile played on his lips.

"My ass."

"Yes, and it's a very fine ass. But what does that have to do with this situation?" A deep chuckle rose from his throat. He leaned up on one elbow to meet her gaze.

Her heart still pounding, she grabbed a pillow and threw it at him. "Don't you ever do that again."

Lathen ducked, caught the pillow and stuffed it behind his head. "Okay, but since I don't know why it happened, I can't give you any guarantees." He smirked and rolled out of bed.

"You go off on secret missions then you come back and this is what happens?" She spread her arms wide.

He sauntered into the bathroom. "Secret missions have nothing to do with it, and you know it, though it was an extremely successful mission. The one I am considering at the moment, requires you to join me in the shower. Should you accept this mission…" His lips twitched trying to keep the laughter at bay.

She rolled her eyes and followed him into the bathroom. "Before I accept this mission. I want some answers." She burst into giggles. "What do you mean, you don't know what happened? You're telling me, I could wake up next to a huge wolf at any time?"

"Apparently." He reached for the shower knob.

"You never woke up in wolf form while in the SEALs?" she asked incredulously.

"Not that I know of, but they were aware of what I was, so probably wouldn't have been a shock."

"I know what you are, and it still scared the bejeebers out of me. You could have warned me."

"What would the fun in that be?"

"And why didn't Tonk and Ember react?"

"Because they've seen my wolf form, to them it was nothing unusual. As far as the SEALs, I didn't share a bed with any of the team, though we slept in close quarters most times. While on an op, deep sleep was a luxury we couldn't afford." He snapped his fingers. "Which may be the reason it happened here. I've nothing to fear and feel completely safe. Otherwise, I have no idea. It's a question I will bring up with Kolby."

"Wouldn't your dad know?"

"Yes, but I'd never live it down and neither would you, if he was privy to that information. Kolby on the other hand can be black-mailed into silence." He turned the shower on, adjusted the water, and flipped a handful of water at Pepper.

She dodged the water as her mouth formed an O when the statement sank in and she nodded. "One more question. The mission was a success, so is that it?"

"Yep, as far as I know. Now let's get you wet and soapy and have a little fun." Lathen growled playfully.

****

The days flew by in a flurry of activity. The tree lighting ceremony in the town square kicked off the Christmas celebrations. Pepper and Lathen meandered through the crowd, visiting with friends they'd not seen in a while, discussing the Thanksgiving holiday in Colorado. For the first time in quite a while at a town gathering, Lathen's handyman services weren't needed.

Pepper reveled walking hand in hand with her man doing nothing more than enjoying themselves. She sucked in the cold air and blew out a breath that clouded around her head then drifted off with the breeze. Christmas carols wafted through town square, thanks to the new sound system Lathen had installed. A loud speaker squawked, interrupting music as the mayor announced Lathen would be lighting the tree.

The honor was his, since he'd repaired most of the light strands, designed and built the new electrical system in the square.

Lathen barked out a laugh and tugged Pepper along with him to the front of the tree. "I'm honored. But the real reason you want me to do it is because if something goes wrong, it's on my head and you have all these witnesses." He leaned over and checked the industrial power strip connecting the light strings and tree topper for the massive pine. Then he swaggered over to the gazebo, and flipped the main power switch. Pepper held her breath as the forty-foot tree lit up in a multitude of shimmering colors without a problem. She clapped her hands together, released her breath which promptly formed a cloud around her head.

Ooohs and ahhhs swept through the crowd before massive applause erupted across the square. Small trees twinkled with red and green lights. Frosted white icicle lights that trimmed the gazebo, shone brightly among the sea of multi-color lights. Sparkling ice crystals floated through the night air reflecting the bright colors, and adding to the festive holiday atmosphere.

Pretending to wipe his brow in an exaggerated gesture, Lathen gave a quick wave. The church choir assembled in and around the gazebo led a Christmas carol sing along until finally the pastor announced pot luck was ready in the church basement.

Everyone rushed toward First Street, with Lathen leading the pack to the St. Joseph's Church basement where the food was being readied.

"If we don't get in line right away, it will be a long wait, and the best home-baked food goes first." Nearly dragging Pepper, he hurried across town square toward

St. Joseph's a block down the street.

She stumbled once, but he steadied her. "We can visit while we are in line," she offered breathlessly trying to keep up with him.

"I'd rather visit with a plate full of food." His stomach growled loudly as if in agreement.

Pepper giggled as he shoved the heavy well-worn wooden door open. Delicious aromas of fresh baked breads, cookies, cakes, and stews wafted out the door along with gales of laughter and dishes clattering as Lathen and Pepper maneuvered their way near the front of the line.

Matt from the Seacrest and his wife were a few people ahead of them. They waved with a knowing smile. He picked up a plate, loaded it full to running over as his wife rolled her eyes and grinned at Pepper.

"See what I mean." Lathen picked up a plate and handed one to Pepper, pointing out who made what and suggesting what she should try. They finished a circuit around the serving table and found seats at a table with several friendly faces.

A fun time was had by all, and when the evening ended, Pepper was glad all she had to do was go home. No one had asked her to help with this shindig. Probably because they knew she was getting ready for the wedding and she was thankful. Her only obligation was three dozen deviled eggs, which she had delivered upon their arrival.

Lathen grabbed the empty serving platter. "Those eggs were the hit of the party. Ready to go?"

"I am. It was nice to have to do nothing but visit, eat, and visit some more."

"Don't get used to it. I heard plans were in the

works for a spring celebration and—you'll be tapped for decorations. That's how it's done in these small towns. People are always planning something."

"Which is what I like about living here. But they're out of luck. We'll be on our honeymoon." She snickered.

"Well there's still time to warn them when we'll be gone," he teased.

She narrowed her eyes. "You do and you're a dead man."

"Got ya."

****

Gwen arrived two days later, sporting aqua highlights rather than the usual pink in her hair last time Pepper had seen her, and happy to help with the wedding preparations. Pepper checked in with Kelly who assured her everything for the reception was ready. Gwen and Pepper stepped out of Wedded Bliss onto Maple and nearly collided with Dr. Brock Scutter.

"Hi Brock, I didn't realize you were still here. Staying for Christmas?"

"Hadn't planned on it, but Dylan came down with a nasty bug. Every time she felt able to go into work, that damn stuff came back. So I'm going to stick around until the first of the year."

"She told me on the phone it was just a cold, nothing to worry about." Pepper frowned feeling bad about the several calls she'd made to Dylan.

"Yep that's what she told everyone, until the doctor said a week of bed rest. I took her phone and car keys away." He shook his head and smiled. "Hard headed that one. But she's doing much better."

"That's good to hear. What about your practice in

Salem?"

"It's slow this time of year—for the most part, and I have two partners and a couple interns. They're handling it fine. Haven't taken a real vacation in several years, so I'm really enjoying this. I like her varied practice. After this experience I'm considering expanding the practice." Brock shifted his gaze to Gwen and back to Pepper, his lips curved at the corners into a gracious smile.

"Oh...sorry. Brock this is my friend, Gwen. She runs a wildlife sanctuary on the outskirts of Salem. I'm surprised you never met."

"My clinic sees mostly cats and dogs, a few reptiles on occasion." Brock offered his hand to Gwen.

She took his hand and smiled. "Nice to meet you. Pepper's told me quite a bit about you. Saved her Thanksgiving vacation."

"Well, I don't know about that, but I was happy to help out. Nothing serious." He reached into his jacket pocket and pulled out a business card. "I'd like to add wildlife and house calls to the practice when I return. Maybe you could give us a try a couple months into the new year?" He handed the card to Gwen.

"Ever worked with a wildlife rescue? What kind of qualifications do you have?" Gwen took the card, studied it, then stuck it in her coat pocket.

"No... Not in a long time. Right out of veterinary school, I worked in a wildlife rehab for a couple years. Then I took over a troubled clinic. With the help of a good staff, we got it turned around. But I never thought about returning to the wildlife aspect, until now."

Gwen rummaged around in her purse and pulled out a tattered business card. "Give me a call and we'll arrange something. A vet that was helping us out retired and moved to Florida." Gwen shivered and sidled over to a patch of sunshine. "I don't see how it can be so cold, when the sun is shining bright."

"I asked Dylan the same thing when I arrived." He chuckled. "Something about being on the coast and the moisture from the ocean."

"Brock, why don't you stop by the Center. Dylan said she'd be by in a couple days to check on everyone, but I didn't know she'd been so sick. Then we can continue this conversation in the warmth of the cabin," Pepper offered, wrapping her arms around herself.

He pulled his phone out of his pocket, scrolled through the calendar. "Gotta get back to the clinic right now. I'll try for tomorrow. If not the next day. Will that work for you?"

"Sure. And thanks again. See you in the next day or two." Pepper started down Maple to where her SUV was parked.

"Nice to meet you, Brock." Gwen waved and hurried after Pepper, grabbing her arm. "What are you doing?" Gwen hissed.

Pepper raised a brow and glanced down to where Gwen grasped her arm. "Having Brock check the rescues rather than Dylan," Pepper said innocently, unlocking the vehicle door. "Don't want to be responsible for Dylan having a relapse."

Gwen released her hold and gritted her teeth, as she jumped into the SUV. "Oh...no... I can see that little brain of yours working overtime. Don't play matchmaker... I don't have time for such nonsense," she warned settling into the seat.

Pepper walked around to the driver's side of the

truck, climbed in. "I don't know what you're talking about." Her lips twitched as she bit back a grin. "Looking out for the best interests of the animals is my job. Brock wants more experience. Why not?" Pepper started the engine and turned on Main Street ignoring the stare her best friend was giving her. When the windows started to steam up, Pepper flipped the heater to defrost, turned the fan on low, and cracked her window. Gwen was sitting silently on her seat, arms crossed.

"Oh come on. You gotta admit he's cute. Dylan said he's very single."

"Ok, he's good looking, smart, and single. So what's wrong with him?"

"Works all the time, according to his cousin. So you two would get along great. Besides, you said you needed a new vet last time we talked. I found you one. You're welcome."

Gwen blew out a breath. "You had this planned all along."

"Don't be silly. How could I know Brock would be walking down Maple as we left Kelly's place?" Pepper turned onto the gravel road that led to the cabin, coasted into the driveway, and cut the engine.

"I don't know." Gwen huffed, opening the door, and hopping to the ground. Ember and Tonk came bounding up the path, raced around the SUV, then chased each other back to the cabin. "But I do know when you are up to something."

Chapter Nineteen
What's the Use of Magic, If You Can't Use It?

A few days later, Lathen's dad phoned to tell Lathen that he'd stopped in Denver to pick up Pepper's mom and dad. Their flight would touch down in Bar Harbor in an hour. He also indicated that the rest of the pack members attending would arrive the day before the wedding. They had rooms reserved at the Sea Crest Inn. Lathen relayed the information to Pepper.

A rental SUV pulled up in front of the cabin as Lathen, Pepper, and Gwen were walking up the path from the office. The back door to the vehicle flew open, Pepper's mom, Klaren, bounded out of the vehicle and down the path to envelop Pepper and Lathen in a hug. Pepper's dad, Duncan, got out of the other side smiling and joined Klaren, careful not to step on Ember and Tonk circling the newcomers. He kissed his daughter and backed away from the fray.

"It's so good to see you again," Klaren declared. "Gwen, when did you arrive?" Klaren pulled Gwen into the group hug.

"Oh, I was able to sneak away from the sanctuary a few days early. So here I am."

"Mom, Dad, it's only been a few weeks." Pepper kissed her mom and dad on the cheek and untangled herself from her mom's grip. She spotted Elijah and Amy standing beside the vehicle looking out across the expanse of the property to the ocean. Lathen's brother, Kolby and his wife Hayley walked toward Lathen, who also had escaped Klaren's grip.

Tonk and Ember barked at the back of the SUV, circled then returned.

Lathen grabbed his brother's hand then drew him into a hug. "Good to see you." He reached over and gave Hayley a quick hug. "Glad you made it." Lathen joined his dad and Amy, who hadn't moved from the side of the vehicle.

"This is quite a place you have here." His dad reached out and clasped Lathen's hand, pulled him into a bear hug. "You did good, son."

"Not me. Pepper is the driving force behind this Center. I'm just the handyman," Lathen said, smiling wide. Leaning over he gave Amy a hug. "You keeping this old man in line?" He clasped his dad's shoulder.

Amy chuckled. "Hardly. As you know, he's a force to reckon with, but I'm doing my best." Her gaze swept affectionately over her husband. She pointed to the various buildings. "This is a lot bigger than I imagined."

"It's growing by leaps and bounds. When we built it, we allowed for growth. Really glad we did. Apparently there was quite a storm while we were in Colorado. Most the habitats are full."

"I can see you love the work. I'm so glad you…"

"Me too, Dad." An awkward silence fell between the two.

Pepper elbowed Lathen out of the way breaking the silence and grabbed Hayley's hands, swung them out to the sides and back. "Do I dare hug you?"

"Oh, very funny. Come here silly girl." Haley

turned slightly sideways to hug Pepper.

"You look great. How are you feeling?"

"Good. Except I can't get behind the wheel of a car, and I haven't seen my feet in what seems like forever. But the next baby, Kolby is carrying," Hayley said with a laugh.

"Then there won't be another one," Kolby said firmly, shaking his head. "No way."

"Wimp." Hayley giggled wrapping her arm around his waist.

Pepper reached out, snagged Gwen's arm. "Gwen, this is Hayley, Lathen's sister-in-law, the one I told you about, and her husband, Kolby."

Gwen clasped Hayley's hand. "So glad to meet you. Pepper's told me all about you and Kolby—well—everyone," she said happily. "And you must be—Eli and Amy."

"Guilty as charged." Eli chuckled.

"Okay, what the heck is in the back of that SUV that has Tonk and Ember so wound up?" Pepper said stalking around to the back of the vehicle. "That's enough you two. Leave it." Dog and wolf quit barking but continued to sniff and paw at the door. That's when she heard the yips coming from inside.

"Oh, in all the excitement, I forgot Timber is in her crate in the back. She couldn't be trusted loose on the car ride here. Chewing issues and she was asleep when we drove up." Klaren waited for Eli to unlock the door. He stepped out of the way a smirk on his lips. Amy grinned at him.

"No wonder Tonk and Ember are going crazy. Let the poor pup out," Pepper insisted.

Klaren opened the crate door and caught the

wiggling bundle of fur as it leaped out of the enclosure. She clipped the leash on and set the pup on the ground.

"Wow. She's getting big." Lathen watched Tonk and Ember greet Timber. "Easy guys. No rough housing with the pup," he said sternly.

Pepper touched dog and wolf, narrowing her eyes. Tonk and Ember settled down and trotted onto the porch, with a couple backward glances.

"Pep we need your talent to corral Timber. She's a little pistol." Pepper's dad took the leash from his wife and picked up the pup.

"Tonk and Ember will keep her worn out. A tired pup is a happy pup. We'll work on a little training while you're here." Pepper laughed and snatched the pup from her dad, held Timber up to her face. "Won't we girl." Timber licked Pepper's face and yipped, four legs flailing in an effort to get down.

"If you don't mind, I'd like to fence your meadow, away from the gardens of course, so Timber could run off her energy. Safely."

"Sure." Lathen glanced around to make sure no one outside their circle was in the vicinity. "Tonk and Ember can help with that."

Duncan snapped his fingers and a chain link fence appeared around the meadow where the witches had spellbound Ben Bonchard on Halloween night. The gate swung open. Tonk and Ember looked to Pepper, who nodded her consent. They rushed in then paused as Klaren unclipped the leash from Timber and closed the gate.

"You two watch out for Timber," Pepper instructed, slipping her arm through Lathen's as they led the way to the cabin.

When Lathen stepped inside, there was a slight feeling of expanding air and a soft groan from the cabin. Somehow the living area seemed more spacious. Pepper cut her gaze to her mom, who was chatting nervously with Amy. Pepper excused herself from Gwen and Hayley, clasped her mother's arm.

"Mom, could I see you for a minute?" she hissed into her mother's ear.

"Oh, no dear, Amy and I were just discussing your operations here. Won't you show the Quartz's the Center before the sun goes down? They'd like to stretch their legs after sitting in the plane for so long."

"That's a great idea," Pepper's dad said loudly. "Hayley, Kolby you up for a walk with Elijah, Amy, and me?"

Pepper narrowed her eyes and shifted her gaze between her mom and dad. "Lathen would be happy to give you the tour."

Hayley held her hand up. "I'd like to just wander around the main area, close to a bathroom. I'll save the outlying areas for another day. If you don't mind."

"Sure thing. Right this way." Lathen whistled for Tonk and Ember forgetting for a moment they were in the enclosure with Timber. Kaylee whistled in return. "Hey, I think someone wants to join the party. I'll go out and release the hounds. Toss me the leash for Timber."

"I'll get Kaylee and let her fly with you on the tour." Pepper jogged down the hall to the osprey's aviary, tugged open the door and Kaylee came soaring through the door, banked left, down the hall and into the living area. She landed gracefully on her perch in the living room.

Lathen donned a leather gauntlet and held his arm out for Kaylee. "Come on girl, you're coming with me."

Kaylee whistled happily and glided to his arm. He wrapped his other arm around Pepper's waist and leaned his lips to her ear. "I know what your parents did, but let them have their way. We needed the extra room anyway. Not worth scolding them over the use of magic for something they see as helping out. Let it go." Lathen brushed his lips over her cheek. "See you later. I assume you're going to stay with Hayley and Gwen?"

Pepper shrugged as a little line dug itself between her brows. "Yep." She waited until everyone else trooped out the back door and eventually down the path to the office, and mammal habitat.

"This place is huge. How do just you and Lathen handle things?" Hayley asked rubbing her hand across her belly.

"Oh, we don't. It's grown a lot, and right now we are almost filled to capacity. Bad storm over Thanksgiving wreaked havoc with the wildlife in Arcadia National Park while we were gone. We have a couple of employees, Alec and Mike that handle a lot of the outside work. A vet, Dylan Foster, from Lobster Cove and her cousin visiting from Massachusetts, helped out while we were gone. He has a veterinary practice somewhere around Salem."

Gwen raised an eyebrow.

Pepper winked at her. "He stopped by here to check on the animals since Dylan's been under the weather."

Hayley nodded and smiled knowingly when Gwen's face flushed.

"No, no, no...any interest I have is purely professional; we need a new vet." Gwen shook her head emphatically. "I don't have time for personal relationships."

"You better make time, or you'll find yourself old and alone with only the animals at the sanctuary to keep you company. They won't keep you warm at night, or care for you when you're sick." Pepper waved her off as her lips curved up in a mischievous grin. "Wait 'til you get to know him. You'll see what I mean."

"At least the animals won't deliberately cause me heartbreak," Gwen shot back.

Knowing full well the heartbreak of rescue, Pepper raised a brow. "Don't they?"

"You embarrass me, and so help me I'll..." Gwen started.

Pepper cut her off. "I won't embarrass you. Fair enough?" She zipped up her coat. "Ready for a short walk, ladies?"

"That sounds good." Hayley re-buttoned her coat and slipped on her gloves.

"Come on Gwen." Pepper tugged her friend by the hand, led the way out the front door and around to the greenhouse.

After touring the greenhouse, mammal habitat, and resting for a bit in Pepper's office, the girls trudged up the path to the cabin. Kaylee whistled high overhead and dove for Pepper just as she encased her arm in leather over her coat and raised her arm.

"That was quick," Gwen commented accustomed to Pepper's use of magic to protect her arm from the osprey's talons.

"Yeah, the parka material protects my arm, but

leather helps avoid replacing my parkas on a continual basis due to the material being shredded by sharp talons." She laughed and touched Kaylee's wing. "She was sitting in her favorite tree outside the office, so figured she'd join us."

"She has grown stronger and more confident here." Gwen removed her boots and hung her parka on one of the pegs by the door.

"Kaylee has. During the summer, she is about ninety-eight percent, but during the winter, the cold bothers her old injuries, so she spends less time outside, unless we are outside working." Pepper started the fire in the usual fashion since Lathen had stacked wood in the fireplace earlier in the day. Flames licked at the logs and soon flickered high above the wood providing additional warmth to the room. Gwen and Hayley stretched out on the recliners while Pepper put coffee on and popped cookies in the oven that she'd pulled from the freezer earlier in the day.

"Hey, Pepper," Gwen called from the other room. "Hayley was just wondering about this wreath of feathers hung on the wall behind the couch. Isn't it the one you made with all the rescued birds we'd taken in at the Salem Wildlife Sanctuary? I don't remember it having this glow about it in your apartment."

Pepper stuck her head around the corner and glanced at the wreath. "Yes, it seems to have taken on a life of its own here."

The back door banged open with a whoosh of bitterly cold wind. Pepper's mom, with ice crystals in her hair, and Amy, rosy-cheeked from the cold, rushed in closing the door quickly behind them.

"The wind whipped up as we walked back from the

apartment." Klaren shivered and toed her boots off. "It's cold in Colorado, but this is different. Burrr."

"It's the moisture in the air," Pepper said out of habit.

The men trooped in with only a few pieces of luggage. "Where's the rest of our bags?" Elijah wanted to know.

"Oh, I took care of them. Yours are in the apartment, and Hayley's and Kolby's are in the other guest room. I didn't know who the smaller ones belonged to so figured you guys could sort them out." Pepper glanced out the window a smile turned up the corners of her mouth.

"I like having a witch in the family." Amy sighed, following Pepper's gaze to the beautiful sunset.

Duncan stood near the doorway hands in his pockets. "We need to open the cottage. Have to stock it tomorrow. So how about we all meet back here in about an hour and have dinner at The Cliffside?" He cut his gaze over to Klaren. "Our treat."

Remembering Lathen's words, Pepper agreed and walked them to the rented SUV. When she set foot in the door of the cabin, Lathen was grinning from ear to ear as was Elijah.

"Dad's agreed to officiate at our wedding."

Pepper threw her arms around Eli's neck then kissed his cheek. "Thank you. It means a lot to us."

"The pleasure is all mine," Eli replied.

Two hours later they were all seated around a large table covered with a crisp white cloth and a lit candle in the center. Pepper warmed her hands around a china cup filled with freshly brewed raspberry tea and watched as a waiter poured steaming coffee into each person's cup.

Another waiter dressed in black with a towel draped over his arm crossed the polished wood floor and paused at their table. "Are you ready to order?"

"I believe so." Pepper glanced around the table as everyone nodded.

The waiter started with Amy and went clockwise around the table taking each person's order. "Wine?"

"Maybe after dinner. We'll peruse the wine list." Lathen turned to Elijah handing him the list. "They have an extensive selection of wines."

"Excuse me." Pepper eased up from the table. "I want to check on our arrangements for the rehearsal dinner."

She'd just stepped away from the table when a manager came up behind her. "Wanted to let you know we're all set for your dinner next week. Did you need any changes to the menu or anything else? Kelly contacted us about the decorations."

Pleased, Pepper smiled. "No not at all, I was going to check, but you've already addressed my questions."

"Our pleasure, Ms. McKay. We look forward to your party."

"It's Pepper and thank you." She returned to the table.

"Looks like you've gotten everything taken care of," Klaren said a bit of disappointment in her voice.

"It was crazy until we decided to hire Kelly from Wedded Bliss. She took care of everything I hadn't, and did a beautiful job with the reception. I didn't want you to run yourself ragged when you arrived." She smiled at her mom and hoped to alleviate some of her disappointment of not being able to help in the wedding plans. *She would have driven me crazy.*

Lathen cleared his throat and gave her a thumbs up behind his napkin with a wide grin.

She winked at him as the corners of her mouth turned up in a saucy smile.

"Okay, what's going on between you two?" Gwen wanted to know.

"It's on a need to know basis." Pepper's lips twitched, then turned up into a mischievous grin. "And you don't need to know." She returned to her seat.

"Well, la ta da." Gwen chortled. Nearby customers turned their heads in her direction. One hand flew to her mouth as red patches bloomed on her cheeks.

After dinner, everyone returned to the cabin. Pepper's parents left for the cottage, everyone else went their own way leaving Pepper and Lathen alone sitting in front of the roaring fireplace.

"See, everything is turning out perfect," Lathen whispered, trailing a line of kisses along her jaw line to the soft swell of her breasts above the plunging neckline of her sweater.

She giggled. "You're right. Nothing to worry about." She tucked her hand under his chin and brought his mouth up to hers. Tracing his lips with the tip of her tongue, she pressed her lips to his, caressing his mouth more than kissing it. He took control of the kiss, parting her lips, slipping his tongue inside stroking, tasting until her senses reeled as if short-circuited.

In a husky voice, Lathen said, "I think we need to take this elsewhere…" He slipped an arm under her knees and swept her into his arms, carried her up the stairs to their room without a sound.

****

For the rest of the week, Pepper was thankful that sunshine was unusually abundant, there was only a gentle breeze allowing family excursions to the ocean, tour of the town and surrounding areas. Several members of Lathen's pack arrived a couple days before the wedding and joined the family outings. Feeding the large group at the cabin was a challenge. But with everyone pitching in, the meals went smoothly and turned into gab fests and planning sessions for the next day's activities. Occasionally, Lathen made advance reservations at local restaurants to accommodate the large group.

Wild stories of life in Alaska circulated as well as embarrassing tales of Kolby and Lathen's childhoods. Pepper along with her parents, and Gwen enjoyed them all. Gwen told a few hair-raising tales of the Salem Sanctuary's early years and what a blessing it was when Pepper joined the staff. She also recounted the story of Kaylee and the ruckus she caused until Pepper arrived to take the osprey with her to Lobster Cove.

A couple days before the wedding, Pepper and Lathen strolled through the town square waiting for the others to finish shopping across the street. She sucked in a breath and pointed to a tall, thin hooded figure, head down walking directly in their path. Suddenly, he glanced up, veered right, and ducked behind the tall decorated tree in the center of town square.

Lathen dropped Pepper's hand and gave chase. Within a couple of minutes, Lathen appeared on the other side of the tree, hands out in front of him, palms up, shaking his head. "He disappeared. As if by—"

"Magic." Pepper finished for him. "It was Ben's brother. He wore the same coat and boots he had on last time I saw him."

"Maybe he works around here, and this is a short cut home," Lathen offered hopefully.

Chewing on her bottom lip, Pepper frowned. "Guess we need to see what Mom and Dad know about the Bonchard family."

Chapter Twenty
History, Friends, and Family

Ember and Tonk sped across the meadow in an effort to beat the other to greet the family as they emerged from their vehicles. The bright sun dried the path and driveway to the cabin, leaving mounds of snow on the other areas. Once inside the house, everyone went their separate ways to stow the treasures and possible presents purchased, except Lathen who stocked the fireplace and Pepper used her flick of the wrist to start it. She took her coat and scarf off, hung both on the peg next to the back door then sprinted down the hallway to feed Kaylee. When she returned to the living room, she settled into the couch facing the roaring fire. Pepper's mom and dad joined them after starting a pot of coffee, their packages left in the SUV.

Shifting in her seat to face her parents, Pepper asked, "Mom, what did you know about Ben Bonchard's brother, Brent?"

"I never knew Brent well. He was a year younger and never hung out with us. Guess he had his own group of friends." Pepper's mom frowned and scrubbed her hand over her face. "Seemed like they didn't get along very well. Ben always complained about him being a pain. At our ages at the time, never thought much about it. Teenagers are so self-absorbed, you know." She waved her hand in dismissal. "Is there a problem?"

"Not really. I've run into Brent in the town square a couple of times. Acts strange, he never says hi or anything. Which seems unusual for this time of year. Merry Christmas or Happy Holidays are on everyone's lips. The last time he appeared in our vicinity, Lathen tried to catch up with him, but he ducked behind one of the pines and disappeared."

"The Bonchard boys—the whole family—were always a little strange." Pepper's dad drew in a deep breath, blew it out slowly. "Until the events of Halloween, I thought they were harmless. But I can't believe Ben would be so stupid to risk the deadly wrath of the coven."

"Me either, but it makes me nervous with the wedding and all."

"Think Ben convinced his brother to cause problems, maybe exact revenge?" her dad asked, his lips set in a thin line. "I don't believe Brent would do it. He left town as soon as he graduated, never looked back."

"So why did he come back—now?" Pepper asked.

"I've no clue. It's probably best to keep an eye out but not do anything else. He's had two opportunities to cause trouble, and he hasn't. I'd take that as a good sign." Her mom tapped a finger to her chin. "Didn't the coven decide to implant a charm in Ben's arm that reports magic activity around him?"

Pepper nodded. "Yeah, after the initial shock of being spellbound wore off, he was quite combative, made threats. Without his ability to wield magic, I didn't give it much thought."

Klaren pursed her lips. "I'm going to call Ravyn,

the coven's high priestess. See if there's been any activity reported. I'm sure you'd have heard from the coven had there been a problem."

Pepper glanced over at Lathen, pointed her thumb in his direction. "He thinks I'm over reacting."

****

Lathen raised an eyebrow. "Noooo. The information I dug up, concurs with your parents. I vote we take a wait and see attitude, until after your mom checks with the high priestess." He planned to do more digging but didn't want to worry Pepper; with the wedding only two days away, it seemed best to downplay any possible collusion between the brothers.

Elijah strode into the room, glanced around. "Why so serious? It's a time for celebration!" he announced. "Unless there is something I should know about."

"Nope. Just nailing down last minute details. We're all set," Lathen said nonchalantly.

The rest of the evening, it was the men against the women in a variety of board games, then everyone for themselves in a cut throat game of poker.

"I've had enough." Elijah glanced at Amy. "How about we turn in and have some fun."

"Yeww. Dad. Too much information." Hayley squealed, her protests turning into gales of laughter at the red patches blooming on Amy's cheeks.

"You'd think I'd get used to this heathen." Amy fanned her face and chuckled.

Elijah caught Amy's hand in his and tugged her to her feet. "Time to turn in and go to sleep." His eyes twinkled with amusement.

Lathen grinned, he never tired of seeing his dad so happy. The long years of being pack leader and raising two headstrong boys had taken a toll long before Amy steam rolled into his dad's life. Covering his mouth, Lathen couldn't stifle the jaw popping yawn.

A gracious smile curved Amy's lips. "Know that feeling well. Days before our wedding, I was exhausted chasing down all the details. And I had most the women of the pack helping out. Naturally, everything pertaining to pack business needed Eli's expertise, day and night. Then you two appeared on our doorstep and things became a lot easier. He was forced to let his assistants handle the day to day, something he should have done long ago"—she cut her gaze to Elijah who glared defiantly at her—"so he could spend time with you and Pepper." She paused. "Don't give me that evil eye, Elijah Quartz. Won't work on me. Where was I? Oh yes, but when we stood at the truck, 'Just Married' written all over it, tin cans tied behind it, a wave of exhaustion overtook both of us. That's why you and Kolby got away with the little escapade."

Kolby cleared his throat, grinning like a Cheshire cat. "Technically, we didn't do a thing to your truck."

"Nope, sure didn't." Lathen smirked, leaning his chair on its back two legs, fingers tented on the edge of the table.

"I don't know what you did to your cohorts in crime, but not a one of the pack owned up to assisting you. I know it had to be…" Elijah roared with laughter. "There were a lot of teen wolves avoiding me in the weeks after we returned from our honeymoon."

"Speaking of honeymoon, where are you two spending yours?" Pepper's mom asked.

"Not taking one until spring." Lathen dropped his chair back on four legs as Klaren shot him a warning glance. "We decided to purchase a fifth wheel trailer. I can pull it with my truck. Pepper arranged for us to take a month off, volunteers covering shifts. Ember, Tonk, and Kaylee will go with us. We plan to visit Rocky Mountain National Park, Yellowstone, and Glacier then meander our way home." A conspiratorial grin passed between him and Pepper. "We might even stop at a certain cabin near Evergreen, Colorado, for a couple nights."

Pepper's mom immediately reached into her purse, took out her phone and scrolled through her calendar touching the screen a couple of times. "I'll make sure spring is clear, though I think we will be taking a trip to Alaska come summer. Your father has always wanted to see Denali National Park. Now we have a professional guide in the family and an open invitation for a place to stay."

Lathen yawned again, this time made no attempt to stifle it, and got to his feet. "I'm for bed."

"Me too." Pepper shoved out of her chair. "You guys are welcome to stay as long as you wish. Lock the door when you leave."

"Better get your rest, or you won't have enough stamina to…"

Amy reached over and punched Eli in the arm. "Knock it off with the innuendos."

Eli held his hand up in a gesture of surrender. "What—I was just going to…"

"I know what you were going to say. Don't." She pushed to her feet and pulled him with her. "Good night everyone."

"It's about time." Eli waggled his eyebrows and grabbed Amy around the waist. "Good night all." He nuzzled her neck.

"Elijah, you are incorrigible."

"I know, but you love me anyway." He reached for their coats and helped Amy on with hers.

Lathen and Pepper crossed the room. The wooden back door groaned in protest when Lathen shoved it open for his parents. Standing in the doorway, Pepper and Lathen watched his dad and Amy amble down the path washed a shadowy silver by the moonlight.

When they returned to the living room, Pepper's parents stood at the front door dressed in their coats, hats, and gloves. Kolby assisted a waddling Hayley down the hallway to their room.

Pepper kissed her mom and dad on the cheek, walked them out to the vehicle her dad had started a few minutes earlier. Tonk and Ember trotted out, did their business, and returned to wait patiently on the porch. After watching the SUV bump down the gravel road, taillights disappearing in the inky night, Lathen and Pepper sprinted into the cabin.

"It's freezing out there." She shivered in front of the fireplace, rubbing her hands together. "Not much heat left to the fire."

Lathen nodded as he pushed her toward the stairs and banked the fire. On his way to the stairs, he turned out the lights and followed Pepper upstairs to the loft.

****

The day before the wedding arrived with a flurry of phone calls, last minute arrangements, and deliveries. Most of Lobster Cove would be attending the reception, with only a few close friends in the know attending the ceremony. Pepper woke up to huge white flakes drifting gently to the ground outside the bedroom window and

Lathen softly snoring next to her. When she tried to slip out of the bed without waking him, he banded a strong arm around her.

"Morning sunshine," he mumbled, rolling to his side spooning his front to her back. "Time to get up already?"

"I was, but apparently you have other ideas." She wiggled her behind against his growing interest and giggled.

"I wake up that way, comes from having a sexy woman sharing my bed." He nuzzled at her neck and breathed several kisses from the hollow of her throat to her jawline.

"Last night's romp in bed didn't keep you satisfied?"

"I've slept since then. You should know by now that werewolves are—"

"Horn dogs," Pepper finished for him.

"By nature we are a carnal species," Lathen said thoughtfully, then chuckled. "Yep, you got it right."

Kicking the covers off, she sashayed into the bathroom. "Wanta share the shower?" she cooed.

"Sure." Lathen swung his legs off the side of the bed, touched his feet to the soft rug, and stood. Arms raised high above his head, he stretched, then leaned from one side to the other.

Resting her shoulder against the doorframe, she waggled her finger. "No time for funny stuff this morning."

Lathen groaned. "You take all the fun out of a shower." With preternatural speed, he jumped in the shower, flipped on the water, and grabbed the soap; holding it above his head, out of her reach, he crowed,

"I get to lather you up."

She giggled and stepped under the cascade of warm water. "Only if I get to do the same," she cooed. One half hour later, they bounded into the kitchen. Lathen grabbed a mug and poured coffee to the rim. Pepper took the cup of orange spice tea Gwen handed her along with a breakfast burrito. "Thanks."

"Hey, where's mine?" Lathen whined, swiping at Pepper's burrito as she took a big bite. Scrambled egg spilled out the side of the stuffed tortilla. He caught the egg and popped it in his mouth.

"Quit squealing before you're hurt," Gwen retorted and handed him a plate with two steaming burritos.

"These are Gwen's famous breakfast burritos. She always made them on Saturday morning, and we had a full staff of volunteers show up early those days." Pepper giggled. "Still doing that?"

"Only once a month and I never say which Saturday, so everyone has to show up, just in case," Gwen said smugly. "It's not the same without you there. Jodie is a quick learner, but she can't boil water without burning it." She shook her head and snickered.

After breakfast, Gwen sat at the table sipping coffee reading the morning newspaper, while Kolby and Hayley stretched out in the reclining sofa in front of the fireplace. Pepper shrugged into her parka, opened the door to see the sun peeking through the mist. It would be a nice day after all. "What's on your agenda today?"

Lathen pulled his coat on, kissed her on the nose. "Make sure the buildings are spotless. Check on our creatures. Go over the schedule with Alec and Mike through the first of the year, so we can spend as much time as possible with family. Oh yeah, I meant to talk to you about offering the kids that brought the bird in the dog crate months back part-time work after school, weekends, holidays, whenever they're available."

"That would be Rick and Judy." Pepper yanked gloves out of her pocket and put them on. "They've volunteered off and on, seem to have a talent for rescue work. Maybe it's time to offer them a paid part-time position."

"Sure could use their help right now." The door let out a nails on a chalkboard squeal, when he tugged it open. Tonk and Ember skidded across the kitchen floor, dived between him and Pepper, bounding outside. "First thing I'm going to do is oil those damn hinges, again."

"Home numbers are in the office, give 'em a call, and set a time to have them come in and talk with us after the wedding. I'm going to check on things at the pond, see if Ashling's around."

Lathen nodded. "Meet up with you later." The door banged shut behind him as he sprinted across the path to the supply room shared with Pepper's office.

She stood for a beat in the doorway, watched Lathen and sighed. *What a hunk.* A tune about a fiddle playing boy startled her. Glancing around, she chuckled to herself and pulled her cell phone from her pocket. Hayley had changed the ringtone on Pepper's cellphone when she was in Alaska. Claimed the simple chime she'd always used was boring.

The number on the screen wasn't familiar. "Hello?"

"Pepper, this is Ravyn, high priestess of the Lobster Cove Coven. Talked to your mom the other day about concerns regarding Ben Bonchard. While the fact his brother is in town might be disconcerting, there's been no magic activity registered around him. He should have reported his brother was here, and we'll have a talk with him about this infraction."

"Okay. So there's not a problem?"

"Don't believe so. I called to remind you that even if there is a problem, the magic emanating from your property is so strong with all the McKay's in residence, that penetrating the perimeter is absolutely impossible."

"I hadn't considered the increase in magic. I feel better already."

"The Lobster Cove Community Center will be protected by members of the coven attending your wedding, myself included. Some members volunteered on the decorating committee for the Center, so there'd be no questions when they arrive early on your wedding day. Enjoy your wedding, there will be no incidents."

"Oh, thank you so much for doing all this and for the call."

"You're welcome. Feel free to join in the coven's activities, when you have time. We miss Ashling's participation and only see Colleen on occasion."

"LCWRRC keeps us pretty busy. But after all you've done for us, Lathen and I will be happy to assist the coven in any way we can. If you could send us the coven's calendar of events, I'd like to coordinate it with ours and see if we can't make it to a few of the activities. Thanks for calling." Pepper disconnected the call and held the phone to her chest for a beat as relief flooded through her. *But why was his brother here?*

Shoving the phone back in her pocket, she scurried over the rock path to the pond and suddenly backpedaled to a stop, her eyes rounded.

Several feet in all directions from the pond's edge piled snow and brown vegetation ceased to exist. Soft green sprouts were abundant with flowering deep purple roses every ten feet or so near the water's edge. The wedding archway gleamed a rich tawny with thin ribbons of mahogany woven through it. Stems with tiny green leaves and rosebuds climbed their way up the sides and over the top of the arch.

Pepper sidled closer, gingerly caressing the wood with her fingertips, surprised to find it warm to the touch as was the ground beneath her feet. Inside the magic induced environment felt like a fairyland in the middle of barren frozen landscape. She stood between enchanted realm and Mother Nature's blanket of winter. She breathed in the warm air and exhaled into the frosty air watching her breath curl in white tendrils caught on the breeze, carried upward. At the sound of snapping twigs, she paused, then called out, "Lathen?" When there was no answer, she whirled around nearly crashing into Brock, his eyes wide, and mouth hanging open. Lemon yellow eyes stared out of the bundle of blankets he held in his arms.

"I—uh—Dylan—uh—told me to bring this..." Brock stammered. "She's got an emergency at the clinic—will be there for..." He froze, stared straight past Pepper to the oasis, clamped his mouth shut for a moment then opened it. "Exotic bird smugglers busted on Hwy 3. Crates of illegally caught birds confiscated. Dylan called in to check them out, most went to a Bar Harbor bird rescue. This little girl is on the critically endangered list, Dylan's sure of it...felt she'd be better off in your care and you're licensed..." He sucked in a breath. "Pepper, what the hell is going on?" He blinked several times and thrust the bundle into her arms as he took several uncertain steps closer to the pond.

Big yellow eyes stared out of the blankets, blinked as Pepper chewed on her bottom lip for a beat. She shrugged seeing Lathen sprinting down the path behind Brock. "I'm a witch. The rest you don't want to know." She flashed a *c'est tout dire* smile in his direction, just as Lathen clasped Brock on the shoulder.

"A lot to take in. Huh?" Lathen peered over Brock's shoulder at the bundle in Pepper's arms. "Another owl?"

Brock said nothing but nodded his head.

"Let's get her to the barn." Pepper took two steps when her cell phone's ringtone went off. Lathen yanked it out of her pocket, looked at the screen, tilted it so Pepper could hear as he said, "Hello Dylan."

"I wanted to let you know…"

Pepper interrupted. "That Brock is on his way here with an…owl?"

"Guess I should have called sooner, but I'm really tied up. She came in with a dislocated leg joint. Repositioned it with a soft splint, gave light pain meds and figured she'd be better off with you in the special cubes Lathen created. Oh, she's a Forest Owlet, critically endangered."

"So Brock told us. Any other injuries?"

"Don't think so, mostly scared. I cleaned adhesive off her wings, probably had the wings taped down. Her legs were taped together too, skin irritation from the tape removal. She may have gotten hold of someone with those ridiculously huge talons. Guess that's why her legs were taped, and I suspect that's how her leg got injured. "

"Bird's alert, starting to struggle at bit, but Brock's in shock. You didn't tell him—about my—talents."

"Damn. Never considered it." Dylan paused for a beat. "Did he walk into…"

"Yep, remember the changes we discussed around the pond? Yeah, well they're in place, and Brock is ash white."

"I'm sorry. Gotta go. They're bringing in more birds. Be in touch."

Pepper closed her eyes and connected to the owlet, feeling terror and hunger. In a soothing voice Pepper cooed. "It's all right; you're safe now. A quick exam and we'll get you fed." She projected calm over the bird. It blinked its eyes slowly, stopped struggling.

"Hey, what's going on? You need my help?" Gwen skidded to a stop a foot from Brock, her gaze sliding between him and Pepper. "He doesn't know?"

Pepper shook her head. "Gwen, would you take Brock back to the cabin, get something hot in him, do a little damage control. As soon as Lathen and I get this little owlet settled, we'll be up to lay it all out for him." Her gaze returned to Brock. "Unless you want stay for the exam and report back to Dylan." She stood waiting for a response.

Rubbing his eyes, he blinked, scrubbed a hand over his face, and tore his gaze from the pond to Pepper, Lathen, and lingered on Gwen, not saying a word.

"Sure thing." Not waiting for Brock's answer, Gwen gently slid her arm through his and guided him up the path toward the cabin.

A thick mist wound itself around the tree, lengthening. "Don't do it, Ashling. I'll get back to you.

Things look great. Thanks." Pepper called over her shoulder, turning back to see Brock walking with Gwen, stopping occasionally to glance backward.

"Oh, boy. Never a dull moment." She breathed, scurrying over the rocks to the old barn remodeled as a seabird aviary. She was almost there when her toe caught a rock and she stumbled.

"Careful." Lathen's hand shot out, caught her elbow as her grip tightened on the bird, and steadied her. Once inside the aviary, Lathen flipped on the overhead lights, turned the heat on in a cube, then slipped on heavy leather gloves. He began unwrapping the blanket, while Pepper held the owl securely over the examining table.

Several birds' surprised cries echoed through the building. The owlet's eyes blinked open wide as it struggled to free itself from the blankets and Pepper's grip. Kaylee's mind touched Pepper's in concern. She sent calming reassurances to Kaylee, everything would be fine, at the same time trying to keep calm over the owlet. Pepper drew in a long breath, let it out slowly, her shoulders slumped. Only a little while longer she told herself and handed the bird to Lathen, sheathing her own hands and arms in leather.

Dylan was right, those talons are dangerous. With the owl relaxed again, taking her time, Pepper was able to gently spread and fold the owl's wings, checking for additional injuries. Deep purple bruises formed on the legs where they'd been taped together, a few feathers missing. The body beneath the feathers showed a wide band of bruising.

From a jar on the counter top, she removed a cotton swab, dabbed on alcohol, and removed a bit more adhesive residue from a few of the primary feathers. The chunky little owl turned its large head to assess her. Grayish/brown feathers covered its head with its primary wings in a darker color. The upper breast was nearly solid brown, and the owl's sides were barred with a white central wedge in the lower breast. The wings and tail were banded with white trailing edges.

Pepper touched the pale cream colored feathers on its face and was rewarded with a slow blink of its lemon yellow eyes, its breathing returning to normal.

"Probably hasn't been fed in a while." Lathen passed by the puffin's cage next to the owlet's cube. "Brought you a friend." He crooned, opening the cube door for Pepper to ease the small owl inside.

Lathen took live food from the enclosure, offered it to the owlet, who ripped into it with its beak, securing it with one talon.

"Bless its heart, this little bird has been through the wringer," Pepper said sadly. "Since it's still willing to eat, there's a good chance the owlet will make a full recovery, thankfully."

"Let's hope we don't have a repeat performance tomorrow." He shifted his gaze from the bird to Pepper.

"Hazards of the business. Rescue never takes a day off."

Switching the main lights off, a soft glow from the night lights cast shadows on the walls as they moved toward the exit. Where had the day gone, Pepper wondered, the sun sinking low in the sky. Lathen slipped his arm around Pepper's waist, she leaned against him as they climbed the path to the cabin.

Elijah stuck his head out the door of the visiting veterinarian quarters, while Amy peered over his shoulder. "Everything all right?" Elijah's deep voice boomed.

"Yep, just a new arrival," Lathen called over his shoulder.

****

A few minutes later, Lathen shoved the cabin door open, a delicious aroma of homemade chili and cornbread welcomed them inside.

Pepper gave her parents a wan smile as she followed Lathen straight to the computer. He flipped though screens until she stopped him at the camera feed inside the aviary. Training the camera on the new addition for a beat, Lathen waited until she nodded then he rotated through the rest of the aviary making sure all inhabitants had settled down. One final check found the little owlet's eyes closed, its breathing regular.

She blew out a breath and leaned against her husband to be. "Feeling a little light headed."

He swept her into his arms and carried her to the couch, easing her onto the cushions gently. Klaren hovered after him, with Duncan behind her.

Gwen and Brock jumped up in alarm. "What's wrong?" Gwen asked edging next to Lathen.

"Overtaxed from wedding preparations and her abilities. Nothing serious." He shot a reassuring look at her parents.

Brock's eyebrows winged up to his hairline. "She's okay? Should I call…"

"A little rest, a good night's sleep and she'll be fine," Lathen assured him. "What about you?"

"Oh, I'm fine. Learning more about the McKay's explains a lot."

"Did you know; he has Gypsy blood in his veins?"

Gwen blurted. "Just like me, well…"

"Many generations back," Brock agreed. "It's not something Dylan or myself acknowledge for various reasons."

"Made it easy for him to understand our—your situation." Gwen smiled wide. "I explained everything with the help of your parents. The McKay land, your heritage, and um, talents."

"Good to know," Lathen said, settling beside Pepper on the couch. "How you feeling?"

"Exhausted, but otherwise fine. Funny I've never done that before." Pepper scrunched her face in puzzlement. An expression Lathen enjoyed.

"Juggling too much over the last couple weeks." Lathen leaned over, brushed a strand of hair from her face.

Pepper's mom poked her head around the corner. "Dinner's ready. Do you want to eat it in there, or gather around the dining table?"

"You two sleep in tomorrow," Gwen commanded. "Plenty of people to help out. I'll handle the Center, everyone else can pitch in, and your wedding will come off without a hitch."

"Tomorrow's the big day, huh?" Brock asked sharing the rocking recliners with Gwen.

"Yep." Lathen got to his feet, pulling Pepper beside him. "Don't think there are any last minute arrangements. We'll leave everything in your capable hands, Gwen."

"Mom, we'll eat around the table. Brock, won't you join us?"

"If it's no bother, I'd love to. Something smells fantastic."

"Mom's chili and cornbread," Pepper said proudly. "Best in the west."

A blast of cold accompanied Eli and Amy when they strode in the back door. Kolby and Hayley wandered into the kitchen.

"Great, everyone is here. Com'on sit down and eat." Pepper's mom slid a trivet to the center of the table, and Duncan placed a huge pot of chili on it. As everyone settled in the chairs, she came around the corner with two large pans of cornbread, dropped a folded towel next to the chili, and set the cornbread on the table. "Dig in."

Her mother eased into a chair, then cursed under her breath. Pepper grinned and padded into the kitchen to retrieve the forgotten butter. The room filled with dinnertime chatter, dishes clattered as food was passed around the table and spoons clinked the bottom of bowls.

After Lathen finished, his chair's legs scraped the floor as he pushed away from the table. "Klaren, that was a wonderful meal. Thank you so much for stepping in. We kinda got caught up with the new addition."

"Sure was. Thank you." Pepper eased up from her chair, began gathering dishes. Gwen rinsed them, and Amy loaded the dishwasher.

After dinner, everyone else meandered into the living room for quiet conversation and to enjoy a glass of wine. Lathen followed them into the living room, Pepper stopped at the computer screens and checked on the owlet, who was asleep.

"Is she out for the night? Aren't owls nocturnal?" Lathen asked standing behind Pepper peering over her shoulder.

"Most are," Brock replied. "According to Dylan, a Forest Owlet is an early morning hunter."

"Interesting." Pepper covered her mouth to hide a yawn and leaned against Lathen.

"Ladies and gents if you don't mind, I believe we are going to call it a night. Got a big day tomorrow." Lathen grinned. "Getting married, you know."

Pepper started up the stairway to the loft followed closely by Lathen.

Gwen popped up, squealed, and grabbed Lathen by the arm, whirled him around. "Oh no you don't. Not tonight. Can't see the bride before the wedding." She sing-songed, tipping her head up to peer at Pepper stopped halfway up the stairs.

"I agree he can't see me in the wedding gown before the wedding, but…it's not like he hasn't…" Her gaze met Lathen who stood one foot solid on the first step, the other poised on the second.

Lathen ran his fingers through his hair, rubbed the back of his neck. He'd spent the last several nights working on a project. After the escapade today, he was nearly dead on his feet. Didn't care where he slept. Snuggled up next to the love of his life was preferred, but right now all he wanted to do was lay down. Gwen stepped up even with him, eyes narrowed. He leaned on the banister wearily. "Tell me where to sleep, and I'll go."

"Now ladies, I didn't listen to all that jazz before our wedding day, and things turned out just fine," Amy suggested firmly.

"Sure did," Eli said, waving his hand dismissively then grabbed Amy around the waist. Pulling her in close for a smacking kiss. "Those are just old wives' tales."

"Let him go on up," Amy said.

Gwen stood her ground, one hand fisted on her hip. "Nope, we agreed. Lathen can sleep in my room. I'll share Pepper's room."

"I didn't agree to anything," Pepper protested, directing her gaze at Hayley standing in hallway. "You two cajoled and badgered me into submission."

Hayley eased closer to the fireplace, nodding in agreement. Her hand rubbing circles on her belly. "But it's for your own good. Gotta start this marriage off right."

His eyes met and held Pepper's bright green ones and saw the concern in them. This morning when he'd looked in the mirror to shave, he'd noticed the dark circles, but judging from her expression, he must look like hell. Lathen shrugged. "It's fine, hon." He stepped off the stair, nearly toppled over, then trudged down the hallway to the guest room Gwen had occupied. He pushed the door open and fell across the bed, fully clothed.

Chapter Twenty-One
No Cold Feet, No Wedding Day Jitters, Just the Best Day of Their Lives.

Pepper held the beautiful cream gown up to the soft dawn light flooding though the open curtains, from here she could see a wide expanse of her property. A light dusting of snow fell overnight, but the thinning clouds brought promise of a perfect day for her wedding.

Not a soul stirred in the cozy cabin full of family and friends. Ember, sprawled in front of the bedroom door as if guarding against unknown intruders, lifted her head to watch Pepper's movements. Pepper reveled in the quiet and smiled when she felt the light touch of Kaylee's mind, a soothing reassurance swept through the bride to be.

She brought the shimmering dress to her cheek; it was so luxurious against her skin. The scents of lilac and honeysuckle permeated her senses, she inhaled deeply as she slipped the dress over her head, let it slide down her body, leaving a shoulder bare as the hem caressed her bare feet. When she turned this way and that, then spun in a circle in front of the full-length mirror, the dress moved with her hugging her curves. The dress split just below her thigh on the left allowed freedom of movement emphasizing her long shapely legs.

Daily walks up and down the rocky paths to the

various habitats on the property kept her in good shape, though this was the first time she'd really taken time to notice. Easing down on the chair at her dressing table, she stroked a brush through her sleep tangled hair until it shone in a cascade of light red waves down her back to her waist.

A quiet tap on the door, brought Ember to her feet. "May I come in?" Gwen asked quietly.

"Sure. You're up early." Pepper shifted in her chair to peer at Gwen then back to the neatly made extra bed, conjured the night before.

"Yes, I snuck out way before dawn, you were still sound asleep. Wanted to make sure everything was taken care of around here. Alec and Mike are doing the rounds. The little owlet had a restful night and is up making woohoo sounds, probably anxious for breakfast. Kaylee's been fed. Tonk and Ember's food is in their bowls." She scratched the dog's ears as it brushed against her on the way out the door.

"Thanks for that." Pepper turned back to the mirror.

"You shouldn't have your dress on already. Might get it messed up, with hair and makeup."

"I couldn't help it. The dress felt so wonderful and seemed to call to me. I'll be careful."

"Okay," Gwen said doubtfully. "I saw this hair style in a magazine and thought it would be perfect for today." She drew out a folded magazine page from her pocket, unfolded it, and showed Pepper.

"It's gorgeous, but my hair is longer around the face than the model's."

"That's what a curling iron is for. We'll take a few wisps of hair and turn them into the long curls around your face. Pull the rest away from your face, let it fall down the back. I brought hair clips that will work great under your tiara of rosebuds, ribbons, and trailing tiny leaves."

She handed the brush to Gwen. "Let's get started."

"Are you nervous?"

"Excited, but nerves are surprisingly calm. It's going to be a wonderful day." Pepper smiled wide.

There was a sturdy knock on the door. Gwen opened it. "Good morning, Elijah."

"Morning to ya. Can I have a moment with Pepper?" He glanced over Gwen's head to where Pepper sat.

"I guess it's all right. Not heard anything about the father of the groom seeing the bride before the wedding." Gwen chuckled, stepping out of the room.

Elijah closed the door behind him drawing out a black rectangle box from his jacket pocket. When Pepper started to get up, he motioned her to remain and wordlessly presented the box to her.

She smiled up at him and took the box. When she opened the gift she gasped, inside lay a gold heart pendant with edges scalloped in silver, a tear drop diamond sparkled in the center surrounded by tiny blue sapphires. Her gaze locked with Eli's, there were so many emotions swirling in the man's eyes, she was speechless.

He cleared his throat and swallowed hard. "Originally, this was Lathen's grandmother's pendant. I gave it to his mother on our wedding day, she never took it off until...Lathen's difficult birth. When she realized...she may not survive..." He paused for a moment, swallowed hard, and cleared his throat again.

"She took it off and requested it be given to Lathen's wife one day. So—today is the day. I understand the bride should have something old and something blue, this covers both."

Still not trusting herself to speak, she swept her hair to one side, nervously moistened her lips and handed the box back to him. "Would you put the pendant on for me?"

His eyes sparkled. "My pleasure." Carefully he removed the delicate gold chain and pendant from the box and clasped it around her neck.

Pepper touched the beautiful necklace and looked at her reflection in the mirror, then raised her eyes to the man's reflection who'd given her such a priceless gift. "Thank you so much. I will cherish it always." She got to her feet and wrapped her arms around him. "Oh, Elijah." She sighed.

****

With Pepper's dad at her side, she stepped out of the cabin and looked down the path transformed from a rocky surface to a lush carpet of moss and flowers. Around the pond gathered her friends, family, and ghosts under a canopy of magic warmth. She touched her dress to make sure the hem floated above the ground, thankful she decided on flat shoes. The air filled with strains of a traditional wedding march. She put one foot in front of the other and felt like she was floating. Kaylee flew overhead and landed in Ashling's tree beside the pond. Ember walked the path in front of Pepper, and Tonk waited next to Lathen. Her father smiled over at her as they reached the wedding arch. Unwrapping her hand from his arm, he put her hand in Lathen's, kissed her cheek, and turned to join his wife.

First Lathen recited the vows he had written, then Pepper repeated the vows she had created. They exchanged simple gold bands engraved inside with "*My Love For Always,*" a beaming Elijah pronounced them husband and wife. "Kiss that woman," Elijah said with a laugh. "And you kiss him back."

Family and friends cheered and tossed birdseed as Lathen's head lowered, his lips caressing more than kissing hers. She quivered at the tenderness of his touch, lingering over and savoring every moment until he raised his mouth from hers and gazed into her eyes. His father said with flourish, "May I present Mr. and Mrs. Lathen Quartz."

The guests formed a line on either side of the path, shaking hands with the groom, hugging and kissing the bride as they made their way toward the cabin. Pepper squealed with pleasure at the horse drawn carriage waiting in the driveway. It was decked out in cream and purple bows, a banner across the front proclaimed "Just Married," and purple ribbons were braided in the horse's mane and tail. Not a tin can in sight.

Lathen swirled a long fleece lined red cape around her shoulders and offered his hand to help her into the carriage. "See you at the reception," he called out to the group following them. Pepper waved from inside the carriage, her lips curved in a dreamy smile as her husband climbed in beside her.

When Lathen tugged open the heavy wooden door to the community center, music and laughter flooded into the early afternoon air. The whole town had gathered to celebrate their wedding, in addition to the friends and family that attended the ceremony.

A white flocked Christmas tree decorated in cream

and purple bows, ribbons, and balls stood in the corner. Several tables were scattered over the entire room, with a stage set up in the opposite corner from the tree. Two tables sat at the front of the room, a huge wedding cake sat on one with additional sheet cakes placed on either side. The wedding party was to be seated at the other.

After everyone took their seats, Lathen cringed as his brother stood to make a toast.

"I'm not very good at this, so it'll be short. My name's Kolby. I'm Lathen's brother and best man. How my brother wrangled Pepper into marrying him, I'll never know." He shook his head and chuckled. "But she said yes, and I wish them all the happiness in the world. They are wonderful people." He sat down with a whoosh and wiped his brow.

Pepper leaned over and whispered in Lathen's ear. "I guess Kolby learned his lesson at your dad and Amy's wedding." She snickered.

Elijah stood, raised his glass. "I'm Elijah Quartz, father of the groom. Welcome to the family, Pepper. Lathen, you are one lucky man. May the magic remain in your relationship forever." He winked at the couple as he eased back into his seat.

Pepper's dad shoved up from his chair. "As most of you know, I'm Duncan McKay, the bride's father." He raised his glass. "Never met a finer man than the one that married my daughter. Never take your love for granted, and Lathen, realize from this day forward you will always be wrong." Duncan roared with laughter as his wife frowned at him.

Laughter rippled through the crowd, with the men smiling and nodding knowingly. Lathen pushed up from his chair. "Enough of this repartee, let's eat."

After dinner, the band played a slow ballad for the bride and groom's first dance. When Duncan cut in to dance with his daughter, Pepper winked at the bandleader, and they segued into a quick Irish jig. By the end of the tune, Pepper and her dad were winded but had managed to put on quite a show for everyone's enjoyment.

"That famous Irish dance troupe has nothing on us, Dad." Pepper giggled, her chest heaving while she leaned against Lathen. Other couples flooded onto the floor as the band struck up a lively tune. "That band is as good as Kelly said." She tapped her toe in time with the tune.

Shortly after midnight, Duncan brushed by Lathen, gave him a wink and a nod. "I'm afraid this old man is worn out. My beautiful wife is going to take me back to our cottage. Talk to you later. The pack has a late morning flight tomorrow?"

"I think you've visited the punch bowl too many times, hon," Klaren said. "We have the pack breakfast at the cabin before they head to the airport."

"Yes, we'll send them off with their bellies full of food," Lathen said. "Thanks for everything."

Pepper hugged and kissed her parents before they left.

Lathen whirled her onto the dance floor for a couple more songs, then whispered in her ear, "Are you ready to go?"

"How? We came by carriage. I'm sure it's turned to pumpkins and mice by now." She snickered.

"That's why I parked my truck here earlier in the day. Fairy godmothers don't come cheap." He chortled.

Lathen, his arm around Pepper as they stopped at

various tables and said their goodbyes to family and friends, before he led the way to his truck. On the drive home, he rested his arm across her shoulders as she cuddled into him.

At the cabin, he unlocked the door, swept her into his arms, and carried her over the threshold and up the stairs to the loft. Ember and Tonk raced up the stairs and sat at the bedroom door. "Tonight, you two sleep out here." Setting Pepper on her feet, he leaned in close, his warm breath caressing her ear. "Close your eyes. No peeking." He stopped to give the dog and wolf a quick ear rub as they circled and settled on either side of the bedroom door.

She closed her eyes and held tight to his hand, shuffling along. He opened the door and tugged her through, closing it behind him. "Stay right here, eyes closed." Leaving her standing alone, sounds of footsteps and a match igniting heightened her curiosity. "Okay, open your eyes."

When she opened her eyes, her hand flew to her mouth. "Oh, Lathen." She breathed, candles flickered around the room casting shadows across the walls.

In place of the old worn bed was a huge beautifully carved king bed. A golden hue of enchanted wood permeated the room. One main large branch with several smaller branches crisscrossed the headboard, which attached to a smooth log on either side at least six foot tall. The framework consisted of medium sized supporting logs that extended a couple feet beyond the foot of the bed, forming the sides of a polished bench. A wolf head had been carved into the top of each foot post while the base splayed a root system sinking into the wooden floor, as did the head posts. Nightstands attached on either side of the headboard columns with a log base of their own. Granite tops with matching logs grew out of the middle of the stands to form lamp poles with cream shades. The bed pulsed a golden hue of the same magically protection afforded the cabin and land.

Pepper caressed the wolf head on the foot post with her fingertips, warmth spread across her hand. "Did you carve this?"

"Yep. Created the whole bed," he said proudly.

"How did you get it into the room?" Her gaze traveled to the door, back to the bed, and finally to her husband.

"Oh, a little magic from your father." Lathen waved his hand dismissively. "Happy wedding day."

"It's beautiful." She slipped her arms around his neck and breathed a kiss at the base of his throat.

His fingers tugged the zipper at the back of her dress until it slipped off her one shoulder and pooled at her feet. "Darling, step out of your gown."

She did as instructed, waved her hand, and the dress flew across to the room landing on the corner chair.

"Nice."

She reached for the bottom of his sweater and tugged it over his head, waved her hand, and again he stood naked.

"No fair." He flipped open the catch of her bra and caught her firm round breasts in his hands as the lacy garment fell to the floor. Bending over, he sucked each nipple into his mouth and teased it with the tip his tongue until it was a hard little berry.

Pepper's pulse raced as her heart thundered in her chest. "Lathen." She breathed, loving his tender touch as raw desire swirled through his expressive eyes.

When his hand slid down across her belly and inside her panties, she sucked in a breath and moaned at the magical touch of his fingers where she was already hot, already wet.

One long thick finger slipped inside her slick channel. She arched against his hand as he slipped another inside, curling them into the sweet spot had her begging for more. He withdrew the fingers and teased her opening then nudged her onto the bed, pulled her underwear off, and spread her legs wide, crawling between them. He paused.

"What are you waiting for, I want you inside me—now." She reached for his erection, her fingertips barely able to caress his slick head. "Let me pleasure you."

"All in good time." He bent his head, his mouth moved lower to her center while his fingers stroked the little bundle of sensitive nerves hidden there.

His sweet caress teased layers of flesh. She writhed underneath him. "Bastard, quit teasing me, or I'll—"

"What?" He chuckled and gripped her ass cheeks, raised her slightly off the bed, his warm breath caressed her core, teasing, exploring with his talented tongue.

She moaned. "Please."

"That's more like it." His finger delved inside, curving at just the right angle sending her over the edge, her breath coming in long surrendering moans as multicolored stars burst in the air above the bed. "Oh, Lathen."

"I love the fireworks with your ecstasy," he murmured. "My little witch. That's why I pleasure you first."

Her body squirmed beneath him. "If I could control

it—"

"But you can't, so I wait until—" He licked his way to her breasts, sucked each nipple, flicking it with his tongue. His weight settled between her wide-spread thighs until he was seated at her passage, slipping only the head inside, holding it there as she pulsed around him.

She shifted rolling her hips so his length filled her, and it was his turn to moan. She smiled slyly as he lost control, thrusting into her over and over, his breathing ragged, until together they reached the pinnacle of ecstasy. Lathen slumped on top of her for a moment then rolled to the side. Tugging her against him, his semi-rigid length nestled against her ass. He pushed her hair aside and nuzzled her neck. She relaxed into him with a little wiggle to tease, savoring the satisfaction they shared. His arm wrapped around her, his hand cupping her breast as she drifted off to sleep.

Chapter Twenty-Two
The Pack Leaves—Nor'easter Arrives—Surprise

The morning after the wedding, a thin line of orange trailed along the edge of ominous clouds building over the horizon. Pepper stared out the window and glanced at her sleeping husband. She whispered the word husband aloud to see how it sounded, smiled, dressed quietly, then padded down the stairs into the kitchen rubbing her eyes. Surprised to see Amy and Klaren already had the buffet set up, Pepper sniffed, fresh coffee brewing and a batch of scrambled eggs and bacon already in the warming trays. *Yum.*

"Wow, how long you two been up?" she asked.

Amy whirled around as Klaren let out a squeak. "We didn't expect you up this early."

"Yeah thought you'd be spending time—uh—cuddling with your new husband." Amy grinned. "I'm so happy you're family." She reached out and hugged Pepper. "Eli is so much more relaxed now that Lathen has found his place in the world." Amy patted her back and turned to the stove.

"Wanted to make sure food was ready when the pack arrived. No one mentioned at the reception who was doing what this morning." Pepper stretched her arms in the air and yawned. "Except that the pack would be here for breakfast before their flight."

"That's because you are the bride. We got

everything under control," Klaren said cheerfully. "Go on back to bed with your husband." She bustled around the kitchen setting out pitchers of orange juice and ice water. Hot water sat on the warmer beside packets of hot chocolate and tiny marshmallows in an airtight container.

"He'll still be here when everyone is gone," Pepper shot back. "Where's Dad?"

"Well that's nice to know," Lathen said in a gravelly voice from the doorway of the kitchen.

"What are you doing in here?" the women said simultaneously, then chuckled looking at each other.

"My wife was missing, and I heard voices. Wanted to make sure the pack hadn't arrived yet." He snaked out an arm, caught Pepper around the waist, and crushed her against his chest. Covered her mouth with his, then trailed his lips across her cheek, teasing a tantalizing kiss at the pulsing hollow of her throat.

The heady sensation of his lips feathering along her neck rekindled the desire of last night. Pulse racing, her heart beat a tattoo in her chest. She couldn't believe the effect his touch had on her this morning especially after their marathon lovemaking last night. "Lathen, the pack will be here soon." She breathed, feeling his arousal pressed against her.

"I know; just thought I'd remind you..." He wiggled his eyebrows in a seductive manner, held her a couple of beats longer in an attempt to avoid embarrassment.

"If you two are not going to help, get out of our way." Klaren swatted Lathen with a tea towel she yanked from the waist of her apron.

Amy stood hand on hips. "Shooo...out of here you

two." She flicked her hands in a dismissive gesture.

"Okay, okay, we're here to help. What do you need?" Pepper said giggling, reluctantly unwrapping herself from Lathen's body. *Maybe we should have had the pack breakfast at Maggie's.* She threw a coquettish glance his way and caught the spatula thrust into her hand by Amy.

Klaren handed paper plates, plastic ware, napkins, and cups to Lathen, pointed to the end of the long table set up in the living room. Folding chairs borrowed from the reception were arranged along the walls. "Duncan and Elijah went to get the rest of the folding chairs. Kelly said we can return them later today."

Kaylee's plaintive whistle echoed though the cabin. Pepper noticed the dog bowls on the floor were filled with kibble. *So that's why Ember and Tonk are asleep at the front door.* She tossed the kitchen utensil on the counter. "Be right back." Pepper scurried down the hallway and skittered to a stop in front of the fireplace. Two paw shaped Christmas stockings with Tonk and Ember stitched across the top hung at each end of the fireplace. Stockings with Lathen and Pepper stitched on them and a red one with an osprey sewn on it, Kaylee stitched across the top hung between them. "Where'd these come from?" she called out.

"Oh…the ladies from the pack made them for you guys, and charged Jan with delivering them. Brought the stockings with us this morning and hung them up so everyone could see their handy work before leaving." Amy stood in the archway between the kitchen and living room.

"Sweet of them." Lathen stopped what he was doing and looked over at the fireplace. "It sure is. We'll make sure and thank her this morning." Pepper sprinted down the hallway when another reminder whistle pierced the air from Kaylee. After feeding the osprey, Pepper rushed into the living room at the sound of gravel crunching on the driveway. Amy pushed the curtain aside and peered out the window. "They're here," she announced following Lathen to the door.

When Jan walked through the door, Pepper grabbed her in for a hug. "So glad you made it. Sorry we haven't had much time to visit." Pepper met Lathen's pack during his first trip back home last August after being estranged from his family and pack for several years. Jan was one of the women she'd met while helping out at Amy and Elijah's wedding in Alaska.

"Me too, but I understand. Welcome to the pack. Several of the other gals wanted to come but had small kids, family obligations with Christmas and all." She motioned to the fireplace where the stockings were hung. "I see Amy brought the stockings we made for your family."

"Yes, they're wonderful. Tonk and Ember already tried to give them the once over. Thank you so much. Better get a plate before the guys eat it all. I'll catch up with you later."

"Pep, before you run off, the gals wanted me to let you know, in case Lathen had forgotten about the big end of winter celebration we have every year. Maybe you and Lathen could come up for it."

Pepper thought for a couple beats. "Maybe…We're not taking a honeymoon until spring. We bought a large fifth wheel and are planning to camp in Rocky Mountain National Park, Glacier, and Yellowstone. If we work it right and we can find a storage place for our RV for a week in Washington, near Sea-Tac, and catch a flight, spend a few days in Alaska for your party. Email me the dates."

"That would be super."

"I'll talk it over with Lathen and let you know. Also depends on things at the Center. We are talking about hiring more staff, so we'd have a bit more freedom."

"I understand. It's quite a place you have here. Took lots of pictures when Lathen gave us the tour before the wedding. Talked with Gwen, that woman's a hoot."

Pepper grinned and glanced across the room where Gwen stood deep in conversation with Brock, who she'd invited to the breakfast. Secretly…well maybe not so secretly she hoped Gwen found a soulmate in Brock. "She is, known her for years."

Jan followed Pepper's gaze and jerked her chin toward the two. "Looks like she's…"

"We hope so." Pepper laughed, pointing to one of the guys with his plate heaped high with eggs, bacon, hash browns, and a cinnamon roll on top.

"I better get food or like you said, it'll be all gone." Jan rushed off to the buffet table.

Pepper visited with several other people and watched as a large knot of men she recognized from Eli's wedding, gathered around Lathen laughing and talking. He'd rekindled the relationships he'd had before leaving the pack.

When she walked over and settled in a chair next to the fireplace, she sighed. His family had grown closer after Kolby and Hayley came to Lobster Cove several months ago. Kolby was looking for Lathen to tell him about their father's impending nuptials. Elijah's first wife died shortly after giving birth to Lathen, and his father had never remarried, until Amy. Pepper grinned watching the interaction between Eli and Amy. They were prefect for each other.

Her gaze returned to Lathen. After he'd been badly injured in the middle east, recovery had been difficult, and he wasn't the same man that left to join the SEALs. Violent and unstable after his physical injuries healed, he'd left the pack and found his own way of dealing with the trauma. Drifting from place to place, he settled in Lobster Cove where the people embraced him and his skills. And where fate had intervened. Pepper shook her head and wove her way through the crowd, touched Lathen's arm, and smiled. He wrapped his arm around her waist, brushed his lips over hers, and continued visiting. *I'm a lucky woman.*

****

By noon, the pack departed to catch their flight home. Hayley begged off to go lay down while Pepper, her mom, Amy, and Gwen cleaned the kitchen and the men brought in the serving dishes and collected the trash.

After checking on his wife, Kolby joined his brother and dad for a long run around the property. Pepper watched the men strut to the barn, probably to strip and shift. Pepper was still uncomfortable seeing her father-in-law and brother-in-law in the nude after a run. So the group usually disappeared before a run and returned fully clothed. Even though nudity was not a big deal in the pack, the cost of replacing clothing shredded by phasing was. Tonk was on Lathen's heels,

Ember remained behind with Pepper.

Gwen would probably enjoy the sight of the naked well-muscled men, Pepper mused as she put away the warming trays and joined the women in front of the fire. The ominous clouds on the horizon this morning spread across the sky, the wind whipped around the cabin howling like a banshee. Small snowflakes swirled down sideways becoming bigger and bigger until the ground was covered, visibility at zero. Pepper stood at the big bay window, her forehead creased. *Where were the guys? They should have been back by now.* She paced the floor watching the snow pile up.

Amy stepped behind her. "Honey, they've played in storms worse than this. Remember we're from Alaska."

"But Lathen isn't—I mean it's only been a while since his abilities…"

"Once a werewolf, always a werewolf. They're fine." Amy patted her shoulder. "Let's play cribbage, Klaren and I against you and Gwen. I know we can beat you this time."

Pepper raised an eyebrow. "And what's changed? Mom, no magic, understand?"

Her mom stuck out her bottom lip in a pout. "I'm shocked you'd even think such a thing." Gales of laughter floated through the room.

"Kolby," Hayley called from the bedroom. "Kollbbby."

Amy sprinted down the hallway, just as Hayley reached the doorway, white as a sheet. "What's wrong?"

"My water broke, and the contractions have started. We gotta stop them. It's too early."

Remaining calm, Amy said, "Awww...babies make the rules, especially first ones. Let's get you settled back in bed. Kolby went for a run; he'll be back any minute."

Another contraction took Hayley by surprise, she leaned against the door jam, dug her fingers into the wood, leaving imprints, while she breathed through it.

"How far apart?" Gwen wanted to know looking over Pepper's shoulder into the room.

"I'm not sure, but they're coming fast," Amy answered. "Where's the nearest hospital?"

"Lobster Cove—a couple miles away. But...I'm not sure..." Pepper glanced out the bedroom window, the snow was falling so hard all she could see was white.

Suddenly, the back door banged open. Pepper rushed to the kitchen. Tonk raced into the room, flinging snow all over as he shook, followed by a snow covered Lathen, Kolby, and Eli.

"That was a blast," Lathen declared. Shrugging out of his parka, he hung it on the peg by the door. His smile faded as he saw his wife's face.

Pepper raced to him, threw her arms around his neck. "I was worried sick. But more importantly, Hayley's gone into labor. Think we can get her to the hospital?"

The color drained out of Kolby's face at the news, and he sprinted down the hall into the bedroom.

"It's just a wall of white out there. The snow is... No. I don't think it's safe. You can't see where the side of the road ends or where the shoulder begins."

"Pepper, got a minute," Gwen called from the bedroom. "I don't think we got time to get her anywhere." She turned as Pepper skidded into the room. "The contractions are two minutes apart."

Pepper turned to Amy. "Do you people have a history of quick births?" As the words left her mouth, her face warmed. "Oh, shit, I didn't mean that the way it came out."

"No worries," Amy said with a nervous laugh.

"What do you mean? What are we dealing with?" Gwen's eyes widened.

"Can't sugar coat it." Amy glanced at Pepper then back to Gwen. "We're werewolves. Yes, the birthing process can be quick compared to human standards," Amy said. "As well as the healing. That's one reason we have our own doctors." She whirled around to face her husband. "Eli."

"Okay. This can't be much different than the deliveries we've handled at the Sanctuary…" As soon as the words were out of Pepper's mouth, the look of horror on Hayley's face caused her to wish she could take them back. *Insert foot, chew vigorously.* Her defense mechanism in a crisis was humor. However misplaced, the creatures she cared for never minded.

Panting lightly coming down from a contraction, Hayley narrowed her eyes. "If you weren't a witch, I'd…"

Pepper straightened, hands on hips and grinned. "What is the big not so bad werewolf going to do?"

Hayley attempted a laugh. "Your bedside manner needs a little work, woman."

Pepper's lips twitched as she patted her sister-in-law's arm. "Gotcha…" Pepper stopped mid-sentence her gaze shifting to Gwen who seemed frozen in place scanning from one person to the other.

"Did yyyou sssay wwerewolf?" Gwen finally stammered.

"Yes, now get a grip. Amy, have you had any experience delivering the pack's babies?" Pepper glanced at Amy who shook her head.

"Not hands on. We do have a doctor in the valley that takes care of our mothers. Eli would have that number."

Eli, stood outside the door, jerked his phone out of pocket, and touched the screen. He brought his gaze to meet Amy's, shifted to Pepper. "Storm's interfering with reception. I'll send a text."

"Try the land line in the living room." Pepper smiled at Hayley, sucked in a breath, then glanced over at Gwen. "We got this. Right?"

Gwen straightened her stance and raised her chin. "Of course."

Klaren stuck her head into the room. "You're going to need blankets, bassinets, diapers." She flicked her wrist and several of the named items materialized in the room. "There, that's about all I can help with. Unless you need something else, I'm going in the kitchen and start cooking."

"That's Mom's answer to everything." Pepper grinned. "Kolby, quit pacing. Hold Hayley's hand, wipe her forehead with this washcloth." Pepper flicked her fingers, a bowl of cool water and washcloth landed in his hand. "Gwen, grab the supplies we'll need from the medical supply cabinet in your room."

Gwen sprinted out the door, nearly colliding with Klaren.

She quickly moved out of the way. "Well everyone is going to need to eat. We aren't going anywhere for a long while, just look at the snow coming down out there," Pepper's mom said over her shoulder. Her footsteps echoed on the hardwood floor as she made her way to the kitchen.

"The bones in my right hand are crushed," Kolby teased, shaking his hand, holding his wife's hand with the other one.

"That's not the only thing you bastard..." Hayley panted on the verge of another contraction.

"Breathe...breathe...breathe," Kolby coached. "Come on Hayley, you know what to do. It's cresting now, relax. You're doing great, my love."

"This one is going to be our only child," Hayley spat out between clenched teeth, then leaned back against the pillows, eyes closed. At once her eyes flew open, and her breathing increased. "Oh God. Another one."

"Com'on Dad, you don't want to get in Pepper's way. She and Gwen can handle it." Lathen tugged his dad down the hall into the living room. "Guess I'd better stoke the fire the old fashioned way."

Eli snickered. "Spoiled already?"

"Hey, I heard that you two," Pepper called out as Gwen positioned Hayley to deliver the baby.

"I can see the baby's head. Here we go," Pepper said squatting down, nodding to Gwen. "Push, Hayley, push." The words barely out of her mouth before the baby almost slid into her hands. "It's a girl." She cleaned out the mucus, and the baby took her first breath. A loud wail followed. Laying the baby on Hayley's chest, Pepper slid her hand over her sister-in-law's belly and started to clamp and cut the baby's cord. She paused. "Oh—Gwen take over here." Pepper wiped her arm over her face and blew out a breath. "We have another one."

Hayley let out a scream. "I gotta push."

Returning to her position, it was only a matter of minutes. "It's crowning, oh—" Pepper supported the baby's head, turned the shoulders slightly, and helped the little boy into the world. He voiced his displeasure loud and long. "Kolby, you got your boy." She clamped and cut the cord, wrapped the baby in a blanket, and handed him to Kolby. "Give him to Gwen for a minute. Have her weigh the boy. Bet he's close to five pounds, the girl's a little less."

"Amy can you let the guys in the other room, know we have twins."

"Of course." Amy turned on her heel and strode through the doorway. "Guess what guys, we got two for one…" Her voice faded.

Gwen took the baby, weighed it on the scales Lathen brought in earlier. "Yep, five pounds thirteen ounces. Good guess, girl." She handed the boy back to Kolby.

"Let me take the little one for just a moment," Gwen murmured to Hayley, weighed the baby. "Five pounds two ounces, a nice healthy set of twins."

Pepper delivered the placenta and determined the uterus was contracting down. Bleeding would not be an issue. Getting to her feet, she tossed the soiled linens in a pile. Peering at the mess for a moment, she frowned and waved a hand. The pile disappeared, in its place clean blankets and sheets appeared neatly folded. "That's better." Leaning against the wall, she heaved a deep sigh, glancing at Hayley. "You did great. How are you feeling?"

"Tired, sore, but happy. So many things could have... You did a great job too." Hayley's gaze flitted lovingly to the little girl in her arms and over to Kolby and her son. He leaned over with the little boy in his arms and murmured something into his wife's ear, brushing his lips across her cheek and lips.

"I'm going to give you two a little privacy. If you need anything, just holler. Amy and Gwen are just down the hall. The others—are probably chomping at the bit to see the babies so make it quick."

The grandfather clock chimed six when Pepper scooted by the window noting darkness had fallen. "I'm going to take a shower and get changed. Be back in a flash." Pausing at the base of the stairs, she sniffed. "Something smells awfully good." She dashed up the stairs.

"I'm going to see if she needs any help." Lathen flashed a quick smile and followed her.

"She's been dressing herself since she was three," Duncan called after him, chuckling.

Kolby stepped into the hallway. "Dad, Duncan, everyone, come see Amber Moon and Colton Elijah."

Chapter Twenty-Three
Christmas Will Never be the Same

Christmas Eve morning, Pepper woke up to a snowplow rumbling up their gravel road. Jumping out of bed, she pushed aside the curtain and saw the snow had stopped. The sky was still cloudy, but patches of yellow sunshine tried to break through. "I think the storm is over." She bounced onto the bed jostling Lathen awake.

He blinked, stretched his arms over his head, and yawned. "Never a dull moment around you."

"Me? It wasn't my brother's wife that decided to give birth to twins in the middle of a snow storm." Pepper balanced on her knees on the bed, hands fisted on her hips.

Raising a butterscotch eyebrow, he stared at her. "Are you sure. I believe a few days ago we were married, so that makes her your sister-in-law too." He shifted on the bed and Pepper toppled over.

She rolled over and sat cross-legged on the bed. "What a whirlwind this last couple of weeks as been." She paused for a beat and threw her arms up in the air. "The whole holiday season."

"That's what happens when you have a wedding for the holidays. Makes for an interesting ending to the year that has brought more happiness than I can ever remember. I love you, Pepper McKay Quartz." He reached over and pulled her on top of him.

"I love you, Lathen Quartz." She settled onto him and kissed his lips affectionately, slipping her fingers through his hair. "More."

A pounding on the door brought her upright.

"Hey guys, hate to bother you, but...doc from Alaska is on the phone. Needs some information," Eli said.

"All the times, weights, measurements anything else he needs is written on the pad next to Hayley's bed," Pepper said.

"Oookay—we're considering going into town to get baby gifts for this evening. Do you think any stores will be open?"

"Since the plow has been here, you can bet some of the merchants in town have their stores open. It's Christmas Eve, but they will close early."

"So...do you want to join us?"

Pepper looked at Lathen, paused for a couple beats then shook her head. "I don't..."

The skin at the corners of his eyes crinkled as a grin spread across his lips. "Family will be gone in a few days, then we can spend all the time in the world with each other. I don't mind going if you want." He whispered conspiratorially.

"I don't know how you do it, know what I'm thinking even before—"

"It's a wolf thing." He shrugged, climbed out of bed, and pulled on a clean pair of jeans.

"Oh, kinda like going to sleep as human and waking up as a frigging huge wolf?"

"Yeah, kinda—but different." He guffawed. "Kolby said it's happened to him, but Hayley didn't think anything of it—well—because—"

"He's married to a werewolf," she interjected, threw up her hands and giggled. "But that situation tends to scare the bejeebers out of us normal folk."

"Normal folk? You?" He gave his head a little shake and pursed his lips. "Nope, not a word I'd use to describe you or the McKay's." He lunged for her, caught her around the waist, and brought her down on the bed, tickled her until she was gasping for breath.

"Okay you two, a no would have sufficed." Footfalls moved away from the door.

Lathen released Pepper, in a blur of motion was at the door, opened it a few inches. "We'll be down in a minute to two." Pepper joined Lathen peeking out.

His dad turned and winked. "We'll wait for you."

Pepper scrambled into her favorite red holiday sweater. She'd bought it at an after-Christmas sale several years ago to squelch Gwen's complaints about her lack of festive attire. Slipping into a black pair of jeans, she brushed her hair and added mascara to her light red eyelashes. "I'm ready."

"Me too." His voice muted as his head popped out of a green fleece pullover with red bands at the bottom and cuffs.

She looked him over and smiled. "Very festive." Nodding approvingly.

"Yep, Lobster Cove is a jolly place around Christmas. You know what though, I heard something about a Grinch award next year." He shook his head. "Wouldn't want to be on the receiving end of that."

"Why…did someone—"

"Don't know, didn't ask." He sniffed. "I don't smell any food; bet we're going to Maggie's for brunch."

"Sounds wonderful. Give everyone a break." She snapped her fingers. "We could have finger foods for Christmas Eve dinner. I have taquitos in the freezer, several kinds of dip in the fridge. We could pick up lobster rolls while we're in town. Ashling used to have lighted candles around while we opened packages on Christmas Eve. They've got to be here somewhere. Afterward, we could relax with family."

"Sounds like a plan." Lathen bobbed his head in agreement.

Pepper scooted downstairs slightly ahead of him and found everyone waiting for them. "We're off to Maggie's?" Lathen asked smugly.

"How'd you know?" Klaren asked. "Kolby is going to fix eggs and bacon for Hayley when she wakes up. We'll leave the house to them for a while." Klaren frowned. "That's okay, isn't it?"

"Sure, Mike's going to take care of the residents this morning and leave by noon to spend Christmas Eve with his family. Alec has a few days off for working over Thanksgiving for us," Lathen said. "We'll be back by early afternoon."

"Speak for yourselves. We got shopping to do," Klaren said, elbowing Amy.

"Fine, you two, Dad, and Eli take the SUV, Lathen, Gwen, and I will take our truck. That way you can shop 'til you drop or until the stores close, whichever happens first." Pepper chuckled.

Duncan and Eli looked dismayed at each other, glanced at their spouses and shrugged. "Guess that will work."

Pepper's lips twitched in an effort to hide a grin.

Better you two than us. I hate to shop; do all mine online. She glanced around. "Where's Gwen?"

Klaren pointed down the hall to the guest room. "She's been on the phone all morning."

Careening out of her room and down the hall Gwen came to a quick stop in front of Pepper, "I'm here, I'm here. What's up?"

"Want to ride into town with us to pick up a few baby things?" Pepper said with a chuckle.

Gwen hesitated for a couple beats. "Sure. We won't be gone too long? Brock is coming over—um—to discuss the needs of the Salem Sanctuary so he can inform his partners. He's leaving day after tomorrow."

"Guess the storm delayed his departure. Didn't he say something about returning Christmas day to avoid traffic, so he could open the clinic the day after?" Pepper mused.

"Apparently. He checked the highway conditions and decided to wait 'til the day after." Gwen shifted from one foot to the other uneasily.

Narrowing her eyes, Pepper couldn't pass up the opportunity to tease her friend. "Gee that decision didn't have anything to do with say a woman he met recently?"

Red crept up Gwen's neck spreading across her cheeks. "Nooo." She couldn't keep the smile off her face.

"You can tell me in the truck," Pepper whispered conspiratorially.

"What are you two girls twittering about?" Duncan asked using a pretend cough to cover a snicker. "Are we ready to go or not?" He glanced at the others.

"Ready," Gwen and Pepper said simultaneously,

slipping into their parkas and boots.

Lathen held the door open as everyone piled out into the winter wonderland. Someone swept the snow off the trucks. They also ran the snow blower to clear a path from the cabin to the driveway and out to the road.

"Hey, who's the elf that did all this work?" Pepper's glance bounced from her dad to Eli. Both grinned wide.

"That's quite a tracked snow blower you have," Eli said climbing into the rented SUV, holding the seat forward for Amy to hop into the back seat.

"I knew where you stored it. Figured that Lathen kept it all gassed up and ready to go. So when we heard the snowplow come by, figured we could make it into town. To make it easier, we made a few passes with the snow blower on the property." Duncan opened the passenger door and boosted Klaren into the back seat. "Lead the way," he called to Lathen.

"Thanks for doing that guys." Lathen fobbed the pickup doors open. Pepper shoved the seat forward for Gwen, then leaped into the front seat. It was slow going; as they drove through town, Pepper sat up straight and craned her neck, pointing to a house they passed.

"Look, there's a "For Sale" sign outside the old Bonchard place. Did you hear anything about Ben moving, Lathen?"

"Nope, but that's a good thing. Maybe he's leaving."

"Or up to something." She blew out a breath, settled back against the seat. "I know, I know, I'm over reacting."

Lathen shrugged as he pulled into the gravel

parking lot behind Maggie's, the parking lot was half-full.

"Guess the last minute shoppers thought they were sunk when this storm hit." Pepper snickered.

Inside they found a corner booth roomy enough for everyone. Sandy brought tea for Pepper and poured coffee for the rest of the group. Sandy came back for the order, and the weather was the conversation of the hour.

In short order, smiling she brought heaping plates of eggs, bacon, hash browns, and sausage. "Can I get anything else for you?" Sandy glanced across the table.

"Nope looks like it's all here," Lathen said scooping up a fork full of scrambled eggs and cheese.

The others ate with gusto and soon the plates were empty. Duncan got up to meet Sandy at the counter, took the bill, and handed her a credit card.

Klaren took hold of Amy's arm. "Time to shop."

She looked dubious. "Think many shops are open?"

"Oh, yes, it's Christmas Eve. If the shop owners could get to their shop, you bet they're open."

"I guess we're off," Duncan said. "Meet you at the cabin in a couple hours?"

"Yep," Pepper and Gwen followed the group out the door, with Lathen bringing up the rear.

"Is this going to take very long?"

"Nope, going to pick out a few baby things and head home." Pepper carefully picked her way along the partially snow-covered sidewalks of Main Street to Hazeltine's. "There is a children's boutique in here, The Pink Lobster. We should be able to get everything we want."

Gwen nodded. "Does everything in this town have something to do with a lobster?"

"Of course." Lathen tugged the door open, a bell overhead tinkled as Gwen and Pepper walked in. "It's Lobster Cove." He pointed to the left where Amy and Klaren stood browsing through the women's department. To the right, Eli and Duncan's attention focused on the leather goods in the men's department.

Pepper hissed out a breath as she elbowed Lathen in the ribs pointing across the room. "Look, Brent Bonchard passed behind Dad and Eli." She grabbed his hand.

Lathen followed her gaze as she yanked him along behind her skirting the tables and other shoppers. She grabbed hold of Brent's coat sleeve. "Could we have a word?"

Brent narrowed his eyes looking coldly at the hand holding his coat and shook free. "Ms. McKay, what can I do for you?"

Stepping between Pepper and Brent, Lathen moved Pepper to his side, holding her back with his arm. She bristled and glared at him, then turned her attention back to Brent. "Why have you been following me?"

He gave a half laugh. "I wasn't following anyone. You seemed to be in my path, no matter where I went. Wanted to avoid contact if possible, so as not to get my brother in trouble."

"What are you doing here?" Pepper asked.

"Obviously as you know, my brother has some issues. Lobster Cove is not good for him. So I came to convince him to move to the west coast with my wife and I. We own a business there, and he could get the help he needs and work for us. That way we can keep an eye on him and out of the reach of the McKay's."

"Wait a minute, your brother caused—"

Lathen gripped Pepper's arm and gave a nearly unperceivable shake of his head. "So when are you planning on leaving?"

"Hopefully in the next couple days. If that's all, I need to pick up a few more things and get back to packing. This whole debacle has put a wrench into my family's holiday season."

"You do realize the coven will have to be informed," Pepper said.

"Already done. His tracking will be done by our coven on the west coast."

"But I just talked to Ravyn," Pepper argued. "She didn't say anything about Ben leaving."

"We finalized the arrangements this morning. Believe me I want my brother out of here as badly as you do. Enough damage has been done to all parties."

Pepper searched his expression and saw the pain in his eyes, along with the overwhelming hurt she now detected from him. "Agreed. It's just that—"

Brent stared at her then a light of understanding glinted in his eyes. "You thought I'd come to revenge my brother's spell binding," he said sardonically. "Nothing could be further from the truth. Best thing to ever happen to Ben. He was headed for trouble when I left years ago, but no one would listen to me. So here I am to pick up the pieces." He shook his head sadly.

She'd verify Brent's story with Ravyn later, but her intuition told her he was telling the truth. "I can't say I'm sorry to see him go, but I do wish you luck in your endeavor."

"Thank you. Now, if it's all right, I'll be on my

way."

As he stepped away, the circle Pepper hadn't seen forming of her mom and dad, Gwen, Eli, and Amy closed in.

Pepper held up her hand. "It's all right. We've straightened everything out. Brent is here to move Ben to the west coast."

Lathen remained slightly in front of Pepper and slipped his arm around her waist reassuringly.

With a collective sigh of relief, the parties returned to shopping. Brent went on his way without a word.

"So you believe him?" Lathen asked.

Pepper slumped against him. "Yes, I do. But—"

"Oh, yeah, we'll be keeping an eye on him and Ben until they leave." Lathen straightened. "Let's get the shopping done. We've packages to open," he said with a boyish grin.

After only thirty minutes, Lathen's arms were full of packages. He followed the girls to the truck as light snowflakes drifted through the dusky sky.

"A successful outing," Pepper declared. "I'm sure glad Kate wasn't working at Maggie's. Didn't want to explain that to your dad."

Lathen shook his head. "Oh, I'm sure Kolby has chewed that little tidbit over with Dad and anyone else that would listen. My brother is not one to keep his mouth shut when he can stir the pot, so as to speak. You'd think she'd give it a rest since we've all moved on."

"Hell has no fury like a woman scorned." Pepper snickered climbing into the truck.

"Yeah, yeah. How many do we expect for dinner?" He closed the door behind her.

Waiting until Lathen climbed into the driver's seat, she said, "The nine of us, plus the twins. Gwen, is Brock staying for dinner and Christmas Eve festivities?"

"I don't know. He may want to spend it with Dylan and her family."

"Yeah, right." Pepper snickered.

"Brock is a nice guy." He put the key in the ignition, turned it, and the engine roared to life.

"I hope it works out for you."

"We're just friends," Gwen protested.

"That's where it all begins." He paused, raised an eyebrow, and glanced in Pepper's direction. "You didn't have anything to do with it, did you?"

"Not exactly—fate had more to do with it while we were busy with the Forest Owlet rescue." She shifted in her seat and looked out the window.

Gwen tapped Pepper on the shoulder. "Hey guys, I'm sitting right here."

The sidewalks were nearly deserted; several shops already had closed signs hung on their doors. Ice crystals mixed with snowflakes shimmered as the street lights blinked on.

"Bet everyone will be home sooner than expected. It'll be dark by four, and they're not used to shops that roll up their sidewalks this early on Christmas Eve."

When Gwen, Pepper, and Lathen walked through the door to the cabin, Kolby had relocated one bassinet into the living room beside Hayley. The twins were nestled together, sound asleep. Hayley lounged on one side of the double rocker recliner, dressed in red sweats, and matching slippers adorned with embroidered holly.

"My don't you look nice," Pepper said leaning over

to give Hayley a hug after peeking at the babies in the shared bassinet.

"I wanted Amber and Colton to be a part of our first family Christmas." Hayley glanced over at the bassinet when Amber fussed a little.

"I'm going to call Brock. Be back in a minute." Gwen hurried down the hall, into her room.

"Be right back." Pepper left the room and returned lugging her aunt's decorations box. She popped the top, rooted around, and found several large red, green, and white candles with festive holders. The few holidays she had spent here as a child with her family, Ashling and Colleen celebrated Christmas Eve with lit candles, and she wanted to recreate that ambiance tonight. Lathen took the candles while Pepper placed the holders. The aroma of cinnamon, bayberry, and cloves lightly filled the room.

Headlights swept the driveway, Pepper peeked out the window. "The shop 'til they drop group are back."

Klaren was the first through the door. "My it's cozy in here and smells"—she sniffed furrowing her brow—"just like when we spent Christmas with Ashling and Colleen. Where ever did you find those candles?"

"In Aunt Ashling's Christmas decorations." Pepper pointed to the box in the center of the room. "I even found the table cloth." She shook out a red and green crocheted cloth with crystal beads attached to the scalloped edges. "Anyone hungry?"

There were nods all around.

"The taquitos are in the freezer. Several types of dip in the fridge and chips are in the cupboard. I've a bowl of fresh fruit…well frozen fresh, thawed out fruit." Pepper giggled.

"I'll help you get things set out," her mom offered.

"Lathen, could you get out the plates, silver, and napkins?"

"Sure."

It didn't take long, and everything was arranged on the dining table. Pepper took out the deep fryer, added oil, and set out a platter piled high with frozen chicken and beef taquitos. "Taking orders, how many of each does everyone want?"

One by one each person filtered past the table filling a plate, most adding a bowl of fruit.

Everyone settled down around the crackling fire, plates in laps and discussed their fondest childhood memories of the holidays. After dinner, Lathen lit the candles and lowered the lights. Flames cast shadows that danced across the walls in a warm orange glow. Ember, Tonk, and Timber lay by the front door, each gnawing on a large meaty bone. Kaylee watched the activities haughtily from her perch across the room. Packages were distributed.

When Pepper's turn came, she tore open the wrapping, lifted the lid from the little jewelry box, and gasped. "Oh, Lathen they're beautiful." A pair of emerald earrings sparkled in the firelight. She jumped up and gave him a big hug.

"Way to go little brother," Kolby said. "Great minds think alike."

Puzzled, she glanced around the room. Kolby tossed a small box to her. "Go ahead and open it."

Catching the box, she untied the ribbon and opened a hand carved wooden box, lifted the top, and nestled inside were a pair of onyx wolf earrings. Pepper's breath caught. Amy had received a pair almost identical for a wedding present. At the time, Pepper had gushed over the workmanship and originality of the design.

"Yeah we noticed," Hayley said gleefully. "One of our pack members designs one-of-a-kind jewelry and sells the pieces on the internet. Makes a damn good living too."

"Oh wow. You have to give me his business card," Pepper insisted.

Kolby pulled out his wallet and handed her a dog-eared business card. "It's the only one I have."

"Way to show me up, bro." Lathen leaned over to get a better look, and his brother handed him a multi-use knife in the original packaging.

"I don't wrap gifts." Kolby shoved his hands in his pockets.

The whole room burst into gales of laughter.

Next Hayley untied the ribbon from her gift, slid a fingernail under the taped edges, and carefully unwrapped the package then folded the paper neatly in her lap. The group gave a collective groan.

"Hayley sometime tonight," Eli chided. "Some of us would like to open our gifts before the new year."

The room erupted with more laughter. Hayley stuck her tongue out at her father-in-law and opened the box in slow motion. She shook out a lilac hoodie with the LCWRRC logo embroidered across the back and her name in pink on the left front.

"Oh, I love it." She unzipped it, rubbed the fleece material against her cheek, then tried it on. "It's so soft and fits perfectly. Thanks so much."

Tired of waiting, Kolby had already ripped open his present and proudly showed off his black hoodie, his name embroidered in silver thread on the front left and the LCWRRC logo across the back.

"We didn't want you two to fight over the hoodies, so we had your names stitched on them." Pepper's lips twitched with amusement, imagining Kolby in the lilac hoodie.

As each person took a turn opening their packages the pile of wrapping paper grew, nearly as tall as the mountain of baby gifts stacked next to Hayley.

Pepper shook her head. "Colton and Amber will be the most spoiled grandchildren on the planet. It's a good thing Eli has a private jet, or you'd never get all the Christmas gifts back to Alaska without paying boocoo bucks for shipping."

As the remaining packages were opened, there were ohhs and ahhs from the group.

After clean up, Pepper handed out wine glasses. Lathen poured the wine, with the exception of Hayley who got sparkling grape juice. He held up his glass in a toast. "The best gift of all tonight is being together as a family." Everyone raised their glasses in agreement.

Pepper wrapped her arm around Gwen and squeezed. "Far cry from last Christmas. Huh?"

Gwen nodded, her eyes glistening. "You are so lucky."

"No, we're lucky. You are a part of this family too," Pepper whispered.

Brock sidled over to Gwen and slid his arm around her waist, bent down, and whispered something. She smiled.

Lathen joined their little knot and rested his arm around Pepper's shoulder. She nudged him in the ribs and subtly tilted her chin toward the couple, silently mouthing, "Friends my ass."

He grinned and brushed his lips over hers. "Stay out of it," he whispered before deepening the kiss.

"Well, I think it's time we hit the road," Duncan said picking up their empty wine glasses, carrying them to the kitchen.

Klaren chuckled. "We'll be here first thing tomorrow morning to help with the Christmas feast."

"Ditto," Amy said slipping her arms into the coat Eli held. When they started out the back door, Timber scrambled between Eli's legs in an effort to escape only to be yanked away from the door by Duncan.

"Oh no, you don't you little scallywag." He swung the pup up in his arms.

Hayley nodded off in the recliner, so Kolby took the twins into their room then roused Hayley and said their good nights.

Pepper and Lathen ambled out with her parents and waved as they got inside their vehicle and started down the plowed road. Snow sparkled in the beams of the headlights giving everything that magical Christmas aura.

Returning to the cabin, they met Gwen and Brock on the porch.

"I'm going to walk Brock to his truck. Be right back," Gwen said, her hand wrapped though Brock's arm.

Lathen nodded and closed the door behind Pepper. After several minutes, Pepper tugged on the door handle to make sure it hadn't accidentally lock. The door flew open. "Oh, geez, I'm sorry." She quickly closed the door.

"Interrupt something?" Lathen raised an eyebrow.

"You could say that." She scurried upstairs tugging an amused husband behind her.

Chapter Twenty-Four
A Christmas Day Surprise and Celebration

The kitchen filled with laughter as Pepper eased the cooked yams in a pan with butter and sprinkled brown sugar over the top. She scooted to the side as Amy took the turkey out of the oven, basted it, and shoved it back inside.

"Another thirty minutes and the turkey will be done," Amy declared.

Klaren wiped her hands on the holiday apron tied around her waist. "The spiral sliced ham is precooked so all we need to do is warm it a bit."

"I just took the pumpkin pies out of the upper oven," Pepper said. "Slide the ham in there; it'll be warm through by the time the turkey is done."

Lathen carried a tray of cut veggies and ranch dip to the table and checked on the rolls in the bread warmer. He reached for a basket and put a napkin inside.

"Don't put those out yet; they'll get cold," she chided.

"I wasn't," Lathen retorted. "See, the basket is all ready for when you need it."

Amy and Eli set the table with the silverware and china plates stacked on the counter.

"Hey, where's Kolby and Hayley and our grandbabies?" Eli stood in the doorway between the kitchen and living room staring down the hallway.

"They had a rough night. The babies slept through the festivities last night, but after everyone went to bed, they woke up and kept mom and dad up most of the night." Pepper snickered. "Got their days and nights mixed up already."

A truck's engine rumbled up the driveway. "Are we expecting someone?" Amy stopped and glanced out the window.

"Yes. We invited Mike and his family since they don't have anyone close." Lathen crossed the room.

"Lynette, his wife is bringing homemade cranberry sauce." Pepper wiped her hands on a towel, followed her husband to the door.

He pulled the door open as Mike had his hand poised to knock. "Merry Christmas. Come on in."

Mike handed two apple pies to Lathen then sprinted back to the car.

"We are so grateful to you and Pepper. I made two apple pies from my granny's recipe," Lynette said, a sleeping child in her arms. "Mike went back to the car for the homemade cranberry sauce in the back seat."

"Thank you," Pepper and Lathen said simultaneously, then grinned. Mike handed Pepper a bowl of ice with a molded Christmas Tree of cranberry sauce. Lathen showed the couple to the dining room and made the introductions.

She set the bowl on the table, turning it this way and that. "How creative." Pepper took the baby from Lynette as she shrugged out of her coat. Mike unfolded a combination crib and playpen against the wall next to the dining area. Pepper eased the child into the padded play area.

"You come prepared."

"It's the first time we've used it," Mike admitted. "We don't go many places." His gaze fell to the floor then back to Lynette.

She smiled encouragingly. "But that is changing slowly. Molly's colic seemed to have eased over the past couple of weeks." Lynette sighed. "Makes going places with the baby so much easier."

"Sleeping too." The corner of Mike's mouth turned up in a slight smile. "We really appreciate the invitation." He shifted from one foot to the other, surveying all the people in the room.

Eli stepped up with an outstretched hand. "Those colicky babies are tough. Lathen cried the better part of two months." He shook his head. "Thought I'd lose my mind."

Lathen gave his father a hard stare.

"But…with the help of a couple of people. We got through it. And look at him now—still a pain in my ass." Eli snorted.

Mike chuckled. "He's a great guy."

"Don't say that too loud. Don't want to feed his ego," Eli whispered conspiratorially, a devilish grin spread across his lips.

A haggard-looking Kolby dressed in rumpled jeans and green sweater shuffled into the room. Behind him, Hayley appeared with dark circles under her eyes and her dark hair pulled back in a ponytail, dressed in black sweats and red and white sweatshirt. "Sorry we're late, the twins were up most the night. They didn't disturb your sleep, did they?" Hayley glanced at Gwen, then Pepper and Lathen.

"Didn't hear a thing," Pepper said. Gwen nodded.

"Hey, did Brock leave this morning?" Lathen asked.

"Nooo—actually, he is going to stay 'til after the new year. Dylan's still weak, especially after helping with the bird rescue. Besides, he wants to follow me back to Salem. Guess the roads are still a bit rough in spots."

"Good idea. Is he coming to dinner?" Pepper couldn't keep the smugness out of her voice.

"I was going to ask if that would be all right. And you can just wipe the smirk off your face Pepper McKay—uh—Quartz." Gwen fisted her hands on her hips.

Pepper raised her hands palms out. "What?"

"Of course, he's welcome. If Dylan doesn't need him to help her," Lathen said.

"No, they are going to the in-laws today. I told Brock if he didn't hear from me, to come on over."

A vehicle pulled to a stop in the driveway.

"There he is now." Gwen took a couple quick steps, then sauntered across the floor.

Pepper giggled. "Gwen just admit it, more than "friends" is going on here."

"Don't you dare say anything." Gwen whipped around standing in front of the door.

Pepper made a zipping motion across her lips, eyes sparkling with mischief as Gwen opened the door.

"Don't you dare," Lathen cautioned. Soft laughter rippled through the group.

"Just in time. Dinner's ready," Klaren called out, rounding the large dining table heaped with turkey, ham, homemade rolls, cranberry sauce, and other scrumptious trimmings.

Chair legs scraped on the polished hardwood floor as everyone sat down. Lathen at the head of the table carved the turkey. Pepper's dad passed the plate of ham slices followed by the bowl of orange marmalade spice glaze. The candied sweet potatoes and deviled eggs were the favorite side dishes of the group.

After dinner, Eli and Lathen arranged additional chairs in the living room around the fire. Klaren and Amy took orders for either apple or pumpkin pie to go with coffee or tea as everyone settled in the living room. Duncan and Pepper put the leftovers away and loaded the dishwasher.

Low mummers of conversation wafted through the room as Pepper sat back and took it all in. She'd never been happier in her life. Her family had more than doubled in the last few months.

Hayley left the room to attend to the fussing twins with Kolby hurrying after her.

Lathen leaned over and kissed his wife's cheek, whispering in her ear then pushed up from the couch. "Mike, can I have a word with you?"

Mike looked uncertainly from his boss to Lynette. "Sure." He got to his feet and followed Lathen down the hall to a tiny office.

****

Lathen closed the door behind them and motioned for Mike to have a seat across the desk from him. Mike stared at the floor and nervously fidgeted in the chair, his mouth set in a thin line.

"You've done a very good job here at the Center. The animals respond well to you. Are you enjoying the work?" Lathen paused waiting for Mike to meet his gaze.

It took a couple of minutes for Mike to raise his gaze to Lathen's. "Yes, I love working with the animals, working with my hands and the income has been a life saver for Lynette and me."

"That's great."

"But…" Mike interrupted in a resigned voice.

Lathen shrugged. "But nothing. Mike, I'd like you to join our team. Pepper and I decided to cut your probationary period short and offer you a full-time permanent position beginning tomorrow, with an increase in pay. You'll be salary rather than hourly. Will that work for you?"

Mike sat silent for a few minutes, shook his head. "A permanent, full-time salaried position?" He repeated.

Lathen relaxed back in his chair, slid several pieces of paper across the desk toward Mike. "Yes, with health benefits, paid holidays, retirement plan, and paid time off—two weeks after the first year. You may have to work a few holidays if Pepper and I take time off, but you'll be well compensated."

Mike's eyes glistened. He turned his face away for a moment. When he turned to face Lathen, a full smile curved his lips. "Yes, sir."

Lathen reached his hand into the desk drawer, pulled out an envelope, stood and handed it to Mike. "Merry Christmas."

His eyes rounded as he carefully took the envelope. He turned it over and over in his hand staring down at it. Then turned his gaze to Lathen. "You have no idea how much all this means to me. Thank you."

"Oh, I've been there, and you're very welcome."

After a soft knock, the door opened, and Pepper

slipped in the room. "Everything all right in here?"

"Perfect." Mike took two steps toward her and threw his arms around Pepper. "Thank you so much!"

"You've earned it. We are proud to have you as part of the team."

As Mike got up to leave, Lathen's phone rang. "Who the hell would be calling on Christmas Day?" Mike exited and quietly closed the door.

Pepper quirked a brow, hand on her hip. "This is a wildlife rescue, twenty-four/seven business. Remember?"

He looked at the screen and blew out a breath. "It's Ray."

"Merry Christmas, Lt. Commander."

"Merry Christmas to you too. Thought you'd like to know. The info your team obtained and the total destruction of the financial conduit your worm shut down has resulted in several insurgents' strongholds falling and hundreds of lives saved. There was no exposure of our forces nor knowledge of who's responsible. Excellent job."

"Of course, you expected nothing less."

"Thanks for your help, though you did uncover deficiencies in our cyber training."

"Now there's a surprise. As I said the military is way behind the private sector in cyber security."

"If you're interested in instructing…"

"I've got my hands full, and you've got some good guys. But if you get in a bind again, we can talk about it."

"Fair enough. Enjoy your holiday."

"You too." Lathen disconnected the call and relayed the conversation to Pepper.

****

There were no new arrivals at the Center, which pleased Lathen. He loved the work, but they were full and would need to add additional staff after the first of the year to accommodate the growth so there would be no lack in care for the residents.

Lathen called a quick meeting the day after Christmas, Alec's first day back. "I wanted to let you know that Mike has agreed to a full-time permanent position with the team. Judy and Rick will be part-time employees during their time off from college, starting today. Pepper and I will be gone for a few weeks in the spring for our honeymoon. By then we should have any new staff trained ready to fill in during our absence. Any questions?"

Alec shook his head. "Your family's still here, so…"

"The Center is in your capable hands for another week. We'll be helping out when time allows."

"Got it." Alec grinned and slapped Mike on the back. "Come on, we got work to do. Judy and Rick, take the seabird aviary and check the marine habitat."

The remainder of the week proved to be peaceful, the melting snow made it easier, but sloppier to get around to the Center's inhabitants, who were doing well.

Chapter Twenty-Five
The New Year Arrives and With It Hope for a
Bright Future

Lathen kicked back in the double rocker recliner
with his arm around Pepper, the flames reached high
into the fireplace as he swirled red wine in his crystal
glass against the firelight. Beside them, the sixty-inch
television screen showed New York Times Square a
few minutes from the ceremonial ball drop. Eli and
Amy sat at one end of the high-back couch, watching
the TV intermittently and talking quietly with Klaren
and Duncan. Hayley sat on the edge of the single rocker
recliner holding one of the twins, as husband, Kolby
held the other while sitting on pillows spread across the
floor in front of the fireplace. Brock and Gwen grabbed
a couple of pillows for themselves. Gwen leaned
against Brock, his arm slung lazily over her shoulder.

Ember and Tonk sprawled out in front of the front
door, snoring softly. Timber lay next to the canines,
ready to pounce each time Ember's tail twitched. A
behavior that had earned the pup a warning growl and a
swipe from the alpha of this pack earlier in the day.

Lathen looked around the room and wondered at
the calm scene around him. Not so long ago, in fact it
was last New Year's, estranged from his family, he'd
finished an emergency repair at the Seacrest Inn,
returned to his sparsely furnished cottage, and crashed

on the bed. He shook his head slowly. If someone at that time would have told him one year from that date, he'd be married, reunited with his family, and co-owner of Lobster Cove Wildlife Rescue and Rehab, he'd have laughed his ass off. Yet, here he was, so lucky. Even when a military special assignment reared its ugly head a couple weeks before the wedding, Pepper had been supportive. Further assignments as an independent contractor would be discussed on a case by case basis, no guarantees, a solution he and Pepper agreed they could live with. Pepper's voice roused him out of his thoughts.

"Okay, so tomorrow after the late brunch, are you all taking off from Bar Harbor airport?" Pepper shifted in her chair so she could see everyone. "Gwen, you and Brock are driving to Salem. Right?"

"Yep," Gwen said.

"I believe that's the plan." Amy smiled over at Elijah. "We are going to take Klaren up on her offer to spend a couple days in Colorado before returning to Alaska. Traveling with the twins, changes things."

"Yes," Hayley said in a hushed voice. "We really appreciate the offer."

"No problem. We have plenty of room." Klaren winked at her husband. "Pep, do you need a hand with the brunch preparations tomorrow?"

"Nope, got it covered." She cut her gaze to the TV and pointed. "Looks like it's almost time."

All eyes in the room turned to the television.

Pepper reached over and caressed Lathen's arm, her gaze catching his and holding it. She mouthed I love you, leaned over, and brushed her lips over his. The music on the TV grew louder to announce the beginning of the ball drop at midnight.

Lathen pushed up from the recliner and took the bottle of champagne from the ice and poured it in seven fluted crystal glasses sitting on the table behind the couch. The bubbly liquid glinted in the firelight as he poured. He took a small bottle of sparkling white grape juice and poured it into the eighth glass, passing it to Hayley. Carefully he extended a glass to Kolby who held Colton Elijah. The baby seemed intent on sleeping through the welcoming of the New Year. Amber Moon fussed in Hayley's arms when she shifted to toast the New Year with the others. The glasses made a tinkling sound when the group touched rims in a toast to the New Year. Pepper grinned and waved her arm above her head, bright colored confetti burst through the air, floating to the floor, magically avoiding everyone's glasses but covering their hair, and clothes. Ember and Tonk raised their heads to glance at the confetti spreading across their fur. They got to their feet, dark eyes narrowed at Pepper, shook, and stood at the front door.

The huge grandfather clock Klaren and Duncan had given their daughter and son-in-law for a wedding gift chimed midnight in deep resonating tones. Lathen's smile was so wide he thought his face would crack. He took a sip from his glass, sighed, and swirled the bubbly liquid around in his glass again. This past week had been a happy whirlwind. He was thankful that Ben had moved to the west coast with his brother, just as Brent had indicated in their conversation Christmas Eve.

After midnight, Klaren and Duncan said their goodbyes, scooped up Timber, and promised to return early morning for the family brunch. Eli and Amy grabbed their coats and wandered out the back door to the cottage on the property. Amber's fussing became a loud wail alerting everyone to her desire to be fed at which time her brother joined in.

"Let's take a walk." Lathen took hold of Pepper's arm and in a flurry of movement grabbed their coats from the pegs on the kitchen wall. After helping Pepper into her parka, he shrugged into his and followed Eli and Amy out the back door. "Goodnight," Pepper and Lathen chorused and turned down the path to the pond bathed in the silver light of a full moon. Ember and Tonk trotted beside them.

The ground around the pond was still warm from the spell cast by the McKay ghosts for the wedding. The heat flowed up the enchanted wood keeping the bench Lathen had made for Pepper warm. He motioned for her to sit down. This was also the bench he'd knelt before her and asked Pepper to be his bride in front of her parents and a crowd of McKay ghosts on Halloween night. A thick mist crawled across the surface of the pond, several ghostly forms appeared on the shore along with Ashling's familiar silhouette leaning against her favorite pine tree near the water. Waves softly lapping at the shore could be heard among the murmurs of the ghosts.

"I'm glad you joined us," Ashling said. "Dusty and Aidan were about to depart along with several of the McKay family ghosts.

Pepper's eyes rounded. "They were going to leave without even saying goodbye?" She shifted on the bench to see her great-great-great and even more greats grandfather and grandmother rise from the mist.

"Absolutely not. We would have found a way to

make ourselves known before our departure." He smiled and made a slight bow, holding Dusty's hand in his. "It's time we returned to the afterlife. I am so happy we got a chance to know you." He glanced at Lathen then to Pepper. "The McKay property and destiny is safely in your hands." The grandfatherly ghost winked. "Along with the werewolf." Aidan chuckled shaking his head slightly causing it to blur. "Never thought."

Dusty moved closer to her husband, their forms nearly intermingled. "Our legacy is safe with you and the family to come," she said with a wink.

Pepper stared wide-eyed at Dusty then cut her gaze to Lathen. "Family?"

"Of course," Dusty stated in melodic voice. "He may be a werewolf, but you're still a McKay." She floated closer until mist surrounded them and whispered. "We're very fertile, you know."

Lathen felt a cold chill pass over them.

"Dusty, that's enough," Aidan said. "We must be off—as they say now days."

"We'll miss you," Pepper said tears glimmering in her eyes.

"Oh, we'll never be far. Ashling knows where to find us." Aidan's form wavered and faded along with Dusty. Leaves rustled as a slight breeze brought salt and brine on the air, the mist thinned and several other ghosts uttered their goodbyes disappearing into the fog.

"Yep, I'm staying put to try to keep Colleen out of trouble until…" Ashling said her voice fading away with the rest of her.

They were alone at last, Lathen wrapped his arm around Pepper, brushed his lips over hers. She cuddled into him with a sigh. "Well, I guess we're on our own."

Thundering paws came down the path, Ember and Tonk raced around the pond, finally settling on either end of the bench, Kaylee's shrill whistle cut through the crisp night air.

One corner of Lathen's mouth kicked up in a lopsided grin. "Somehow—I doubt that. Happy New Year—my little witch."

"Happy New Year, my werewolf." Pepper giggled.

A word from the author…

With the majestic Rocky Mountains just outside my window, I sit at my computer with vampires, demons, witches, faeries, and a variety of paranormal creatures gathered around telling me their stories! I write paranormal romance novels. Remember the magic to happily ever after!

Colorado is home. I share my life with a wonderful husband of many moons, our brilliant Chow Chow, a terribly spoiled companion parrot, and a forty-year-old box turtle. We enjoy hiking, biking, and camping, also love water sports including kayaking and whitewater rafting, especially on the Arkansas River through the Royal Gorge.

You can find me any winter evening curled up in front of a crackling fire with a good book, a mug of hot chocolate, and a big bowl of popcorn. While growing up if I didn't like the ending of a book, I'd rewrite it, which led to writing my own books.

http://www.tenastetler.com

Thank you for purchasing
this publication of The Wild Rose Press, Inc.

If you enjoyed the story, we would appreciate your
letting others know by leaving a review.

For other wonderful stories,
please visit our on-line bookstore at
www.thewildrosepress.com.

For questions or more information
contact us at
info@thewildrosepress.com.

The Wild Rose Press, Inc.
www.thewildrosepress.com

Stay current with The Wild Rose Press, Inc.

Like us on Facebook

https://www.facebook.com/TheWildRosePress

And Follow us on Twitter
https://twitter.com/WildRosePress

www.ingramcontent.com/pod-product-compliance
Lightning Source LLC
Chambersburg PA
CBHW051516260626
47170CB00003B/646